How to Tame a Human Tornado

Also by Paul Tobin and illustrated by Katie Abey

How to Capture an Invisible Cat
How to Outsmart a Billion Robot Bees

HOW TO TAME A HUMAN TORNADO

PAUL TOBIN

BLOOMSBURY
CHILDREN'S BOOKS
LONDON OXFORD NEW YORK NEW DELHI SYDNEY

*To Colleen Coover, and to every child
with questions*

BLOOMSBURY CHILDREN'S BOOKS
Bloomsbury Publishing Plc
50 Bedford Square, London WC1B 3DP, UK

BLOOMSBURY, BLOOMSBURY CHILDREN'S BOOKS and the Diana
logo are trademarks of Bloomsbury Publishing Plc

First published in Great Britain in 2018 by Bloomsbury Publishing Plc

A catalogue record for this book is available from the British Library

ISBN: PB: 978-1-4088-8181-1; eBook: 978-1-4088-8182-8

2 4 6 8 10 9 7 5 3 1

Typeset by Westchester Publishing Services
Printed and bound in Great Britain by CPI Group (UK) Ltd,
Croydon CR0 4YY

MIX
Paper from
responsible sources
FSC® C020471

To find out more about our authors and books visit www.bloomsbury.com
and sign up for our newsletters

Chapter 1

I was on high alert.

Ready for anything.

It was the middle of the afternoon and I was in the center of the sidewalk in the heart of downtown Polt. There were people everywhere. Everyone else was walking casually, but I was on tiptoes, looking in all directions, and knowing that it was almost entirely useless.

My phone rang.

It was Nate.

"Do you see him?" Nate asked.

I looked around at all the people. There was a college-age couple walking by. He had huge sideburns and she had pigtails and they were looking at something together on her phone. There was a businessman in a striped suit, balanced on one foot, checking the bottom of his left shoe to see if he'd stepped in something unpleasant. There was a group of three high school boys kicking a soccer ball. There was a man with a remarkable mustache just ahead of me on the corner, holding a signboard advertisement for a mattress store, bellowing "hello" to everyone and trying to shake their hands. There was a very young girl holding her mother's hand and *earnestly* explaining the differences between apes and monkeys. There was a woman trying to text with one hand while eating a meatball sandwich. Her blouse was white. She was holding the sandwich away from her, worried about stains.

The meatballs smelled *so good*.

"I don't see him," I told Nate, on the phone. "What should we—?"

But it was at that moment I heard the roaring hum. The air began to vibrate. There were crackling noises from everywhere, like tinfoil being crunched. A Corgi began nervously barking. An old woman in a blue hat clutched a tiny dog to her chest, saying, "Hush, Jeremiah. Hush." Even so, I could tell she was worried. The air didn't feel right. There was . . . too much of it. Pigeons were suddenly flying away. A crow that was on the awning for the All-Winners Art Museum began cawing, hopping along the awning, head swiveling nervously. The hum was growing louder. The crackling rising in intensity.

It felt like the whole world was starting to shiver.

And then . . .

. . . I saw him.

He was only there for a second.

Moving much too fast to see.

He was a blurred line, a thousand flickering images, racing around everyone, racing past them, the air sizzling around him. A few bits of trash . . . newspapers and fast-food wrappers . . . simply burst into flame.

The couple toppled over in the sudden gust of wind. Their shared phone dropped to the sidewalk, tumbling along, bouncing again and again, caught in the blustering wake. The businessman's shoe was ripped off by the pure force, so that he was hopping on one foot, gazing around, bewildered. The high school boys were frowning at their soccer ball, which had popped from the intense air pressure. The woman with her meatball sandwich was looking at her blouse in horror, because it had been simply *painted* with meatball sauce in the sudden wind that'd lasted for less than a second, but had been faster than any tornado, stronger than any hurricane.

The man with the signboard was frowning at it, clearly puzzled. The edges of his sign were tattered and smoldering. And . . . written on the sign with the remains of a meatball sandwich . . . it said, "Nate! Delphine! Help me! *Please!*"

I looked down the street to where the blur had disappeared, then picked up my phone from where I'd dropped it in the sudden chaos.

"Nate," I said. "Chester was just here. We have to save him."

Chapter 2

Two hours previously I'd been in the Next Page Bookstore on Trillip Avenue and Nate Bannister had been chastising a confused employee because the quantum physics section had fewer books than the one for celebrity diet tips. The clerk's name was Lucy and she was at least thirty years old, meaning almost twenty years older than Nate and me, so you'd think she'd be wiser (my mother *assures* me that wisdom comes with experience), but Nate, as it so happens, is the smartest person on earth. His IQ is immeasurable. His hair is brown and flopping. There's no connection between these two facts, at least I don't *think* there is, though Nate says there's a connection between ALL facts, if you know how to find them.

Anyway, poor Lucy was just staring at Nate and his floppy brown hair, which he kept having to brush out from behind his glasses, because he has a big nose, meaning that it holds his glasses too far out from his face, meaning his hair can fall behind them. There *is* a connection between all these facts.

"I was hoping you'd have *Brinkman's Theory of Transitive Kinetics in Orbital Molecular Vectoring*," Nate complained.

"Maybe . . . we could order it?" Lucy said. Her blond hair was almost as curly as my red hair. She was tugging on a few strands, looking around in that manner people have when they think they're being pranked. Her lips (she was wearing green lipstick, which made me jealous) kept squinching up like chewed bubblegum. There was a computer terminal just a few feet away, and she beckoned Nate and me closer to where she typed for a moment before saying, "Oh. Oh, *wow*."

"What?" Nate said.

"That book is, like, really expensive."

"It is?" Nate asked, clearly disappointed. "But I've seen it listed for cheap. Only around four thousand dollars."

"Four thousand dollars is *not* cheap," Lucy said. Her eyes were wide and her lips became chewed bubblegum again.

"Knowledge is worth any price," Nate said. "I'd like the signed copy, if one's available. It doesn't matter if it costs more." He was taking his gold elephant credit card out from his wallet. It's the rarest of credit cards, only three of them in the entire world, because Nate is apparently one of the richest people on earth, though he won't tell me *how* rich. As for me, I have a part-time dog-walking job. I make seven dollars an hour. Per dog. Sometimes three or four dogs at a time. I do okay.

"Here," Nate said, holding up his credit card. "Do you know what this is?"

"Uh, a shiny credit card?" Lucy said, clearly not impressed.

But, then . . .

"G-GOLD! G-g-gold ELEPHANT CARD!" the store manager shrieked, bellowing out from three aisles away. He not-very-adeptly leaped over a display of books on Greek mythology, scurried through an aisle of romance books, then skidded to a stop in front of Nate. He trembled. I thought he was going to salute.

It was at that moment, when everybody else was watching the commotion, that I saw Bosper sneak in through the front door.

Bosper is Nate's Scottish terrier.

Bosper is also the smartest mathematician in the world, excepting only Nate, and possibly Jakob Maculte, the leader of the Red Death Tea Society, a cult of super-smart villains who do super-evil things.

Maculte's top priority is to take over the world, and his credo is . . . *Whatever works, as long as it's EVIL.* (I made that last part up, but it's basically true.)

Anyway, we weren't talking about the Red Death Tea Society, even though Maculte had recently escaped from custody and was calling Nate multiple times every day, swearing all sorts of revenge, making an amazing array of threats, and sporadically inviting me over for tea, invitations which I have *politely* and *not-so-politely* declined.

No. We were talking about dogs.

Nate's dog, in particular.

Bosper can talk.

And he was *not* supposed to be in the store.

Because he forgets he's not supposed to talk when he's in public.

I had to do something.

"Be right back," I told Nate.

"Oh, okay, Delphine," he said. The bookstore manager was stupidly grinning at Nate and babbling about how it was an honor to have him in the store, meaning it was an honor to have a *gold elephant card* in the store. Some people are *way* into money. It's kind of sad, really. They're so focused on money, they miss the bigger questions in life, like . . . is there anything better than climbing a tree to watch a sunset with a friend? Or, why do some people think *pie* is better than *cake*? Or, of course . . . why was a talking dog sneaking into a bookstore?

And Bosper *was* sneaking. No doubt about it. He was darting between bookcases, peering around them, acting like a spy. Like an especially *incompetent* spy. You know that thing in horror movies when people are scared of the monsters, so they tiptoe into rooms or along darkened corridors, but they never look *up*? That's what Bosper was doing. Forgetting to look *up*. Which isn't very smart if you happen to be a Scottish terrier and therefore only about a foot tall.

I secretly started following him.

It wasn't very hard to do.

All I had to do was stay behind the bookcases, one aisle over, because he was in the children's picture-book section where the shelves were only about three feet high. I could easily peer over them at Bosper.

He was whispering, "The dog is quiet. No barking for Bosper! I am a sneaker." I should've mentioned that while Bosper can do math and can also talk, he's much better at math than he is at talking.

I followed after him, keeping out of sight, listening to what he had to say.

"No time for farting," he said. "Because Bosper is

a sneaky dog." He stopped at the end of the aisle and looked left, and right, and then he farted.

"This has happened and the dog has regrets," he said. His tail slunk low. But, then he regained his composure and scurried forward as fast as he could, dodging a group of children looking through picture books, then skidding out on a tile walkway at the edge of the carpeted children's area and thudding into a bookcase, knocking over a display of Robinson Crusoe books and a cardboard pirate ship.

"The dog has tumbled," Bosper said. "But no one has noticed." This was decidedly untrue. Several first graders had been listening to a bookstore employee (Ms. Chrissy) reading from the *Polka Dots vs. Angry Spots* picture book, but had turned around to stare at the Scottish terrier. Those who were close enough had even heard Bosper speak. They were staring at one another in amazement, but it wasn't very *deep* amazement, because first graders still believe that everything is possible and therefore aren't too surprised when they hear a dog talk. I still remember being that age. It was fun. It was only later that I began to understand how the world works, and that dogs do not talk, which is why it was such a shock the first time I heard Bosper speaking on the day that I met Nate and discovered that everything *was*, in fact, possible.

Bosper was again trotting through the bookstore. Now and then he would look back to make sure he wasn't being followed, but he would always murmur, "Bosper is checking for spies," before turning around, giving me ample time to hold a book in front of my legs so that Bosper wouldn't recognize me. I wasn't holding the books in front of my face, because Bosper still wasn't looking up.

We moved through all the math books, just an aisle away from where Nate was talking with the store manager. Bosper pawed at some of the books, whispering about "inter-universal Teichmüller theory," but then moved on.

I followed him through the romance section.

And the section for westerns.

And into world history.

I was only a few feet behind him when he turned into an aisle, let out a happy yelp, and said, "The dog discovers you! His tail goes wagging!"

I couldn't see who he was talking to.

I edged closer.

I was in a shelving area for bookstore merchandise. There were various coffee cups and water bottles and shirts emblazoned with the store logo, as well as other items like action figures of famous authors and an assortment of calendars, including a display calendar turned to the proper date.

Saturday the fourteenth.

Wait.

What?

Uh-oh.

I'd lost track of time again, and since it was Saturday the fourteenth that meant that Nate had done three dumb things yesterday. That's what he does. Dumb things. Every Friday the thirteenth. He's explained to me that since he's so intelligent, things rarely come as a surprise to him. He's figured out all of life's equations, all of the various probabilities, and so on. It's exciting for him to solve problems, to make incredibly accurate predictions, but at the same time it bores him, because everything moves steadily along a path that his amazing brain has already predetermined. Because of this, he plays with the equations. What I mean is that he messes them up.

He does three dumb things.

Every Friday the thirteenth.

The first time I met him he'd transformed his mother's cat into a dangerous giant. At other times he's taught the orangutans at the zoo how to build skateboards, taught a mouse how to sword-fight, and accidentally unleashed a swarm of robot bees.

I heard a small noise at my feet.

A tiny thump.

Looking down, I saw one of Nate's notes, the ones he leaves in places where he predicts I'll be. I had to make a decision: either sneak around the corner to see who Bosper was talking with, or read the note. Normally, this wouldn't have been a major decision, because I was shivering with anticipation about discovering Bosper's secret, but this was no ordinary day. This was one day *after* Nate had, without doubt, done three incredibly dumb things.

I leaned over and picked up the note . . .

. . . just as Bosper peered around the corner.

Meaning that our faces were at equal levels, and the terrier didn't need to look up in order to recognize me anymore.

"Delphine?" Bosper said.

That's my name. Delphine. Delphine Cooper.

"Bosper," I said. "Why are you here?"

"Bosper is not here," he said in a solemn voice. His eyes keenly searched mine, hoping I would believe him. Whatever he saw in my eyes wasn't belief (it was much closer to *disbelief*, and also dizziness, because I'd been bending over for far too long), and so he abandoned that tactic and enacted one of the most commonplace plans in all of history for when things are going wrong.

He ran.

I looked around the corner to see who he'd been talking with, but there was no one, and Bosper was already gone and the note was just *burning* in my fingers, so I shrugged and opened the note, which was folded in an intricate pattern so that when I unfolded it there was a pop-up swan with my name on it, followed by, "Don't be mad."

"Uh-oh," I said.

I unfolded the note a little more.

It read,

"You forgot that yesterday was Friday the thirteenth, but by now you'll have remembered, and you'll be wondering what I've done. So I thought I'd tell you. If you promise not to be mad."

I unfolded the note some more.

But there was nothing. No more words.

I looked around for more notes.

Nothing.

I stared at the note, reading it again. The last sentence was underlined. I glared at it. It said,

"If you promise not to be mad."

"*Piffle*," I said. "I *won't* promise not to be mad."

As soon as I spoke, the line wavered, and the under-lining faded away.

A folded note fell on my head, bouncing off my hair onto a shelf in front of me. It said,

"Delphine."

Unfolding it, I read,

"You probably noticed how the underlining on that previous note disappeared. That's because you said the words 'promise not to be mad,' which means I'm safe, because you promised."

"How did you know I said that?" I whispered, not mentioning how I'd only almost-but-not-quite said that. Then, with a thought, I added, "Wait. How did a *note* know that I said that?"

Another note fell on my head. I looked up this time before grabbing the note. I didn't see any more notes lurking above me. Still, I moved a step to the right.

The new note said,

"The previous note was on a type of touch paper that I've invented. It's like a touch pad, except it's paper, and it was able to measure the wind currents caused by the pronunciation of certain words, like 'promise,' and 'not' and 'mad.' So when you said them, the note knew to trigger the next stage. You should look at the original note now."

I picked up the original note, where there was now more writing. It was a thankfully short list of the dumb things Nate had done the previous day.

"ONE: I made some mini-ostriches.

TWO: I invented an infallible truth-telling serum.

THREE: I took all the science vials out of my book bag and hid them around town."

"You hid *what*?" I hissed, looking at the last entry. "Nate, those things are dangerous!" Nate's "science vials" are almost like magic potions, or pills that have incredible side effects, such as invisibility, or chameleon powers, or having lightning breath, the last one of which sounds so dangerous that I've always been too afraid to even *ask*.

"Oh, Nate," I whispered. "You just *can't* have scattered these around Polt. This could be catastrophic!"

Another note fell on my head.

It said,

"I know. Really dumb, right? I feel pretty good about it, too! Also, nearly ninety percent of people step to the right in order to avoid perceived danger, so it made it easy to predict that you would step to the right to avoid any more notes."

I swiveled in place and stomped off in the opposite direction, entirely ignoring how three notes fell to the floor behind me, and how another one dropped in front of my face.

"Nate!" I almost-nearly-shouted as I stomped closer to him. "Did you *really* leave your science potions all over town?"

"Yes," he said. "I did." The bookstore manager was grinning at us. I've noticed that whenever Nate has his gold elephant card in view, certain people turn all mushy-brained. We could've been talking about blowing up the moon, and the manager would've happily nodded and tried to sell Nate an umbrella for when all the moon-chunks started falling from the sky.

"But that's insane!" I told Nate. "Think of the chaos! *Anything* could happen! This could go *horribly* wrong!"

"I know," he said, beaming with pride. "I've really outdone myself this time!"

"This thing about the science vials," I said. "Tell me what you've done, and you'd *better* tell the truth." Nate and I were standing outside the bookstore and he was twitching, probably because of the way my Nate-punching fist was in Nate-punching position, right next to his shoulder.

"Oh, I'll definitely tell the truth," he said. "No choice, there." Usually he sounds confident and talks very quickly, but this time it was as if the words were being pulled from him, like a boot from mud.

I asked, "Nate, how many of your science vials did you hide around Polt?"

"Fifteen."

"Fifteen," I said, thinking of how that was more than enough to destroy the world sixteen times over. "Which ones?"

"Oh, there were 'Toad Finder' pills. And 'Lightning Breath' pills. And a 'Crayon Summoning' potion, and 'Handsome Day' pills. And 'Speed Runner' pills. And 'Chameleon' pills. And a 'Make Any Animal a Zebra' potion. And a 'Speed Reading' potion. And—"

"*Piffle!*" I said. Every time he named one of his inventions it hurt my head to think of all the trouble they could cause. The only one that sounded harmless was "Toad Finder." Well, "Crayon Summoning" didn't sound too horrible, either. What could go wrong with that? I like crayons.

I said, "Nate, we need to find these magic pills and potions of yours."

"That would probably be for the best," he said. "But I have to tell you the truth. They're not magic.

They're scientifically blended chemicals stabilized with micro-emulsions and mixed together at precise temperatures in a centrifuge."

"Fascinating," I said. "But what do you mean you have to tell me the truth?" Had we finally reached the stage of trust where Nate would tell me *everything*?

Nate said, "Remember how I said I invented an infallible truth-telling serum?"

"Yes. Although, honestly, that doesn't sound very dumb. You've invented *far* more questionable things in the past."

"Well . . . I drank it."

"Okay, *what*?" I hissed. "Nate, honestly, that *does* sound very dumb." Nate, with all he has in his head, is not a person who should be telling the truth.

He said, "It seemed reckless, and like something I would terribly regret, so obviously it was something I needed to do."

"We have different theories on the word 'obviously,' " I said. But . . . then, "Wait a minute. You *have* to tell me the truth? About *anything*? No matter *what* I ask you?"

"That's true. Although, now I'm nervous about that look in your eyes, so I almost wish I wouldn't have told you. But, you asked, so I had to answer as truthfully as I—"

"OH, THE POWER THAT I HOLD!" I yelled, startling everyone within hearing, meaning the entire block in this case, including people, birds, dogs, insects, cats, and in fact the only person or creature of any type that I didn't frighten was . . . Nate.

"I expected you to yell that loud," he said. "There was almost a hundred percent chance."

"Of course I yelled loud," I said. "You're the smartest person in existence, maybe the smartest person who's *ever* existed, and now you have to tell me the truth about *everything*. I can ask you the most important questions of all time, and *you have to answer honestly*."

"That's true," he said. "But I should point out that—"

"Which do you like more? Cake or pie?"

"Neither," Nate said. "And, that's the most important question you can think of? Never mind. I should have calculated that. Anyway, I have to point out that—"

"How can you like pie and cake *equally*? That's mathematically impossible."

"No it's not. Fifty percent of my preference goes to pie, and fifty percent goes to cake. There are variables involved, such as how I prefer apple pie over Bundt cake by a margin of eighty-two percent, and I like chocolate cake more than peach pie by a factor of three, but when the entirety of all known pies is matched against the vast wealth of cakes, I find that I'm exactly even."

"But that's not fair," I said.

"Math doesn't have to be fair."

"It never has been," I agreed, thinking of certain math tests that I'd not particularly enjoyed.

"Anyway, Delphine, there's something I should tell you before you continue yelling at me."

"It's true that I'm not done yelling at you," I admitted. "How could you do something so idiotic as to put your science vials all over—"

"Oh. My phone's ringing," he said.

"Nate," I all but growled as he started to answer his phone. "I'm talking to you. This is important."

"This is, too," he said, holding up his phone. "Not answering your phone is like pretending you're not available, and that would be dishonest." He moved the phone to his ear and said, "Hello?"

There was nothing I could do but wait. Well, I could also be irritated. And I could poke him in his arm several times while saying "*piffle*," rolling my eyes at him as he listened to whoever was on the phone.

"Who are you talking with?" I finally asked. Nate hadn't been saying anything except a few statements of "yes" and "no" and "I'm with Delphine."

"Maculte," Nate answered. "The leader of the Red Death Tea Society."

My skin went cold. My face flushed. I could feel my stomach tighten and my fingers begin to twitch.

"Wh-what?" I said. "You're not serious!" He had to be joking.

"I'm telling the truth," he said. "Have to." Then, into his phone, he said, "The first pills I hid were taped below Mrs. Isaacson's desk in her classroom at Polt Middle School."

"Why are you *telling* him that?"

"I have to," Nate said. "It's the truth." Then, into the phone, he said, "It's a small silver packet containing 'Speed Runner' pills." Nate listened for a bit, wincing, because I was hitting him in the shoulder at half strength while glaring at him with full power. After a moment, he told Maculte, "Okay. I understand. But Delphine and I are going to try to beat you there and get the pills *first*, and, to tell you the truth, I hope you lose."

He disconnected the call and slid his phone into his front shirt pocket. Most people don't like to carry their phones there, because they slip out when you lean over. But, most don't have a pocket made of intelligent fabric that will grab the phone if it starts to fall out, squeezing shut like a hand. So, Nate was well ahead of the game in that area, but then again most people don't tell their archenemies where to find dangerous technologies. So Nate was both the smartest boy on the whole planet and also, without a doubt, completely and utterly brainless.

"Why did you do that?" I said. "Nate, you just told the world's most maniacal criminal where you hid one of your inventions."

"That's what I was trying to tell you before," he said. "It's not just you that I'll be forced to tell the truth to, it's everyone."

"*Piffle*, Nate. Completely *piffle*." I couldn't even express how mad I was. I felt like there was steam coming out of my ears.

"This is the stupidest thing you've ever done!" I said.

"Yes. It is," Nate answered, telling the truth.

Before we even made it to the car, we saw Kip Luppert, one of our classmates. Kip was carrying four gallons of red paint to his parents' car, struggling with the weight, because Kip is about as muscular as Nate, which is not a compliment.

"How are you today?" Kip asked, sweating with his efforts.

"Not good," Nate answered. "I've done a really dumb thing, and also I think I drank too much cinnamon-radish lemonade, which is a drink I'm experimenting with, and in addition to that I bumped my head on a particle accelerator that I constructed out of soup cans and the remains of a robot I built in third grade."

"Huh?" Kip said.

"Nate's just kidding," I said, grabbing Nate by his arm and dragging his truth-telling butt away from our classmate.

"No I'm not!" Nate yelled back to Kip.

"Any money you can spare?" a panhandler asked us. He was no more than twenty years old, wearing hipster glasses and boots that were obviously so expensive that he had no need to be asking strangers for money. He had short hair, a girl's name (Celia) tattooed on his neck, and a mustache that twirled into complete circles at the tips.

"I *do* have rather a lot of money I don't need," Nate told him, reaching into his pockets and taking out what seemed to be hundreds of dollars, giving it all to the panhandler, who gasped in surprise as I quickly moved on, tugging the world's most honest boy along with me.

We'd only taken about five steps when Melville, my pet bee, came in for a landing on my shoulder.

"Bzzz?" she asked.

"We're going to the school," I answered, glaring at Nate. "Nate did something . . . not so very smart."

"Bzzz," Melville said.

"*So* true," I told her. "It's *not* like the first time ever."

Together, my bee and I frowned at Nate.

Bosper was at our car, staring at the door, wanting inside.

"Bosper is here by the car but not being inside," he said. "Why does the girl smell like bad adventure?"

"I smell like bad adventure? What do you mean?"

"The dog has a nose that says things," Bosper said.

"Okay," I said. He'd explained . . . nothing. No wonder he's Nate's dog.

"Girl smells like yelling?" Bosper said, trying again.

"That would make sense," I said. "I've been doing some yelling. I probably reek of it."

Nate said, "Bosper's nose is talented enough that he can smell moods and feelings, like that day when I put on my mechanical dog's nose." The first time I'd ever met Nate he'd strapped on an invention of his, a technological wonder of a nose, and he was able to actually *smell* that he and I were going to be friends. I wondered if I smelled very friendly just then. I probably did. Just because your friends do idiotic things doesn't mean they're not your friends. They're just your idiotic friends now.

I said, "I thought Bosper could only smell peanut butter." I knew he could smell a lot more than peanut butter, but I was making a joke about the impressively single-minded focus that Bosper sometimes has about peanut butter.

"Peanut butter," Bosper said in a voice as if he'd just fallen in love, which was farcical, because he had *long* since fallen in love with peanut butter.

"Oh," Nate said, suddenly acting very uneasy. And he was trying to avoid eye contact with Bosper.

"Something wrong with peanut butter?" I asked. I was speaking to Nate, but Bosper was the one who answered, because terriers always barge into conversations about peanut butter. It's genetics.

"Peanut butter is bad for dogs," Bosper said. His voice was full of sorrow and woe, and many other words that mean much the same thing.

"It is?" I said. I hadn't thought it was. I've heard chocolate is bad for dogs, and of course that's an unspeakable tragedy in their lives, but as far as I knew they were good with peanut butter. In fact, I'd once watched Bosper eat a glob of peanut butter bigger than he was.

"No," Nate said. "Peanut butter isn't bad for dogs."

Bosper went suddenly still. Terriers normally keep moving, as if they're constantly hearing music in their heads and can't help but shake their little rumps, but now, Bosper was like a statue.

Except for two . . .

. . . slow . . .

. . . blinks.

"The dog was told peanut butter was bad for him," Bosper said. He was definitely holding back a growl.

"Ahhh, yes," Nate said. "That." He adjusted his glasses.

"*Is* the peanut butter bad for dogs?" Bosper said. There was that lurking growl again.

"No," Nate said. "Not really. It's just . . . I told you that because you kept eating all the peanut butter."

"That is what the peanut butter is for!" Bosper said. "The peanut butter is for the peanut eating!"

"Enough of all this," I said. "We're in a race." I started to explain that we were racing Maculte to Polt Middle School, to where Nate had hidden the packet of "Speed Runner" pills, but apparently you should never mention a race to a talking terrier, because they *love* it. They just *love* racing.

"Race!" Bosper yelled, and he spun around in a tight circle, and then dashed off down the sidewalk at top speed, yelling, "The dog can be winning the race!"

"Should we get him back?" I asked Nate.

"No need. He might even beat us there."

"Did you really lie to him about peanut butter?" I asked, getting into the car, grinning, because I also love racing.

"I did," Nate said. He was getting behind the steering wheel, whispering. I wondered why he was whispering. Maybe because Melville, my bee, had curled up in the backseat and was sleeping?

"Okay," I said. "First of all, now that I know you've lied to Bosper, have you ever lied to *me*?" It was a merciless question, but he'd been foolish enough to drink his honesty invention, and I felt duty bound to discover certain truths, like if Nate had ever lied to me, or if he thought I'd looked awesome the time I was riding

28

a hippopotamus like a horse. I highly suspected I knew the answer to that last one, because *of course* I did.

I said, "And, another question, why are you whispering?" When I'd spoken my first question Nate had grimaced, and when I asked my second question he slumped over and thumped his head on the steering wheel, like you do when you feel overwhelmed. I've literally seen Nate wearing a nuclear bomb and the pressure has never been too high for him before.

"I've lied to you twenty-seven times," Nate said. His eyes were closed and he was still slumped forward against the steering wheel, so it was not a fair time to punch him in the arm.

"**Piffle!**" I said, unfairly punching Nate in the arm. "Twenty-seven times! We're supposed to be friends!"

"Sometimes it's friendlier to lie," Nate said. "And sometimes it would be too embarrassing not to lie." I thought about that, and I supposed it was true. I wondered how many times I'd lied to Nate. It was more than twenty-seven, I'd bet.

I said, "We'll talk about this later, when we're not in a race. I'm guessing you regret ever drinking your honesty-potion-thingy, don't you?"

"I do," Nate said. "I don't think I've ever regretted one of my Friday the thirteenth dumb things more than this." We were driving down Alabaster Street, past a row of food carts, like Polly's Pastry Palace, and Thai High, and Burrito Angels, which is run by three Spanish women who dress like angels and serve what I honestly do believe to be heavenly burritos.

I said, "You didn't answer my question about why you were whispering." Nate groaned and his head slumped even farther forward against the steering wheel. Despite how we were zooming down the street, I wasn't worried, because we don't actually *drive* when we're in the car. This is because Nate's car is actually intelligent. Her name is Betsy and she's pretty great, although she has a bit of a crush on Nate and . . .

"Oh," I said, realizing what was going on.

I told Nate, "I'm sorry," and put an apologetic hand on his shoulder, right at the spot where he's usually deserving to be punched.

Nate, forced to be honest when he answered my question, said, "I was whispering because I didn't want Betsy to know I'm now scientifically programmed to tell the truth."

"You are?" Betsy said. Yeah. She can talk.

"I'm *so* sorry," I told Nate again, finally understanding why he'd been whispering. Betsy is great and I completely love her, but . . . she can be difficult.

"How do you feel about me?" she asked. There. See? It was a difficult question.

"Uhh," Nate said.

"Saying 'uhh' does *not* count as telling the truth," Betsy said. Her voice comes from the glove box. It was rattling the entire car. "I spend my days driving you everywhere, utterly devoted, and I think it's only fair that you answer my question. So, Nathan . . . how do you feel about me?"

"Oooh," Nate said. He sounded like a duck with a raging stomachache.

Luckily, it was at that moment that we were attacked. Yes, I do know that "being attacked" is not generally noted as being wonderful, but if you'd seen Nate's face in those moments . . . tottering as he was on the edge of being scientifically forced to answer Betsy's question . . . you'd understand why, when the laser beams began to shoot out from the buildings all around us, it really *was* for the best.

"Oooch," Betsy said as the lasers focused on her. Other laser beams, barely missing us, were cutting swaths through the street, gouging holes in the sidewalks, cutting a fire hydrant in half, and slicing off the top of a mailbox, even chopping over a streetlight that crashed among a group of pedestrians, sending them scrambling for safety.

"Oh boy!" Nate said. "We're being attacked!"

See? It *was* for the best.

But I did worry about Betsy, because I'd seen what those lasers could do, and if they could slice through a streetlight and mailboxes, then where did that leave *Betsy*? Also, where did that leave Nate and me, since if the lasers cut through Betsy, they would also cut through . . .

"Uhh, Nate?" I said. It no longer seemed quite so wonderful that we were being attacked. In fact, I was fully prepared to vote against it.

"We'll be fine," Nate said. "Betsy's variable atomic structure is designed to absorb light, even that from lasers. You see, the photonic wavelength will—"

"Hey, Betsy?" I said.

"Yes?"

"You okay?"

"It tickles, but I'm fine."

"Good," I told her. "Nate was starting to go on about science, and I really didn't understand what he was talking about."

"He's difficult to talk to sometimes."

"Yeah."

"But he has a nice smile," Betsy said. "It makes my tires squeal."

"Yeah," I said again, mostly because I had no idea what else I could have possibly said.

"We *are* being attacked here," Nate mentioned,

truthfully. The lasers had ceased firing from all around us, but men and women were now rushing out from various doorways and crashing out from windows, all of them wearing the distinctively colored suits of the Red Death Tea Society.

There were possibly as many as twenty of these men and women, each of them with a laser-shooter-thingy that looked like a chubby spear, except the ends had fiercely glowing blue lights instead of being sharp and pointy. The assassins were also all carrying tea-cups, sipping from them during the attack. This made the attack seem slightly more casual, although not any less lethal.

"Hmm," Nate said. "We can't let them delay us. They're just trying to slow us down so that Maculte can reach the school first. That's *not* going to happen."

He stopped, and his eyes narrowed, like the way a gunfighter's eyes do in the western movies.

"Betsy," he said. "I am authorizing *Rocket One Mode*." His voice was grim.

"Rocket One Mode?" she said. The glove box vibrated. Her voice was breathy.

"Rocket One Mode?" I asked. My voice was con-fused. What was Rocket One Mode? Were we going to fire rockets at the assassins from the Red Death Tea

Society? I wasn't sure if that was the smartest thing to do, because there were other people around and—

CLICK.

It was a loud noise, and it was also *more* than a noise, because some weird seat belts sprang out from my seat and wrapped around me before I could blink. The seat belts were like tubes, with some sort of liquid inside them.

"What is—?" I asked, but that was as far as I got before . . .

CLICK.

And then . . .

GLURGLE GLURGLE.

My seat suddenly came to life, gone soft and liquid, with the whole seat wrapping around me as if I'd fallen into a big tub of warm jelly.

And then . . . **RUMBLE**.

"Rumble?" I said. My voice was still quite confused.

"Rumble," Betsy said, and then I was slammed back into my tub of jelly (meaning, my seat) because we were suddenly *blasting* forward at speeds that made the buildings around us blur.

"Rocket Three!" Betsy said, the most excited I've ever heard her.

"T-t-take th-this p-pill," Nate told me. He was

holding out a blue-colored pill, stuttering because the acceleration was making it difficult to talk, difficult to do *anything*. It felt as if a giant hand was pushing at me, and also like there was a giant gas bubble being squeezed out of me.

"BURP!" I told Nate. That was the "gas bubble" thing.

"Wh-what?" he said.

"I m-meant o-*okay!*" I was fighting to raise my hand and take the pill, but it felt like there was an anchor tied to my arm. It was lucky I'd been doing my adventure exercises, having built an obstacle course in my backyard so that I can work out every day and get into "adventure" shape. My obstacle course has a row of hurdles (which I can totally jump over, even backward) and a series of ropes that I either swing from or climb up, and there's a punching bag on which I've painted the faces of Jakob Maculte and Luria Pevermore, the two leaders of the Red Death Tea Society. All in all, I *rule* that obstacle course, so my arms were powerful enough to lift that blue pill of Nate's despite the way gravity was hugely increased (and immensely annoyed) by the speeds Nate and I were traveling. It was an effort, though, so I hoped that things wouldn't get any worse, because—

"Rocket Two!" Betsy yelled.

"**Guhh**," I gurgled.

We were moving even faster now, zooming through Polt at speeds that made the blocks go by in heartbeats.

I swallowed the blue pill. It was difficult. The sheer force of our speed was increasing the pull of gravity, and gravity gets irritable when you make it work that hard. It fights back.

But, I instantly began to feel better. The pressure eased off, and I even began to feel comfortable. The bubble seat was quite cushy.

"What was that pill?" I asked Nate.

"'Gravity Adjuster.' It works by enveloping each of our molecules in a protective bath of neutrino barriers, the force of which pulsates with billions of micro-explosions that counteract the pull of gravity by—"

"Got it, Nate," I said, which was a lie, but I've never been personally troubled by any need to tell the truth, as my parents have so often noted.

"So, we're good, then?" I asked.

"We are," Nate said. "But I can't make the micro-explosions too powerful without endangering molecular bonds, so while we're safe at Rocket Three, and even Rocket Two, it's going to get uncomfortable again when Betsy goes to—"

"Rocket One!" Betsy yelled. Everything turned into light. Just . . . whooshing lights. Streams of color. Nothing made any sense. I had that tingling sensation of when you've been sitting in one place for too long, and you get up quickly and take a few steps and then your blood goes all whooshy and your body says, "Hey, *whoa*! I wasn't ready for *that*!"

I was slammed literally into my seat, enveloped by the liquid, and I have to say that I no longer felt like I was floating in a tub of jelly; I felt like a doughnut being dipped into scalding hot coffee.

"**Gahh**," I told Nate.

"The pressure *is* rather intense," he agreed. "Luckily, it won't last long. Now that we've left the Red Death Tea Society behind and can travel uninterrupted, we should be at the school in seven seconds. Make that *six* seconds now. Five. Four. Thr—"

And then we were attacked.

There was a look of surprise on Nate's face, which is something I don't see very often. He once told me he's only truly surprised five times a year, on average, although he added that this calculation doesn't account for what he calls the "Delphine Factor," because my actions apparently don't fit into mathematical formulas and I'm too difficult to predict. It's one of the reasons he likes me.

"**Gahh!**" Nate said as our car suddenly veered sideways. There'd been an impact.

A big one.

"*Piffle!*" I said. A crack appeared in my window. Then a face was there, emerging from the brightly streaming colors. It was only there for a moment, like a ghost. Then it was gone and Betsy started shaking and shuddering.

"Guh gug guh," I said, trying to form words, but the car was shaking too violently and more faces were appearing outside the windows. They were evil, leering faces. With eager, malevolent smiles.

There was a distinct smell of tea.

The windshield began to break.

One thing I admire about Nate is that he remains calm during stressful situations. He doesn't panic. We've gotten together to watch scary movies, like *Hotel of a Hundred Zombies*, and *Motel of a Hundred Zombies*, and *Tree Fort of a Hundred Zombies*, but I have to say that I don't think I'll be inviting him over to watch the recently released *Tennis Court of a Hundred Zombies*. I'll most likely invite Liz, and Stine, and Ventura, because *they* know how to watch zombie movies. Whenever the zombies attack, Liz will shriek and throw marshmallows at the television, and Stine starts trembling and hugs her pillows, and of course Ventura gets up and runs around like there's a zombie in the room and she needs to escape. What I mean is, they act *properly*. Nate, on the other hand, begins to . . . analyze.

"Their best chance of survival is to flee," he'll say when the people open their hotel room to find a zombie waiting behind the door. Then he'll show me some equations he's scribbled on his pants, or on his hand, or that he's doodled with his finger in our pizza sauce, despite how I've told him that pizza is sacred and that he could literally go to prison for life.

Or, other times he'll say, "Since a zombie's decaying flesh will emit a distinct odor, why aren't these people constructing any mechanical sensory apparatus that could detect this scent, and therefore the zombies, from a safe distance? Failing that, why not just befriend a dog? Because a dog could sense the zombies from as far as five miles away, and even provide protection."

Nate said this, incidentally, when Bosper was shivering beneath a blanket, meaning he would've been useless in any attack that didn't *specifically* involve a zombie's favorite blanket.

The point is, Nate doesn't ever panic. It's just not who he is.

"**Gahh!**" Nate said, totally panicking. It was up to me to take charge.

"**Gahh!**" I said, totally panicking.

Sometimes panic is like a virus. It can spread from person to person and suddenly there's an epidemic, except instead of sneezing and coughing and wondering what to do with your tissues, you're shrieking like a terrier hiding beneath a checkerboard blanket.

"This shouldn't be possible!" Nate said. "*Nobody* can catch up with Betsy during Rocket One!" Despite Nate's words, there was ample evidence to the contrary, meaning there was a man standing on the hood of our car, even though we were moving so fast that everything else was just a stream of frankly nauseating colors. The man was seven feet tall with a big muscle-bursting chest and cruel eyes. He had a sneering mouth and long black hair that was whipping around in the wind created by our speed. His arms were covered with horrible scars and intricate tattoos of teacups and tea packets. He was carrying a weird mechanical device about the size of a small microwave and . . . with his muscles straining against the pull of gravity . . . he twisted a dial on the side of it and then slammed it down onto Betsy's hood so forcefully that it left a huge dent. It stuck there on her hood, despite how the roaring winds should've torn it away.

"What's *that*?" I yelled. "Some sort of magnet?" To be entirely honest, I'd caught the panic virus in a bad way. I wanted to hug pillows and toss marshmallows and I wanted to run around in fright, but that's very difficult to do when you're strapped into a car seat.

"Oh," Nate said. "Hmm. A magnet." He'd calmed down. Entirely. He looked thoughtful and even . . . happy. Unfortunately, I myself did not catch the Happy Virus. I was still caught in the grip of the Panic Flu.

"You're right," Nate said. "They have to be doing this with magnets. You're so smart!" He looked over to me with eyes that made me blush. I didn't feel smart, right then. I felt foolish. But I also felt a flood of relief and I wasn't panicked anymore, at least.

"I was right?" I said.

"Yes. You see, Betsy achieves Rocket One speed by oscillating back and forth between S-Pole and N-Pole, playing them off against each other to accelerate."

"That's very nice of her," I said. I'm often at a loss to respond when Nate starts talking about science.

"What I mean is, it's like magnets. Betsy is manip-ulating magnetic fields, or at least manipulating her place in them, fluctuating her atomic structure so that the earth's magnetic field is acting as a slipstream accelerant."

"Ooo!" I said. "I almost understood that one." Being friends with Nate, listening to what he has to say, is like running the obstacle course in my backyard. The more I do it, the better I'm getting.

"But the Red Death Tea Society is using it against us," Nate said. "They're linking magnetic waves, coupling them, so that they're stuck to us like glue."

"So we can't outrace them?" I asked. This was *not* good news. The cracks in Betsy's windows were spreading outward. The faces appearing through the blur of the colors were staying longer, peering in through the windows. The man on our car hood was assembling another device.

"No," Nate said. "We can't outrace them." His voice was grim, but almost even before he'd spoken, Betsy started laughing.

"Ha ha ha ha ha," she said.

"Why's she laughing?" I asked Nate.

"I'm not sure," he said. "Neat! This day is full of surprises!" It was at that moment that our neat day, full of surprises, became even neater and more surprising. My eyes went wide. Nate's eyes went even wider. The eyes of the assassins from the Red Death Tea Society went widest of all.

"Rocket Zero," Betsy said.

"Rocket *Zero*?" Nate said. "There *is* no Rocket Zero!"

But there was. Betsy, already going faster than I could possibly conceive, began accelerating. In fact, she was accelerating at an accelerated rate.

"Ha ha ha ha ha!" Betsy yelled. "Rocket Zero!" The man on the hood started flapping like a flag in a tornado, his feet anchored to the hood by the power of magnets. It did not look comfortable. He was thumping back and forth on his face and his butt. Meanwhile, the magnet-machine was sliding toward the edge of Betsy's hood. The faces in the windows were becoming distorted.

"This is amazing!" Nate said. "Betsy is learning on her own! I hadn't predicted this!"

"I do have a few secrets, Nate," Betsy said. "Even from you." She made it sound like a challenge.

"Are you using a photonic drive? A magnetic monopole to catalyze proton decay into a positron and a pi meson, harnessing the energy release and transforming it into acceleration?"

"Maaaaybe," Betsy said.

"I'm impressed," Nate said. Our whole car turned red and shivered. The faces in the windows were beginning to fall away, one by one, sucked away into the winds. The giant man on our hood was whisked off into the colorful void. Our speeds were inconceivable. We were whooshing through clouds. We were whooshing over treetops. My stomach was whooshy. I saw Polt Middle School, but we whooshed right past it. And then, there it was *again*, even though I'm pretty sure we hadn't turned around. I tried not to think about how fast we must be going.

"Please prepare for impact," Betsy said, which is never a line I favor hearing, though it's becoming surprisingly commonplace in my life.

And then . . . *impact*.

We landed in the parking lot. *Hard.* Just before we hit, I could see that Betsy's sides were smoking, like we were a comet, or a meteor. Betsy's wheels touched concrete, caught for a second, and then the rear of the car came up over the front and we began to roll and bounce and crash and do a bunch of other things that I found to be disagreeable.

"I was clearly not prepared for impact!" I mentioned. Betsy kept bouncing. Tumbling. Rolling. Nate and I were being flung all over, and everything in the car was whooshing around us. Nate's messenger bag, the one where he carries his science vials, now mostly empty, kept thumping off my face. And there were five bottles of mustard being flung around, and a pair of shoes, and several books, and some socks that smelled like they either should be in an emergency laundry basket or, even better, an incinerator.

"*Piffle!*" I yelped, on the third, fifth, and twenty-seventh bounces. I was shouting loud enough to be heard over the car crash, because I wanted my opinion to be known. There was a constant barrage of shuddering impacts. My body felt like it was buzzing. Like I was full of electricity. Like I was surrounded by fireflies. Like . . . ʰᵐᵐᵐ. I actually *was* surrounded by fireflies. Tiny metal fireflies.

"What's this?" I said, pointing to one of the fireflies during the thirty-first and thirty-second bounces.

"Barrier gnats," Nate said. "Robots. Protecting us from impact."

"And, how are they doing that?" I asked. I was bouncing all over the car as Betsy rolled and tumbled, but I definitely *had* noted that I wasn't being hurt. It was like an amusement park ride, where everything seems to be chaos, but you're safe for the most part, except your stomach is questioning why you ate so much cotton candy.

"They're like little catchers' mitts," Nate said.

"Every time we almost smack into something, they catch us, and push us the other way."

"Tiny helpers," I said. "Got it."

"Would you like to know how they work?" he asked.

"Gosh no," I said, then, "C'mon, Nate!" because the car had finally rolled to a stop and the race was on to beat Maculte and the Red Death Tea Society to that hidden vial. I checked on Melville (my bee woke up when I shook her, looked around, and then went back to sleep), and then Nate and I crawled out of Betsy.

She was still laughing.

"That was fun!" she told me, even though she could clearly see that my hair was a mess and that I'd squished an entire bottle of mustard against my leg. Nate, in the past week, had been running an experiment on mustards, and there were several squeezy bottles in the back of the car. Apparently, the whole of his experiment was, "Which mustard tastes better?" That sounds like a rational bit of research, but I was relatively certain the experiment would turn weird. That's just Nate.

"Are you okay?" I asked Betsy. The cracks in her windshield were already fixing themselves, and the dents were popping back out into proper shape. That's one of the benefits of being a talking car made of unstable molecules.

"I'm fine," Betsy said. "But you have mustard on your leg."

"I do." There was no denying it.

"Mustard?" Nate asked. "Is that my mustard?"

"I rarely carry my own bottles of mustard, Nate, so, yes . . . I'd say it was probably your mustard."

"This could be a problem," he said.

I told him, "There are these wonderful devices called 'washing machines,' Nate. I bet they could solve this 'mustard stains on my pants' dilemma." I was already running toward the school. Luckily, it wasn't in session right then, so we were unlikely to be disturbed, except for a few of the janitors.

"I know about washing machines," Nate said, jogging along with me. "They're primitive. Ion bombardments are far more effective at cleansing materials, but the particular problem that I was talking about is—"

"Dog smells mustard?" Bosper said. The terrier was on the front steps. How he'd made it there before us, I have no idea, but I've learned not to ask Bosper how he does things, because he's worse than Nate at explanations. He gets too excited talking about math, the shifting planes of reality, and quantum alignment, and—

47

"Rarr rarr rarrr!" Bosper said. Or, actually . . . he *barked* it.

"Hmmm," Nate said.

"Unfortunate," Betsy said.

"What?" I asked. But it was at that moment that Bosper, snarling mad, came running for me.

"Bosper?" I said. It almost looked like he was going to attack me.

"Attack!" Bosper yelled, so that settled that. The terrier was racing after me, snapping at my leg. At my *mustard leg* in particular.

"Why is he attacking me?" I shrieked. "This is entirely **piffle!**"

"He's allergic to mustard!" Nate said. "It makes him crazy! And it interferes with his acceleration!"

"It does *not* interfere with his acceleration!" I said. "He's too fast!" I was trying to get away from the terrier, but Bosper was far too quick, thanks to that unfair advantage that four-legged creatures have over us lesser-legged beings. Four legs are faster than two.

"I meant it interferes with the way I accelerated his brain!" Nate said. "With the method I used to make him smarter. And . . . oh! You shouldn't let him bite you!"

"Why not?" I shouted, trying to keep Betsy between Bosper and me.

"Because it would hurt," Nate said.

"Oh, *duh*. I thought you meant something *extra*. Like, you'd given him anti-matter teeth or something." I was crawling on top of Betsy, where Bosper couldn't reach me.

"He can totally reach you up there," Betsy said, as if she could read my thoughts, although I might point out that she didn't read my mind in time to stop me from crawling onto her hood, where Bosper easily jumped up and started biting at me. Luckily, he just sank his teeth into my pants leg.

"Nate," I said. "If it isn't too much trouble, could you do some *genius* thing? Your dog is attacking me, and while I don't mean to cast any blame, this is *entirely your fault*."

Nate began fiddling with an odd device that he took out of his messenger bag. It looked like a transparent can of tennis balls, except the balls were bright red and spinning around. Plus, there was a small keyboard on the side. Quickly tapping on the keys, Nate said, "No problem! I can solve this! I'll project a hologram of a cat, and that should distract Bosper long enough that we can get into the school, where he can't follow."

Tap tap tap. This was the noise of Nate's fingers on the keys.

"Quack?" This was the sound of a perplexed duck that had suddenly appeared in the parking lot.

"That's a duck!" This was the noise of *me*, an outraged seventh grade girl named Delphine Cooper as she was being attacked by a dog.

"Ooo." This was the sound of Nate, a boy I oftentimes consider to be a genius, and oftentimes do not.

Nate said, "My holo-projector must have been damaged in the accident. It's showing the wrong images. Here, I'll try again."

Tap tap tappity-tap. That was the sound of Nate's fingers on the keyboard, again.

"That is not a cat!" This was me, again, deciding that Nate was definitely not a genius, because while the duck *had* disappeared, there was now a huge crowd of bears all over the parking lot.

"*Piffle!*" I said, leaping off from the car, with Bosper hanging from my pants leg and growling at me.

"Give me that!" I told Nate, grabbing the device from his hands. I spelled out "cat," on the keyboard, then looked up. There was a giant watermelon. Useless. So I spelled out "feline" on the keyboard, then looked up. There was a giant picture of Susan Heller, the girl Nate has a crush on. She was blinking her eyes in an alluring manner.

"*Really*, Nate?" I said, glaring at him. He had the

decency to blush, and I would've gone over to him and delivered a well-earned punch on his shoulder, but his dog was chewing on my pants, and if I didn't deal with it soon, then Bosper was going to start chewing on my leg.

So I spelled out "peanut butter" on the keyboard.

"Hmmm," I said when I looked up. There were three jars of peanut butter on the parking lot. Two of them were of the chunky variety, and the third was creamy. The hologram was so complete that I could even smell the rich aroma. Nate's inventions truly are amazing. It was almost as if there really *were* three actual jars of peanut butter on the parking lot.

Although they did have spider legs.

"Ick," I said. What else do you say about spider legs?

"Hmm," Nate said, which is not what you say about three jars of peanut butter scurrying away on spider legs.

"Oh, ick," Betsy said. Properly.

"Is butter of peanuts?" Bosper growled out. His voice wasn't anything near normal. He sounded like his throat was full of potato chips. He let go of my pants leg and stared at the peanut butter jars racing away on their icky disgusting spider legs.

Then hurried off in pursuit.

"Hooray!" Nate said. "It worked!"

"Ugg," I said. "I will never again eat peanut butter without thinking of spider legs."

"A certain number of arachnids fall into the peanut butter vats during peanut butter production, anyway," Nate said. "So, *whenever* you eat peanut butter, there's a small chance you're actually eating spider legs."

I stared at him.

I *so* stared at him.

Betsy rolled back away from us, giving me punching room.

"**Piffle**," I said. Low in my throat. Like a growl.

Chapter 3

Our school's front door was locked.

That was no problem for someone like me, who has an adventure kit and who trains in her backyard obstacle course, meaning it was simply a matter of shimmying up the side of the nearest tree, balancing myself while walking along a branch, jumping onto a second-story ledge of Polt Middle School, and then opening a window to slide inside.

Where I found Nate waiting for me.

"How'd you get in here so fast?" I asked.

"My shirt can unlock doors," he said, tapping on his shirt.

"Okay," I said, totally accepting Nate's answer, because it seemed highly probable that an explanation would either take too long or make me crazy, and either way we didn't have time. There was a race to be won.

We ran out into the hall. We needed to make it

to Mrs. Isaacson's classroom, where Nate had taped the packet of "Speed Runner" pills beneath her desk. And we needed to do it before . . .

"Uh-oh," I said.

There were two teacups on the hallway floor.

It could only mean one thing.

"They're here," I said, pointing to the teacups. My voice echoed in the empty halls. It sounded ominous.

"And recently, too," Nate said. "They put down those teacups two minutes and thirteen seconds ago."

"How can you know that?"

"The temperature of a human body is 98.6 degrees, so it's just simple math to measure the residual warmth on the teacups and calculate how long they've been cooling since human contact."

"Nice," I said. "You're like one of those cowboys who can track horses across the wilderness. Can you tell which way they went? How many there are?"

"Yes," Nate said. "There were four of them. And they went down the hall that way."

"Cool!" I said, looking to Nate in amazement. "How did you know that? More temperature measures? Air displacement? Something to do with scent residue or vibration patterns on the floor?" I like to think that I'm beginning to understand Nate's mind.

"No," he said. "I just looked down the hall." He pointed back over my shoulder.

I turned around.

There were four of them. Red Death Tea Society members. Two women walking together, and, a bit farther back, another woman and a man pushing a tea trolley.

The man with the tea trolley said, "Hey. Is that Nate and Delphine?"

I said, "No." But, since I did not think my amazing subterfuge would last very long, I decided to run.

Clop clop clop! That was the noise of my shoes against the hallway floor. It was a noise that was not, unfortunately, accompanied by the noise of Nate's shoes running along *with* me. Instead, it was *tap tap tappity-tap* as Nate quickly typed something on his malfunctioning holographic projector and then . . .

There were bears all over the hallway. I'd guess there were about twenty bears on the floor, and during any normal day that would mean there were twenty bears *total*, because bears are floor-oriented animals. Mostly, bears stay on *forest* floors, but very occasionally and very unfortunately they're on a hall-way floor. This time, however, there were also bears bounding along on the walls and even crawling across the ceiling as if they were spiders. If you've ever looked above your head and seen a spider on the ceiling, you've probably thought to yourself, "*Gahh* and *ick* and *piffle*! I do not like having a spider above my head!"

I can assure you that it's preferable to having a bear on the ceiling.

The assassins began yelling in fright, but at the same time mobilizing into action, activating their force fields and energizing their disintegrator pistols and being careful not to upset their tea trolley, because their tea was almost prepared and they were thirsty.

"C'mon," Nate whispered to me, leaning in close to be heard over the roar of what I hoped were illusionary bears. I mean, I knew that they were being projected by Nate's hologram device, but . . .

. . . well, they *smelled* like bears. All musty and muddy and sweaty and stinky, like raw meat in mud.

And they *sounded* like bears, all roaring and heaving and panting, filling the air with their bellows of rage.

And they *felt* like bears, because I could feel them brushing against me as they charged around, hurrying here and there, and I could even feel the drops of slobber from the ones on the ceiling, which is exactly as gross as it sounds, and maybe even a little more.

So they smelled like bears and they looked like bears, and they sounded and felt like bears, so maybe they *were* bears? The only remaining one of the five senses was taste, and I did not want to taste the bears, and I especially did not want them to taste me.

"C'mon, to . . . *where?*" I asked Nate. "And . . . are these bears *real?*"

"We need to get to Mrs. Isaacson's room. And the bears are only forty percent real."

"You just one hundred percent terrified me," I noted. But by then he was taking my arm, picking me up, and tossing me over his shoulder.

Which was unexpected.

First, this is not the way that Nathan Bannister acts. Second, while I only weigh about ninety-three pounds, that's about ninety-three more pounds than it looks like Nate could lift. And yet he tossed me over his shoulder like I was nothing and began running down the hall at top speed, occasionally leaping over bears.

"If you're wondering how I can carry you," he said, "it's because I'm wearing power gloves." He was indeed wearing gloves. They were paper thin and skin-colored, so I hadn't noticed them at first, but now they were softly glowing.

"What—" I started to say, but then he ran up onto the side of the wall, so that we were running along the wall as if it were no big deal. My sense of sanity thought it was a big deal, and it closed its eyes.

"Power shoes," Nate said.

"There they are!" one of the assassins yelled as we began to race past them. She was in her early thirties, with long blond hair. She drank from a teacup, one finger pointing out to us. The other three assassins all pointed their guns in our direction, which I found to be disconcerting.

"Go away!" Nate yelled.

It was like an explosion. The cult members, the tea trolley, even some of the bears . . . they were all flung into the air by the force of Nate's shout, with fur flying and tea spilling and limbs flailing and teacups shattering. One of the women hit her head on the wall and was knocked unconscious. The man was all tangled up in the tea trolley. Another of the women was flung through the door to Mrs. Isaacson's classroom, smashing it down. The last woman managed to stay on her feet for a moment, but then fell as unconscious as the others.

"Power tongue!" Nate told me, showing me his tongue, which had what seemed to be a rubber band around it, glowing a neon green. It was rather gross, but . . . as Nate once told me . . . science is *often* gross.

"Power tongue?" I said. "What's that?"

"Oh. I can speak different languages with it."

"Okay."

"And shout really loud."

"So I noticed."

"And spit over a hundred feet."

"Nice! You totally *have* to make me one of those." My brother Steve was suddenly in *serious* trouble. He'd recently made up songs about how poorly I dress and how sloppily I eat, but soon he would fall to my wrath . . . from a hundred feet away. I was well into daydreaming about spitwad cannon fire when Chester Humes peeked out from the classroom and said, "Hello?"

Chester is a year younger than Nate and me. He's in sixth grade, and always wears blue shirts and yellow pants, usually with red socks, meaning he's rather colorful. He enjoys singing and often does so in the halls, where it is not generally acceptable to sing and where many people make fun of him, despite how he has a nice voice. He doesn't mind when people make fun of him, though, because he says that he enjoys singing more than he's bothered by jerks, so why let them stop him?

I respect him for that.

"Hello?" he said again, looking outside in the hall. "What's going on?"

"We're playing soccer," I said. Again, my skills of deception are not always at the top of their game.

"Are those bears?" Chester said. His voice was squeaking.

"No," I said.

"They look like bears."

"Why are you so fixated on the bears?" I asked, pushing Chester into the room, yanking Nate inside. "And why are you here? I thought the building was closed."

"It is, but I'm on cleaning duty. This room is a mess! Bubblegum under the seats. Dust everywhere. Scuff marks on the floor. And somebody taped *this* under Mrs. Isaacson's desk." He held up a silver packet. It was clearly labeled "Speed Runner" in Nate's handwriting.

"That's mine," I said. "I left it here by mistake."

"Really?" Chester said. He looked to Nate for confirmation.

"No," Nate said. "Delphine is lying." I'd forgotten about Nate having to tell the truth all the time. A bit inconvenient now.

Nate said, "It's a packet of 'Speed Runner' pills. They enrich your metabolism a thousandfold, super-charging your atomic structure, effectively making you as fast as lightning. I hid it under the desk because

I schedule myself to do dumb things, just to keep life adventurous."

Chester was simply staring at Nate.

Nate said, "We came here because the Red Death Tea Society is trying to steal as many of my inventions as possible. We can't let that packet fall into their hands. The fate of the entire world is at risk. Your clothes do not match."

"What?"

"Sorry. That last bit slipped out."

It was at that moment that the windows exploded. In fact, it was not only at *that* moment that the windows exploded, but also several *following* moments. It was the slowest explosion I've ever seen, with the windows bursting and glass flying everywhere, with the desks being pushed away from the walls with the concussion of the blast and the ceiling tiles rippling and shattering as the explosion reached them, but instead of it happening fast, it was slow as molasses.

"What's happening?" I asked Nate, taking a few steps back.

"Slowstorm," he said.

"Snowstorm?" I asked. There wasn't any snow. And it wasn't cold.

"No. *Slow*storm. One of Maculte's inventions. It slows time by a factor of almost a thousand. But there's a tremendous energy outlay involved. Look at your hair."

"It got messed up during the car crash! You can't blame me for what it looks like! And it's none of your business!" I was getting ready to punch Nate in the arm again. Secretly, I'm almost always ready to punch him in the arm, but I was double-ready, right then.

"No. I mean, look at the way it's starting to stand up."

"Oh." He was right. My red hair was starting to rise up into the air, sticking straight out, like I was some Medusa-type creature. I was studying some strands of my hair when a piece of window glass went strolling past my eyes. Hundreds of other pieces were nearing me, and thousands of other pieces were following behind them. Slow or not, we were right in the middle of an explosion. It was time to leave.

"Let's go!" I told Nate and Chester, grabbing Chester's arm so that I could pull him along. We would have to find some way to get past the Red Death Tea Society assassins in the hallway, and then sneak past whoever had triggered the slow-motion explosion, and then we'd have to—

"Oof!" I said. Chester hadn't moved at all.

I mean . . . *at all*.

It was like yanking on a statue. He wouldn't budge.

He was frozen into position, caught in the Slowstorm, but standing right in the path of the oncoming explosion.

"This is bad," Nate said. "We won't be able to move Chester. He's . . . stuck. A Slowstorm uses gravitational warps to alter the cadence of time. Time grows . . . heavy, I guess. More ponderous. Slower."

"Is that even possible?" My opinions on what I'd once considered impossible had changed a lot since I'd become friends with Nate. I now knew that science could conquer almost anything. Nate had made giant cats, talking dogs, sword-fighting mice, friend rays, robots, and an app for my phone that could detect the nearest clown so that I can always avoid them, because clowns freak me out.

"It's possible," Nate said. "Time can be slowed or accelerated by manipulating gravity. You and I are immune because of the micro-robots I have protecting us, but . . ." He looked over to Chester.

"We can't just *leave* him!" I said, picking up a math textbook from Mrs. Isaacson's desk, using it to push back some of the glass shards that were nearing Chester. "He'll be caught in the explosion if he stays here!" I grabbed Chester's arm again and starting pulling at it, but he wouldn't budge.

"Hmmm," Nate said. "Maybe if I can destroy the

power source." Then, he went down on one knee and stared at my legs.

"Nate?" I said. "What the *piffle*?"

"I'm gauging the amount of mustard on your leg."

"Okaaaaay," I said.

"If I can gather enough mustard, I could shoot it toward the machine that's warping time, and destroy it by—"

"Whatever! As long as we'll be able to move Chester again. But how will you shoot the mustard toward—"

Nate licked my pants.

On the mustard.

This was not something I expected, so I can hardly be blamed for how I jumped back, or for how my knee jerked upward and slammed into the side of Nate's head.

"**Guhh**," he said.

And then toppled over.

Unconscious.

"Oh dang," I said, looking at Nate unconscious on the floor, with a smear of mustard on his lips, and at Chester frozen in place, and at the windows ever-so-slowly exploding inward, and at several members of the Red Death Tea Society running into the room and pointing their guns at me.

"Oh *piffle*," I said.

"Time out!" I yelled, in case it would work.

It did not work. Instead, one of the assassins fired his disintegrator pistol at me, and if I hadn't spent so many hours practicing on my obstacle course to hone myself into "adventure" shape, and if I hadn't also spent so many hours eating cake to fuel my body with so much energy that it's honestly surprising I don't glow, I think the ray would've hit me. As it was, it went whooshing over my shoulder with a sound not unlike a flock of gossiping ducks, and a wide swath of the incoming glass from the exploding windows suddenly ceased to exist.

"Time out!" I yelled again, because I *really* did want it to work.

It still didn't.

So I kicked a desk toward the nearest of my attackers, a man in the usual red suit with black trim of the Red Death Tea Society. Honestly, if you're going to be a secret society, you shouldn't dress in matching uniforms.

The sliding desk hit his legs, and there was a

pained grunt and then some impressive cursing and then he toppled to the floor, glaring at me. I dodged to the right when his gun came up, and then rolled to the left, and then I leaped out for the rope that was hanging in front of me.

"**Piffle**," I said when I realized there *wasn't* a rope hanging in front of me. That's the problem with practicing for adventures on an obstacle course; you get used to the obstacles, and there's a part of my practice where I do a dodge to the right and then a roll to the left and then I grab the rope hanging from my tree. Except there was no tree in Mrs. Isaacson's classroom, and most definitely not a hanging rope, so I probably looked like some cartoon character who's walked off a cliff, with that look of stupid realization on my face that I was about to fall.

I fell.

I bounced off the floor in a not particularly charming manner, and then rolled to a stop.

There was a note on the floor.

Addressed to me.

Written in Nate's handwriting.

For once, it wasn't folded, for which I was very grateful, because I was in the middle of a battle and didn't have time for Nate's intricate folding techniques, which can be a puzzle to unravel.

The note said,

"Delphine. According to my calculations, it's been 234 hours and 17 minutes since you've accidentally knocked me out, so it's ninety-nine percent probable to happen soon. By now I'm almost certainly unconscious and you're likely in a fight with the Red Death Tea Society, meaning you don't have time to unfold a note. That's why I didn't fold the note, even though I've found a way to fold paper into a seven-dimensional form, which you really should see some time, so if you survive this battle, remind me!"

In the time it took me to read Nate's explanation of how he was saving me time by not folding the note, I'd had to dodge seven disintegrator rays and five attempts to grab me, not to mention a desk that had been hurled at me, and do it all within the rapidly shrinking space where the oncoming explosion hadn't reached.

Leaping behind Mrs. Isaacson's desk, I read more of the note. It said,

"Oh. I should hurry up. I get distracted. Sorry. I'll make it up to you by inventing a better pizza. But, for now, you have to wake me up. The easiest way is . . . I've put a packet of Expand-o-Water in your pocket. Just open it up and splash it on my face."

"Expand-O-Water?" I said, reaching into my pocket. There was indeed a small packet of something, wrapped in dark green tinfoil with an image of a raindrop. I opened it up and a small drop of water emerged, clinging to the edge of the tinfoil.

"Here she is!" a woman's voice called out. She was standing on top of Mrs. Isaacson's desk and carrying a disintegrator pistol. The gun was pointed at me, which unfortunately seems to be their natural state. I tried to scramble around the right side of the desk, but was blocked by somebody's legs. So I tried to scramble around to the left, shuffling on all fours, but another of the Red Death Tea Society assassins cut me off.

"Heh heh," one of them said.

"Ha ha," said another.

"Hee hee," said the third.

They were having an excellent time, but I was not.

It's a good thing I created my obstacle course. I'm in very good shape these days. For instance, when I first started, I could barely hold on to a swinging rope. Now, I can easily Tarzan my way through a forest, swinging from vines. And I can jump hurdles and do handsprings, and I can open a door using my feet as long as I'm not wearing shoes. All very important skills. When I was first building my obstacle course,

Dad asked why I needed to hone these abilities of mine.

I'd said, "College," which made him happy, because he wants me to go to college, though I'm not exactly sure what college has an entrance exam where you have to open a door with your feet.

Anyway, my answer satisfied Dad and he let me build the course, which includes such things as an old bathtub where I've been practicing to hold my breath for long periods of time, and a limbo rope where, through long hours of exercise, I've been steadily decreasing the smallest space I can squeeze under.

It's all paying off.

I slid under Mrs. Isaacson's desk and out the other side.

"Where'd she go?" I heard a voice call out from behind me, because the members of the Red Death Tea Society did not expect me to be a limbo champion. I was still clutching the tiny packet of Expand-O-Water, and the droplet was still stubbornly clutching to the edge of the torn tinfoil. I raced first for Nate, but stopped when I saw that the exploding glass from the Slowstorm was only inches from Chester.

I *had* to do something.

He was caught in time, moving too slow for him to escape the blast. What I needed was for him to be moving as quickly as I was, but he didn't have the tiny robots in his system, like me and Nate, so unless I could get him to speed up in some other way, he would . . . he would . . . *hey.*

Oh.

I grabbed the packet of "Speed Runner" pills from his fingers, tore open the packet, and tucked a pill inside Chester's mouth.

His eyes blinked.

Slowly.

Then quicker.

And he said, "Delphine? What's happening?"

"The bears aren't real. We're in a slow-motion explosion. The people with the guns are assassins from the Red Death Tea Society. I've accidentally knocked Nate unconscious. Your clothes do not match."

"What?"

"Sorry, that last one slipped out. The important thing is that you should run."

"Okay," he said, and he ran right out of the classroom. It was, I must admit, refreshing. Usually if I tell Nate to do something, it takes minutes of explanation for *why* he should do whatever I'm asking, and then he likes to consider *alternate* solutions for whatever problem he's up against, and it's no wonder that I punch him so many times.

"Good job running!" I told Chester as he disappeared out the door.

Then I turned around.

To see all the Red Death Tea Society members pointing their disintegrator pistols at me.

"Bad job standing still," I told myself. Then I dove forward toward their legs, hoping to maybe bowl a couple of them over, either to mess up their aim or at least give them a good knock on their shins, because that *really* hurts.

I had the open packet of Expand-O-Water in my outstretched hand.

It hit the floor first.

The waves hit me next.

BUHH-LOOOOOOOSHHHH

The moment the drop of water hit the floor, it expanded. *Fiercely.* It did not expand into two drops, or four, or eight, or any other trivial gradation like that. No, it exploded into an *ocean* of water. The entire classroom was instantly filled with raging water, with water surging out into the hall and bursting out from the windows, with all the desks and everything else hurled back by the force of the expanding water. I was thumped up into the ceiling on a geyser-like current. The Red Death Tea Society's pistols short-circuited in tiny explosions that made all the assassins jerk and twitch with bursts of electricity.

They passed out.

So . . . it looked like I was going to win, except for the part where I was drowning, which would certainly be an asterisk to my victory.

The water was still expanding, making it very difficult to swim anywhere, since the current was roaring in all directions and it felt like riding a bike uphill against a fierce wind, with the addition of that part about the drowning. I'm sorry to keep mentioning the drowning, but it was a central part of my thought process.

Another important thought: Where was *Nate*? I'd managed to swim to the bottom of the classroom, but Nate wasn't where I'd last seen him. Maybe he'd been washed out one of the windows? The currents were even stronger near the windows, because not only was the water still expanding, but it was gushing out through the windows, and every time I got too close to one of the windows it felt like a big watery hand was grabbing at me. I couldn't just *leave*, though, because it's considered impolite to knock a boy out and then abandon him in the middle of a submerged classroom. I *needed* to find Nate. My lungs were burning, though. It felt like they were being squeezed, or roasted over hot coals, or like a cat was using them for a scratching post. The desks were all jumbled together in one corner of the room, and I decided it was possible Nate was buried under them. I had to check.

My lungs HURT.

I moved a couple of the desks aside, but they just tumbled about, sinking back where they'd been. It was like trying to dig in sand.

My lungs were quivering and my throat was tight.

I picked up a desk and shoved it toward the closest window, where the current grabbed it and washed it outside.

I did it again with the next desk. And the next. And the next. My arms were tiring from all the effort. I would definitely have to add "desk-throwing" to my adventure training course. All the sounds in the classroom were muted, like that roaring hush you have when your head is underwater and the rest of the world sounds like a pounding drum, distant voices, the noise of your own heart beating in your chest, water rushing past your ears, a silence that is somehow an overpowering roar.

I kept digging through the desks. Hurling them

toward the currents. Desks were flowing out the window in a surging stream. One after the other. But there was never anything beneath them but more desks.

C'mon, Nate! Where are you?

My whole chest felt like a block of wood. My heart was pounding. I was digging through the desks, but I couldn't find Nate. I was almost entirely out of breath. If I didn't leave soon, it would be too late.

I needed to leave.

I *needed* to.

I stayed.

Hurling desks.

The water seemed darker.

Thicker.

I could barely lift the desks.

The water was cold. So cold. Getting colder.

I felt like I was drifting.

Fading.

"Here," Nate said. "Take this."

"**GRUB-BUBBLE!**" I yelled, which is the sound you make when you're trying to yell "**Gahh!**" . . . but ninety-two gallons of water surge into your mouth.

Nate was floating in the water next to me, entirely unconcerned with all the chaos. Frankly, Nate is rarely all that bothered by chaos, which is probably one reason the two of them hang out together so much.

He was holding a pill. Gesturing toward my mouth.

I was about to ask what the pill would do, but the moment I opened my mouth Nate flicked the pill through the water. It tumbled and turned and curved in the current, and then shot down my throat. I instinctively swallowed.

Nate smiled.

Almost instantly, my strength began to return. Energy flooded through my veins, surging into my muscles. I heaved a sigh of relief, which isn't something you're supposed to do underwater. But, somehow . . . I could breathe.

"Breathing pill?" I asked.

"'Underwater Adventure' pills," Nate said. "But, yeah, pretty much the same thing. Except with these we can even talk underwater. I invented them by . . . GUFF!"

Nate's words were cut off by impact. For once, it wasn't a horrible impact, like falling from a helicopter or being swatted by a giant cat. This time, it was me. Hugging him. I'd thought I'd lost him. I've oftentimes wondered what life would be like without Nate, and the only possible conclusion is that it would be dumber. It would be boring, mundane, and utterly commonplace.

"I would miss you," I said, accidentally aloud. The current was pushing us closer, holding us together. The water felt warmer than when I'd been searching for Nate. Probably a side effect of the pill I'd taken.

"I would miss you, too," Nate said. The water was still whooshing around us, like the classroom was a series of geysers, reverse waterfalls, pressure jets, all of them whirling the waters so that it felt like we were dancing through the room. Nate was looking into my eyes. I'm not sure what he was seeing. Something that made him happy, though. There was a wonderful smile on his lips. Then, he moved his right shoulder forward, looking at it meaningfully.

"Why are you showing me your shoulder?" I asked.

"Because you always punch me when you get embarrassed."

"I'm not embarrassed!" I said, punching him.

The act of punching Nate sent me floating backward in the water, floating just far enough for the violent currents near the door to grab me, so that I was washed out into the flooded hallway and sent speeding past the history room, and the teachers' lounge, and whooshing past the English room where I was scheduled to read my short story wherein Frankenstein defeats Dracula in a game of checkers. There were musical instruments spewing out of the band room, caught in the raging currents, tubas and trumpets and flutes and so on. They were clanging together, rebounding off the walls, swept down the hallway. A saxophone whacked me on the side of the head. The water had filled the hall, and I began to wonder just how much water Nate had unleashed on the school . . . or even on the world. This could be a flood of epic proportions.

The current was carrying me toward the study hall, in room 1A, the central area from where all the hallways branch off.

The big doors were open.

Maculte was standing there.

Luria was next to him.

The two leaders of the Red Death Tea Society.

"Uh-oh," I gurgled.

Sir Jakob Maculte is in his late fifties and his cheeks are sunken like potholes. He has gray hair and eyebrows like puffed-up caterpillars, and he mostly looks like a plant in bad need of watering.

Luria Pevermore, irritatingly enough, is quite beautiful. Her hair is red, but even darker than mine, and hangs straight down to her shoulders whenever it's not doing that "shampoo commercial" thing of billowing outward in an entrancing fashion. She has high cheekbones, a good number of spotted freckles, and green eyes that shine like stained glass. She's almost always smiling, but it never *feels* like a smile.

They're both normally holding teacups, but right now they were clutching onto the frame of the double-wide study-hall doorway, fighting against the flow of the water, watching me as I was coming closer, ever closer, helplessly caught in the current.

I tried to swim the other way, but it was useless. The rushing current was too strong. I could see Nate swimming toward me, looking grim, and swimming much faster than I would have thought possible. Honestly, he's a bit scrawny, but whenever it comes time to do something athletic, he seems to surprise me.

"How are you swimming so fast?" I asked as he caught up to me, slipping an arm around my waist.

"My shoes are submarines," he said.

I said, "I must have heard wrong. I thought you just said that your shoes were submarines."

"My shoes *are* submarines. Or at least my shoes work on the same principle as a submarine, creating propulsion by means of a steam turbine that's powered by the nuclear reactors in—"

"Stop! I don't want to know that you have steam-propelled nuclear sneakers. Just . . . tell me how we're going to avoid those two!" I pointed to Maculte and Luria, who were braced against the sides of the door, struggling to hold their positions against the current, which was slowly drawing us closer to them.

"Won't have to," Nate said. "The count is seven and ten."

"Nate, that makes less sense than when you were talking about submarine shoes. What are you talking about?"

"One," he said. "Two. Three. Four. Five. Six. Seven."

The whole time he was counting, I was watching Luria struggle with her grip on the doorway. The ferocious current was an endlessly bulldozing wave of water storming throughout the entire school. And then, just as Nate counted to seven, Luria lost her grip and was instantly washed away, disappearing into the depths of the study hall like a leaf blowing in the wind.

"Eight. Nine. Ten," Nate said. And then, with a grunt of rage heard even over the surging drumbeats of the water smashing into the lockers and the ceiling tiles, Maculte lost his grip on the doorway and was whisked away into the darkened watery depths of the study hall.

He was gone.

"We need to get outside before my shoes lose power," Nate said, as if that was a perfectly reasonable thing to say. He was still holding me around the waist, using the power of his submarine shoes to keep the water from washing us away.

"Okay!" I said. I was literally in his hands.

"Trombone," he said.

"What?" I asked.

A trombone, caught in the current, bounced off my head. It made a non-musical noise. I did, too.

"Trombone," I said. "Got it."

Nate began swimming toward the front door, with the two of us zooming through the halls of Polt Middle School like sopping wet birds. We whooshed past the gym, which was cluttered with soccer balls and basketballs and shin guards caught in the currents, along with a volleyball net we narrowly avoided. Then we shot through the cafeteria, soaring majestically through a flock of floating bread loaves.

Finally, we were outside, spat out through the front steps in an ongoing gusher and sliding halfway across a parking lot that was inches deep in water.

"How much water did you *make*?" I asked Nate, looking at the school, where every single window and door was doing a spit-take.

"My calculations were that there would be enough water to wake me up. Just . . . a bit of water splashed in my face. But I failed to take the Delphine Factor into account." Nate was standing ankle deep in water, slowly breathing in, slowly breathing out. It looked like he was trying to avoid passing out.

"The Delphine Factor?" I asked, looking around for Chester, trying to make sure he was okay.

"The Expand-O-Water increases by a factor of one thousand when it impacts a hard surface," Nate said. I looked around, thinking of how there'd been a single droplet of Expand-O-Water in the tinfoil packet. By my rough estimate, there were infinite drops of water around us now, which is considerably more than one thousand droplets.

"But," Nate continued, "you must have smacked the droplet into the floor *really* hard."

"I did. I smacked it pretty good."

"Yes. That's something you do. That's the Delphine Factor. You smack things."

"That is indeed something I do," I said, agreeing with him, bursting with pride. My brother Steve says that girls shouldn't smack things. I have smacked him for this. Girls should do whatever we want to do.

Nate said, "It would've caused a *much* greater chain reaction than I'd originally intended. So instead of increasing the water by a thousandfold, it did it by a thousand-thousand-thousand-thousand-thousandfold."

"I have folded a lot of thousands," I said, looking at the school. The water was just beginning to slow down, with the windows and doorways now only *spewing* water, instead of *gushing* it out. For one moment, I thought we might be returning to normalcy, but . . . no.

Of course not.

The water froze.

Not that it turned to ice or anything like that. It just . . . quit moving, the way a bunny will do when you spot it in your yard, nibbling at the grass, and the bunny realizes you're watching and it goes motionless. The water coming from Polt Middle School was just like that, frozen into position, except that it wasn't furry or adorable with big floppy ears.

"Uh-oh," Nate said. I do not like when he says it. When my regular friends say "uh-oh," it usually means something like when Liz Morris gets the hiccups, or when Wendy Kamoss forgets her homework, or when Ventura León and Stine Keykendall accidentally wear identical clothes on the same day, such as their Scuba Bunny shirts. At the worst, an "uh-oh" means something like when my brother Steve is pretending he's at a friend's house when he's really at a concert, and Dad finds out.

But with Nate, an "uh-oh" has a far wider range of possibilities, many of them in the categories of "dire" or "dreadful" or "whoops, I guess that's the end of the world."

"What?" I asked Nate. "Why did the water stop moving?"

"It's the Red Death Tea Society again. Their Slowstorm machine is still operational." Nate's breath was still heaving in and out, like he was on the verge of panic. I do not like it when the world's smartest boy panics. It panics me.

"What are they trying to do with it?" I asked.

"If they can slow time in this area, it will eventually overcome the robots in our bloodstream, and we'll be frozen. Easy to capture. Or worse."

"I'm not in favor of being captured or worse. Didn't we have plans to break that machine? We should get on that, right?"

Nate nodded, breathing in, breathing out. Slowly.

"Let's see," he said. "If I was going to hide the machine, where would I do it?"

"Maybe make it look like a car?" I said, pointing to the cars at the far end of the parking lot. Since school wasn't in session, there weren't many vehicles in the parking lot, just a few cars for the grounds-keepers who were working on the lawns and hedges. There was an old Chevy truck. A Ford truck with a trailer attachment for lawn-mowing equipment. A battered old Volkswagen. And a red truck with a tea-cup symbol painted on the side, and an exposed engine with an incredible array of weird tubes and rubber hoses, bristling with antennae that had arcs of electricity zooming between them.

"There!" I said.

"The Volkswagen?" Nate asked.

"No!" I said, adding in a punch. "The one with the teacup!"

"Oooh!" Nate said. And then he started doing that breathing again. The deep breaths, quickly taken, speedily exhaled, again and again.

"Are you okay, Nate?" I asked. "You keep—"

PHH-THOOOOEY!

Nate spit.

Tremendously.

That's why he'd been doing the thing with the breathing; he was getting ready to spit a big loogie, using the neon-green power tongue rubber band he was wearing.

We were at least a hundred feet from the somewhat-disguised Slowstorm machine, but Nate's wad of spit arced way up into the air, *soaring* through the skies, and then sloshed into the side of the Slowstorm machine with a noise like when a huge frog farts underwater.

But nothing else happened.

Except that the spit started grossly sliding down the side of the machine, and I was looking to Nate, and then back at the machine, wondering what was *supposed* to happen, wondering if Nate had finally failed at something.

"Wait for it," he said.

"Wait for *what*?" I asked.

"Do you remember when I licked the mustard off your pants?"

"Yes," I said, not adding that it wasn't something *anyone* would ever forget, or that anyone sane would ever think to *do*.

"Well, the mustard was in that spit," Nate said, as if everything was now explained, but I was wearing sopping wet clothes and standing in what amounted to a brand-new marsh, and I was on the verge of asking Nate at least fifty more questions, but then . . .

"Is mustard?" I heard. The voice came from what looked to be a floating hairball with whiskers and a furry snout.

It was Bosper.

He was paddling furiously through the waters toward the Slowstorm machine.

"Is mustard!" he snarled. As soon as he reached shallower waters he was racing as quickly as he could, and then he was biting and snarling at the mustard-stained machine, chomping on the wires and the tubes, tearing them from their moorings, avoiding various arcs of electricity, ripping the delicate parts of the machine to bits.

"You sicced your dog on a machine?" I asked. "Why couldn't you just walk over there and break it yourself?"

"Because this was more adventurous."

"Watching a terrier attack mustard-laced spit-stains isn't a common definition of adventure."

"Adventure is never common, Delphine," Nate said, which was annoying, because he was right.

"The dog is attacking!" Bosper said. A few more wires were ripped loose.

Bosper snarled, "Here comes more teeth!" He tore off one of the antennae.

"The dog is a good boy!" Bosper yelled, tearing off an electrical plate and pawing at the exposed circuitry. The machine was pulsing with electricity, but slower and slower, almost entirely destroyed. Nate and I were walking closer, sloshing through the shallow water. It seemed safe enough, because the machine was almost dead, with lights blinking out, and Bosper couldn't be mad at me anymore because I no longer had any mustard on my pants, thanks to how Nate had licked some of it off, and the rest of it had been washed away in the flooded school, as if it were the oddest washing machine of all time.

I said, "I hope Chester doesn't hear Bosper talking." I was looking around, trying to see where Chester might have gone. He shouldn't have been too hard to spot, not when he was wearing that blue shirt and those yellow pants, along with his bright red socks. He normally stuck out like a parrot in a sand pile.

"He'd have to have really good hearing," Nate said.

"Why?"

"Well, because he's all the way up in the classrooms," Nate said, gesturing back to the school. "But as soon as Bosper breaks that machine, Chester won't be caught in time, and we can—"

"Oh. That's right. You didn't know. You were unconscious at the time, but I already saved Chester. Since he was caught in time, all I had to do was speed him up. So I gave him a 'Speed Runner' pill and he ran outside. He should be around here somewhere." I was still looking for Chester. Maybe he'd run all the way home? Not a bad idea, really. I could use some "home time" myself.

"You . . . *what?*" Nate said. His flopping hair was halfway down over his eyes, but even so I could see them, because they'd grown suddenly large.

"I gave Chester one of your pills."

"You . . . *what?*" Nate moved his hair back. Yep, big ol' eyes.

"The 'Speed Runner' pills," I said. "I gave one to Chester. Pretty smart, huh?"

"Oh." Nate's voice was odd.

He turned from me and looked to Bosper, who was still tearing the Slowstorm machine to pieces, currently yelling a battle cry involving "cupcakes" and "quantum equations," two of his favorite things. The machine was now a wreck. There'd originally been hundreds of blinking lights, but now there were no more than ten.

"Hmmm," Nate said, grabbing a pen from his shirt pocket and doing some quick calculations on his pants, scribbling numbers and symbols and a cartoon likeness of Chester circled several times, with lightning bolts surrounding him.

"Hmmm," Nate said.

Then, looking sharply up, Nate yelled, "BOSPER! STOP!"

Bosper looked back to us. The mustard-induced madness had faded from the terrier's eyes, but it was now replaced with anxiety.

"The dog is not a good boy?" he whimpered in question. Behind him, the remaining lights of the Slowstorm machine winked out, one after the other, until there was only one left. It pulsed with a dull green color, slower and slower. Then it blinked red. And went black.

From somewhere in the distance, beyond the football stands, possibly three hundred yards away, I heard Chester scream.

And then there were lightning bolts crashing all over the field, crackling down from the skies and crackling back *up* from the ground, and the football stands exploded into bits and pieces and there was a blur of blue and yellow and red and then Chester was standing right in front of me, appearing as if from nowhere in a brutal rush of wind.

"Huh?" I said, but Chester was already gone.

There was a smell of ozone in the air, and there were thousands of flickers of electricity, like snowflakes, tumbling all around.

The noises were deafening.

From everywhere there was the blur of blue and yellow and red. It was complete pandemonium. There were random explosions, like the toolshed where the lawn equipment is kept, and also a tree, and even portions of the lawn, all of them just . . . exploding. There was lightning striking all around. Bosper barking. Howling winds. Me diving for cover but not finding it, so mostly I was just sloshing around in the waters, which kept erupting in straight lines, like a gargantuan knife was cutting repeatedly through the water, and the colorful blur just wouldn't stop; it seemed to be everywhere at all times, a keening whistle as the air itself burst into thick lines of flames, and the only thing that wasn't a part of the chaos was Nathan Bannister.

He was just standing there.

He tapped the equations on his pants and said, "Yeah. That was gonna happen."

Then, more lightning from the skies.

Chapter 4

Chester was the lightning.

He was the blur of blue and yellow and red.

He was the tornado-like winds and he was the lines of fire appearing through the air. He was the explosions happening all around. Chester was everywhere, and everything. He kept running past us at speeds too quick to see, speeds that burned away the water in the parking lot, sending it skyward in bursts of billowing steam, as if Nate and I were sweltering in a colossal sauna.

"I," Chester said, running past us. His speed left behind a thick black line of charred pavement.

"Can't!" Chester said, zooming past us. The remains of the Slowstorm machine exploded into a thousand pieces, and tiny droplets of molten metal.

"Stop!" Chester said, racing past us at unfathomable speeds. Bosper was barking at him, spinning in circles as he tried to keep up with Chester's pace, which was entirely futile. Chester's speeds were simply beyond comprehension.

"Help me!" I heard Chester yell as he sped off into the distance, his speed blazing a furrow across the football yard. The goalposts at the far end were caught in bursts of lightning, and then a small grove of oak trees exploded into wooden splinters as Chester Humes raced off into the city, unable to stop his amazing run.

The silence began to settle.

Everything smelled like burning tires.

The hair on my arms was standing up.

I had the taste of dust and metal in my mouth.

"Hmm," Nate said after Chester was gone and the storm had subsided. There were raging clouds in the distance now, though. The skies above Polt were churning with violence, spewing lightning, with storm clouds being tugged along after my speedy schoolmate as if connected with a leash.

"What . . . the . . . *piffle*?" I asked.

Nate said, "It's because of the 'Speed Runner' pill. Chester was frozen in time when you gave it to him, so for a bit . . . *after* it was in his system but *while* the Slowstorm machine was still working . . . he was being super-charged, like when you rev an engine but the brakes are on."

"Chester doesn't appear to have his brakes on."

"No," Nate said. "The moment Bosper destroyed the Slowstorm machine, fully releasing Chester from its effects, his metabolism accelerated enormously. When the machine was still operational, it was holding him back, slowing him down to what we perceive as normal speeds. But, so much energy was building up inside him that, now it's been released, he's like a super-charged race car."

"What do we do?"

"We have to catch him. Help him. If we don't . . ." Nate's words trailed off, like they sometimes do when he's avoiding telling me something unpleasant, but for once he was going to have to tell me the truth.

"What could happen?" I asked.

"The excess power could prove too much for Chester," Nate said. "It would burn him up. Like a spent match."

"We can't let that happen," I said. "We just *can't*. But, how can we catch someone who's moving that fast?"

"Hmmm," Nate said, scratching his chin.

Betsy had healed enough that she could drive again, although she couldn't shift into any of her "rocket"

modes. Still, she could drive us around like a normal car, so we raced downtown as fast as we could, searching for Chester and finding him easily enough, but failing to do anything other than watch the woman get her meatball sandwich all over her white blouse as Chester raced past.

"This isn't working!" Nate yelled, waving for me to get back into the car. We needed to go to his lab so he could invent something.

"Maybe some sort of net?" I asked as we drove along. Bosper was in the backseat, his face stuck outside the window with his fur ruffling in the wind. I'd moved Melville, still sleeping, to the front dash, making sure she wouldn't get swept out by the breeze.

"I might be able to create a molecular bond net," Nate said. "But, I don't think it's a good idea to simply catch Chester in a net. Right now, all the running he's doing is siphoning off some of the excess energy. If we were to simply *stop* him . . ."

"Yeah. I see what you mean. The energy could burn him up."

"This dog-face likes winds," Bosper said. The winds were pushing his fur back.

"How about you invent some sort of super-treadmill?" I asked. "That way, at least Chester could run in one place, and we would know where he was."

As we drove along, we could see clear evidence of Chester's passing. There was a whole street with trees that'd toppled over, and a wall where Chester had written, "Delphine! Help me!" possibly a hundred thousand times. I wondered how long it had taken him. Probably no more than a second.

"There's no material that could withstand the strain," Nate said. "A super-treadmill would be destroyed almost instantly. And, even if it wasn't, you've seen what happens around Chester. The storm, I mean. You're beautiful today."

"What?" We seemed to have moved on to a new topic. Had I heard Nate correctly?

"Oh," he said, turning away from me. "Dang it. I said you're beautiful today. Aargh." Nate was blushing horribly, like someone had used a paintbrush to color him a very dark red.

"Is this the honesty potion at work?" I asked.

"Yes," Nate said. "Though I always think you're beautiful. Aaagh! Dang it!"

"The dog has ridden in a helicopter," Bosper said. "And he eats peanut butter, if someone has some. Does someone has some?"

"Always?" I asked Nate, ignoring the terrier.

"Always," Nate said. "Ahhh! Dang it. I didn't know this honesty thing would be so troublesome."

"The dog is moving at 36.789 miles per hour," Bosper said. "He is a passenger."

I was settling back into my seat. My skin was tingling as I listened to Nate talking about how beautiful he thought I was, how beautiful he *always* thought I was. It was weird that my skin was tingling so much, because of course I've *never* thought of Nate as being anything other than a friend, despite how he's handsome in his own way, and I feel comfortable around him, and his eyes are nice, and it's amazing how he can make me feel safe even when everything around us is chaos, and I *do* enjoy how the smartest person in the world always has time to listen to *my* ideas, and of course he takes a punch well. But, despite how I would *never* think of letting him be my boyfriend, I was blushing. I was as red as Nate.

Ridiculous.

"The dog sees a zebra," Bosper said, staring out the window.

"I'm not just some pretty girl, you know," I told Nate. Sometimes, boys think a girl is *all* about how pretty she is, as if she's defined by her looks rather than her accomplishments. But I'd be willing to bet there isn't *anyone* in Polt who can go through my obstacle course as fast as I can, or who knows as much about cake as I do, or who can hold her own against the Red Death Tea Society, or who can—

"Of course not!" Nate said. "Part of the reason we're . . . friends is because you're not afraid of my intelligence. It doesn't intimidate you, not the way it does with everyone else. In fact, in lots of ways, you're just as smart as I am. The way you look at the world, the way you see things, it's amazing. You have insights I could never understand. And you make me laugh, and you make me *think*, and you rode that hippopotamus, and you fought a giant cat. You're the most amazing person I've ever known. It's true that I'm the smartest person on earth, but it's just as true that you're the most adventurous!"

"The dog is still looking at the zebra," Bosper said.

Somehow, Nate and I were holding hands. Why was I holding my breath?

"The zebra is Steve," Bosper said.

I felt a little like I had in Mrs. Isaacson's classroom, when I'd leaped out for the rope that hadn't been there. It was that same feeling of unexpected falling. Sudden weightlessness. The wind was whipping in through the open car window, the window where Bosper had his head stuck out. I was hyperaware of everything, the way my wet clothes were sticking to me, the way water was dripping from Nate's hair, those bright red cheeks of his, the intense brown of his eyes. His fingers were in mine and his hand was so warm. My hand felt warm, too. It felt burning hot. I hoped it didn't feel weird.

Nate slid closer to me, or maybe I was moving closer to him, but either way some of my bright red hair was blowing across his face, fluttering against his cheeks, because of the window where Bosper had his head stuck out, and was seeing a zebra that was Steve.

Wait.

Huh?

"What did you say?" I asked Bosper, taking my hand from Nate's and turning to the terrier.

"The dog eats peanut butter if someone has some," Bosper said. "Does Delphine has some?" His eyes were wide and hopeful.

"No. I don't has some. *Have* some. I don't *have* any. And I wasn't asking what you said about the peanut butter. I meant, what was that about a zebra that is Steve?"

"The Steve was on the sidewalk. Two blocks ago."

"My brother?"

"Yes," Bosper said. "Does the brother has some peanut butter?"

"What did you mean about my brother being a *zebra*?" I asked.

"Uh-oh," Nate said.

I am seriously going to put that on his list of forbidden things to say.

So, as it turns out, my brother had drunk the "Make Any Animal a Zebra" potion that Nate had hidden in town. And humans definitely *do* count as animals, especially if they are brothers.

So now he was a zebra.

A crowd had gathered, thinking Steve was an actual zebra rather than my annoying older brother. Although, I suppose he was both now. A few people were trying to catch him, and others were warning the crowd to stay back, saying that zebras were dangerous and that he could stampede at any moment. Nate . . . burdened with his truth-telling . . . was endlessly explaining that it takes more than a single animal to stampede.

"We have to get him back to my house," I told Nate, trying to coax Steve closer, waving an apple I'd hurriedly bought from a nearby fruit stand.

"Do you think your parents would want a zebra in the house?" Nate asked. "Wouldn't they ask questions?"

"We have to get him back to *your* house, then," I

said, waving the apple to Steve, who incidentally smelled like a sweaty horse, which is basically normal for him.

Nate said, "The most important thing is, we need to discover where your brother came across my 'Make Any Animal a Zebra' potion."

"Why?" I asked, taking cell phone photos of Steve for later blackmail purposes. "What difference does it make?"

"Because I hid the potion in Susan Heller's garage," Nate said. "Why was your brother in Susan's garage?"

"Oh," I said, narrowing my eyes. "You're jealous!"

"Yes, I am!" Nate said, forced to tell the truth, though in this case through gritted teeth and with clenched fists.

Susan Heller is our classmate, and she enjoys going shopping and being pretty, both of which are particular talents of hers. She's also quite skilled at irritating me, and at smiling, the latter of which she gets paid to do by several modeling agencies, and the first of which just seems to come natural to her. She smells, in my infallible opinion, like a rotten peach. Her voice is that of a squirrel on helium and she barely knows that Nate exists. What Nate sees in her I will never know. Maybe it's that thing about "opposites attract," because Nate is very smart and she is very *not*.

"Can we ask him about the potion?" I said as Steve ambled closer, intrigued by the apple. His hooves made the *clip-clop* sound along the sidewalk. People were hurriedly stepping out of his way. Kip Luppert, our classmate, was among them. I gave him a quick wave. He gave a nervous shiver and melted back into the crowd, as if afraid to be seen. Weird.

"We can't ask him," Nate said. "Zebras can't talk."

"Well, *brothers* can talk. In fact, they seem to do a lot of it, and Steve might be a zebra, but he's also my brother."

"True, but zebras don't have the ability to talk. It's a matter of structure, the jaws and tongue and so on."

"Then how come Bosper can talk?" I asked, pointing to the terrier.

"Bosper is not supposed to talk," Bosper said. "It is a secret!" He was bouncing up and down, the way it's no secret that terriers are always doing. Luckily, everyone was so focused on my zebra brother that nobody overheard Bosper speaking.

"I had to make some modifications," Nate said. "And insert some nano-bots." The nano-bots are the microscopic robots that help protect Nate and me from all sorts of things, like detection by the Red Death Tea Society, or the League of Ostracized Fellows, or other pesky things such as mosquito attacks.

I asked Nate, "So, my brother is a zebra now. But is he still Steve? I mean, is he thinking like Steve, or like a zebra?"

"A little of both, according to my calculations. He'll be like your brother, but not quite as intelligent."

"Check your calculations," I told Nate. "It is scientifically impossible for Steve to be less intelligent."

Kip was peeking out from the crowd again. He's about five feet tall. A tad skinny. A bit gangly. He's often the lead in our school plays, such as *Werewolf Versus the Math Test*, which we staged last fall, and *Helga Has Meteor Fists*, which was cowritten by me and Liz Morris and which concerns the adventures of Helga Throttle, who, as you might have guessed, has meteors for fists. Kip played the part of Fred McLente, an astronomer with an interest in meteors.

Kip's eyes are green. He smells like a baseball mitt. His nose is thin. His voice is strong. He does not look like someone who would be very decisive, but he is, except when he's distracted, which is often.

Right then, he looked like he wanted to say something. He also looked very much like he did *not* want to say something. It reminded me of my dad's expression the time Mom came home and he had to explain how he'd been practicing rock climbing on the side of our garage and accidentally torn off the gutter.

But whatever Kip wanted to say wasn't important. Having a brother who is a zebra takes priority, although luckily the problem rarely comes up.

I told Nate, "It doesn't matter *why* Steve was in Susan's garage or *how* he took your potion; what matters is how we're going to *fix* him. Don't you have an antidote? A 'Make Any Zebra into Delphine's Brother' formula?" Steve was nibbling at the apple in my hand, but couldn't decide if he actually liked it. I was trying to decide if he was going to eat my fingers and . . . if so . . . how I could possibly tell Mom that I was missing fingers because Steve had grown hooves and developed stripes.

Something bumped against my leg.

I looked down.

There was a toad at my feet.

I moved a bit to the left, not wanting to squish it.

"I could probably make a quick antidote," Nate said. "Help me get Steve to the car." He walked over and grabbed Steve by one of his ears and started yanking on him, trying to lead him toward our car. This was not a genius-level thing to do. Steve took enormous offense. Zebras don't enjoy being grabbed by their ears any more than brothers do, and the combination of being a zebra and a brother seemed to magnify his irritation at having his ear pulled.

Steve bucked.

He kicked and whinnied.

He reared back.

Nate was still holding on to Steve's ear, dangling from it, looking surprised. It was interesting to see Nate surprised, because it doesn't happen very often. His amazing brain calculates everyday events to such a degree that I sometimes think he knows the future.

"Should I let go?" Nate asked as Steve began to race off. Nate's question seemed obvious to me, but he was out of hearing range before I could answer, meaning I could do nothing but stand and watch as my brother and Nate quickly trotted off down the street, sending cars into skids as drivers tried to avoid this unexpected zebra.

Something bumped against my legs.

There were several more toads at my feet. Lots of them.

I was staring at this unexpected crowd of amphibians when I heard the footsteps.

"Delphine," Kip Luppert said, walking up to me. "I think it's time I told you something. I've been spying on you for the Red Death Tea Society."

He handed me a business card.

It just said, "Spy."

I only looked at it for a moment before it was torn from my hands by a tremendous burst of wind. The entire street began shaking. The hair on my arms stood up. There was an electrical crackling from all around, several bursts of lightning, and then a blur of blue and yellow and red as Chester went racing by so fast that the concussion of his passing charred the side-walk and collapsed the outside wall of the Chandler grocery store. Cans of beans and corn came spilling outward. A jar of olives rolled by, as if it had some-where important to go.

It was at that moment that a helicopter swung low over the street, flying between buildings. It was red and had a teacup painted on the side. It was bristling with strange weapons, and I could see Maculte at the con-trols, with Luria flying along beside the helicopter, wearing a jet-pack harness and carrying pistols in each hand.

She began shooting.

The toads began scattering.

My shoes were still soggy from the flood.

"Nate! Let go!" I yelled out to Nate, who was still hanging from my zebra-brother's ear, flapping like a flag as Steve trotted away, but there were so many cars honking their horns or screeching their tires that Nate couldn't hear me. Plus there was the way the winds were roaring against everything, and the lightning was crackling, and there was gunfire, and people were screaming, and Bosper was barking. It was all very loud. I watched Nate recede into the distance and I heaved a sigh.

My sigh was the loudest of all.

"What's with the toads?" I asked. Even *more* toads were hopping closer to me, leaping along the sidewalk in their ungainly fashion, emerging from sewer drains and squeezing out from manhole covers. They were making guttural whistles, and there was that booming toad noise of "**grrr-roak grrr-ROAK**" and also a soft "**frhh-flump**" noise as the toads leaped along the sidewalk, gathering closer.

"Too many toads!" I said. "Way too many toads!"

Bosper was barking at them.

I was sweating.

Ankle deep in toads.

I started to run.

But I slipped on a jar of pickles and tripped on a

can of corn, and then I squished a package of cookie dough, which at first I worried was a toad.

"**Gahh!**" I said as a disintegrator ray hit just behind me, sounding like a crackling bonfire and smelling like a cauldron of heavily spiced chili.

The ray vaporized three cans of corn, a jar of pickles, and a huge chunk of the sidewalk.

And I was no longer worried about the toads.

Bosper was barking.

He was also shouting, "Bosper is the attacking dog!" while leaping up for the helicopter, with his terrier legs propelling him a good three feet into the air, only missing his target by fifty feet or so.

He kept barking and shouting, and he was also dodging incoming disintegrator rays. The toads were making that "*grrr-roak grrr-ROAK*" sound, and they were hopping and leaping and tripping me up, and also dodging incoming disintegrator rays.

My phone rang.

It was Liz Morris.

I answered while dodging a disintegrator ray.

"Hello?" I said, leaping over some toads and then trying to hide behind a garbage can, which was quickly disintegrated.

Liz said, "Can you come over tonight? I want to discuss space travel."

"Space travel?" I asked, hurling a bottle of ketchup at a helicopter.

"We should do it," Liz said, emphatically. "I am in favor of space travel."

"Me too," I said, dodging a disintegrator ray, and also a bottle of ketchup that was falling back down from the skies.

"Why do you sound out of breath?" Liz asked. "You on your obstacle course again?"

"Something like that," I said, leaping over a fire hydrant that disintegrated only a moment later, sending a gushing column of water across the street, blasting a bearded man off his motorcycle and causing a general round of what I assumed was applause from the toads.

"Are you with Nate again?" Liz asked. There was suspicion and mirth in her voice. There was a toad on my head.

"No," I said. "I mean, *kind of*, but he and Steve went off together, and I'm fighting a helicopter piloted by an evil genius."

"Nice," Liz said.

"Bosper makes more attacking!" Bosper said, leaping over me in another attempt on the helicopter.

"Who was that?" Liz asked.

"A dog," I answered.

"Delphine Cooper," Liz said. "You are the best friend ever."

Liz hung up after praising my imagination and making me promise we could talk about space travel.

"Imagination," I said, snorting, looking around.

I hadn't even told Liz about the toads.

Or the disintegrator rays.

Or how my brother had turned into a zebra.

Or how Chester Humes was running through Polt at unimaginable speeds.

And I hadn't so much as mentioned our classmate Kip Luppert.

The spy.

"What do you mean you're a spy?" I asked Kip, holding out his "spy" business card, waving it in his face in an accusing manner, although it was probably too late for any accusations, considering how he'd already confessed.

"I've been spying on you for months now," Kip

said, stepping away from some toads. "And I've been spying on Nate for years, working for the Red Death Tea Society. Sorry."

"Sorry?" I asked. He really did look sorry. Also, he looked squeamish about the toads. I couldn't blame him for that. One toad is a toad. Two toads are still just toads. A hundred toads is a total nightmare.

"Earlier, you almost caught me," he said. "When I was carrying the red paint? I'm supposed to paint the warehouse where Maculte stores his titanium rockets and sugar cubes. I was so nervous! And it got me thinking . . . I can't live like this. I can't keep lying to you."

A toad looked up at him, shaking its head.

"Kip!" I shrieked. "Why would you spy on us? Why would you work for the Red Death Tea Society? Who *else* has been spying on me? Do you have anything to do with my brother being a zebra? Look out for those toads!" He was about to step on some toads. This is because he was staggering backward, possibly intimidated by my questions or by the fact that Luria was still shooting at me, and, quite honestly, some people are squeamish about incoming disintegrator rays.

Anyway, about those toads. There was suddenly nowhere to step without stepping on a toad.

"My dad is Spectro-9," Kip said. The toads now

numbered in the hundreds. They were gathered around my legs. They were racing toward me from all directions. They were perched atop a newspaper dispenser for the *Polt Pigeon*, our free weekly newspaper, and there were at least twenty toads hopping all over the roof of a parked car.

"Spectro-9?" I asked. The toads all croaked at the same time. Maybe in response?

"Head of spies for the Red Death Tea Society," Kip said. The toads all croaked again. They were not very musical. They were comparable to our Polt Middle School Orchestra, which has won several awards, such as the "Good Try!" award and the "At Least Nobody Cried" award, the last of which was not strictly true.

"Why are you telling me this?" I asked Kip. Was this a prelude to a kidnapping? Were the toads working for the Red Death Tea Society?

"I don't want to be a spy anymore," Kip said. "I've been watching you and Nate, and I feel bad. It's almost like Maculte and Luria are trying to kill you."

"It's *exactly* like that," I said, dodging a disintegrator ray, nudging some toads aside.

"So, I want to be on your side now," Kip said. A traffic light, no more than three feet away, was caught in one of the rays from the pistols Luria was firing, and was disintegrated. I dove behind a parked car so fast that I thumped into it and dislodged several toads from its roof. Two of them fell on my head. And stayed.

"You want to be on *my* side?" I asked Kip. It didn't seem to be a wise move on his part. My side was wearing soggy shoes on its feet, and toads on its head.

"The side of justice!" Kip said, making it sound *dramatically* noble. He raised one fist into the air and shook it at Luria, yelling, "The world does not tremble at your treachery, you scoundrels! We shall prevail!" He used the same voice he uses when acting in our school plays, such as when he'd played the lead in *Loch Ness Locker Room*, another play that Liz Morris and I wrote, this one concerning the Loch Ness monster trying out for our football team, the Crimson Pterodactyls. The play was a musical and should be considered a classic, even considering the fire that broke out, which was mostly not our fault.

The point is, Kip was obviously suffering from a bad case of overacting, and he had toads all around him, although I could hardly blame him for the thing about the toads, since I myself was suffering through the exact same crisis.

The car behind me fell to dust, victim of a disintegrator ray.

The helicopter swooped lower.

The winds were vicious.

More toads fell on my face.

Clip clop. Clip clop! CLIP CLOP!

It was the sound of my brother the zebra coming back down the street. *Fast.* I could only assume that Nate had somehow gained control of Steve and was riding to my rescue, seconds away from defeating the Red Death Tea Society's helicopter and more importantly getting all the toads off my face.

Clip clop. Clip clop! CLIP CLOP!

"Delphine! Help me!" Nate yelled, hanging from my brother's ear as the zebra raced past, disappearing into the distance.

The winds from the helicopter were almost battering me over. A motor scooter that was parked along the sidewalk tipped over, nearly crushing a group of toads that were forced to jump onto my face in order to avoid the toppling machine. There were *so* many toads. *Too* many toads. Hundreds of toads. All of them gathering around me. Gathering *all over* me. They smelled like wet toast, and I felt like I was sinking in quicksand, except it wasn't sand: it was toads. Is "quicktoads" a thing? It seemed like it was, and that I was destined to be the world's first victim.

"Get these toads off me!" I yelled to Kip, with the webbed feet of several toads slipping into my mouth when I spoke. Kip leaped to my rescue, or at least he tried, but the wind from the helicopter was so strong that it was blowing toads like leaves in the wind, and while it's somewhat enjoyable to stand in a strong wind and let leaves whoosh all around you, it's less fun when the leaves are replaced by irritated toads. Again and again, Kip was knocked back by all the toads whirling in the tremendous winds. He stretched out a hand, trying to reach me, but I was sinking lower, lower, plummeting into a pile of toads that was at least six feet deep, and I am five feet and two inches tall.

The math was against me.

The toads were against me.

I couldn't breathe.

I was struggling.

I was drowning.

My breath was . . .

. . . hey.

I *wasn't* drowning?

So, as it turns out, if you take a pill that protects you against drowning in a flooded school, it also protects you against drowning in a pile of toads, should such an occasion arise. Still, I couldn't move, because I was packed tight in the writhing mass of toads, trapped in a vise of toad legs, and toad bodies, and toad mouths making toad noises, none of which seemed to be the toads saying they were sorry for all the bother.

"*Piffle!*" I said, when more toad feet slipped into my mouth.

"Seriously?" I said, when a toad, waddling across my face, put its foot up my nose.

"Haa-chooo!" I sneezed, because I am apparently allergic to having a toad's foot up my nose.

I went into a sudden burst of sneezing that scooted some of the toads back, allowing me to momentarily surface just in time to see that the helicopter had landed and Maculte and Luria were walking closer, carrying pistols in one hand and teacups in the other, and since they were drinking from the teacups I guessed I knew where I stood.

It wasn't the *tea* for me.

It was the guns.

"Hello," Maculte said.

Sir Jakob Maculte, the twenty-seventh lord of

Mayberry Castle and the leader of the Red Death Tea Society, would look very distinguished except for the odd gleam in his eyes. It's the same gleam as that of a boy pulling wings off flies or tossing cats into a river, those same eyes you see in the documentaries about crazy dictators who destroy entire nations in their mad quest for power.

Maculte has gray hair.

Green eyes.

High cheekbones, with a wide, thin mouth almost forever in a smirk.

The fine teacup was held in long, almost skeletal fingers.

His skin is gray. Not pale, though. Just . . . gray. Like it absorbs light.

His voice sounds rather monotone, but with traces of a sneer. It's a voice that makes me shiver. It's a voice that grates on my nerves like toads on my face.

That's what his voice *normally* sounds like, anyway. But right then as he opened his mouth to speak, his voice sounded like the high-pitched wail of a newborn baby. Or, more precisely, Maculte sounded like a man who'd been *about* to say something but was interrupted when a terrier leaped up and bit his butt at the exact same time that a bee landed on his neck and began stinging.

Bosper and Melville had come to my rescue.

"Thanks, you two!" I said.

And then sank back down beneath the toads.

My phone rang.

Liz again.

"Were you serious about that stuff before?" she asked.

"Yes. And I'm drowning in toads."

"Hmmm," she said.

It was then that I saw the note. It was one of Nate's notes, the ones he writes and then leaves in places he predicts I'll be. It was a struggle to reach it, because I had to move my arm through a huge mound of toads that was shifting in every direction, which is something . . . you will have to believe me . . . that a huge mound of toads does *constantly*. This meant the note was forever moving as one toad kicked it to the left, and then another toad kicked it to the right, and there was one toad that nibbled on it for a couple of seconds before I finally managed to grab it.

"You still there?" Liz asked on the phone.

"Yeah," I said, unfolding the note.

Liz said, "Are there things you haven't been telling me?"

"Yeah," I said, spitting toad legs out of my mouth. The toads were glaring at me like it was my fault.

"It's okay to have secrets," Liz said.

"Is it?" I said.

"Yes. But not from your best friend."

"Oh," I said.

"So," Liz said. "I want to know what's been going on in your life. Why did you make that obstacle course in your backyard? Why did I find that 'adventure kit' beneath your bed? Why do you always warn me against drinking tea? I have more questions. Millions of them. You *will* come to my house and answer them. I can serve cake if you like. And we can talk about space travel. And we can talk about if Nate is your boyfriend, and we will—"

"**Nnay uzz nahh buyy boyfwehh!**" I said.

"Uh. What?"

"Sorry," I said. "I had a toad's leg in my mouth. I was saying that Nate is not my boyfriend. And I *will* explain everything. Especially if you serve cake. But right now I'm sort of fighting a deranged madman, so can it be later?"

"Tonight," Liz said. And she hung up.

"Tonight," I said. "And you guys aren't invited." I was talking to the toads. They squirmed in response.

Or at least they squirmed. They were extremely talented at squirming and it was making me feel squirmy. They smelled like soggy cereal and they felt like, well . . . soggy cereal. They certainly didn't smell or feel like anyone who should be invited to a "cake and confessions" party with my best friend.

I heaved a big sigh.

It was relief.

Ever since meeting Nate, I'd been hiding things from Liz. It would be good to get them out in the open, even if she thought I was crazy. Which she would.

Speaking of crazy, I read the note in my hands.

It said,

"Delphine, I've calculated a 96.8 percent chance that you will be buried in toads when you read this."

"You . . . *calculated* . . . this?" I said, the exasperation in my voice making the toads stir uneasily. I was of the opinion that if you believe one of your friends is going to be buried in toads, you do something to *stop it* from ever happening; you don't just write notes about it.

The note said,

"By now, you're also probably being attacked by the Red Death Tea Society. They are a nuisance."

"Yes," I said. "They are. But at least they don't let their friends get buried in toads." Outside of my mound of toads, somewhere in the *non-toad* distance, I could hear Bosper calling my name, and I could hear the distinctive cry of Maculte being stung on his left arm (it sounded like . . . "Grgargh!") and Luria on her right leg (it sounded like "Flargrah!") and also of Maculte being bitten by Bosper on his right leg, which sounded like, "Argggh! This dog just bit my right leg!" Past these various cries of agony I could also hear the disintegrator rays being fired, several police sirens wailing, an assortment of car alarms, a roaring wind, Kip Luppert yelling, and the clip-clop sounds of a zebra running past.

It all sounded very chaotic.

I kept reading the note.

It said,

"I'm sure you've figured out by now that I dropped the 'Toad Finder' pill in the orange juice that you drank this morning."

"I had not figured that out," I confided to a toad whose leg was in my mouth.

"So that's why you're covered in toads,"

the note said. There was a drawing of a toad, in case I did not know what a toad looked like, even though . . . as Nate had correctly predicted . . . I was entirely covered in toads and therefore had an excess of available reference.

"There's a reason for this,"

the note continued.

"It better be a good one," I told the note.

The note said,

"For the last week, I've been putting carefully structured bosons in Polt's water supply. Bosons are subatomic particles, and I created these particular ones so that they'll adhere to toads. Now that the toads are covered in bosons, the particles will act as a force field geared so that the toads can't be harmed by any disintegrator weapons from the Red Death Tea Society. And, since the toads are now attracted to you by the 'Toad Finder' pill I put in your orange juice, you're effectively wearing a disintegration-proof coat!"

There was a smiley face on the note.

"I'm wearing a toad coat," I told the note, wishing I had a pen so that I could draw a frowny face.

"Oh,"

the note said.

"And, one more thing. Here's a 'Power' pill, so that you'll be strong enough to move around in the toads."

There was a pill adhered to the note, with

"take this"

written next to it.

"Oh," I said. "And, one more thing for *you*, Nate. If these boson things can deflect disintegrator rays, maybe you could, I don't know . . . give them to *ME*, instead of giving them to toads and then making the toads *stick* to me."

Still, it was nice to know that I was immune to the disintegrator rays, even if that meant I was covered in toads. I swallowed the "Power" pill and immediately felt a surge of strength bursting through my veins, making my muscles quiver with delight, as if I could bust down walls. I'd been stumbling along the sidewalk, barely able to stand, but now I felt like I could leap over a building or kick a car through a wall. A toad coat was no problem.

Wiping a few toads from my face, I thought about how it truly *did* feel like I could kick a car like a football, and I thought about how Maculte and Luria were firing their pistols at me, and it seemed like I could combine these two seemingly unrelated facts into one big solution.

I could kick a car at them.

"Incoming!" I yelled out to Bosper and Melville. Bosper immediately went bounding to the side and Melville buzzed herself a few more feet into the air, though I could hear the reluctance in her voice, because she really does enjoy stinging people.

Then, I kicked a car.

It made a noise like "*brrrCRUNCH*" and slid back a couple of feet, no more.

But now my foot was caught in the car door. I'd kicked right through it.

With my foot stuck, I tumbled onto my back, irritating a few toads.

A zebra went racing past my head, clipping and clopping, stepping on my hair.

"Steve!" I yelled.

But then I saw another zebra. And another. There were zebras all over. Well, there were only five of them, but that's a lot of zebras to find on the streets of Polt on a warm sunny afternoon, or really anytime at all.

"What *now*?" I said.

"Stripy horses!" Bosper said, bouncing in place, excited.

"They're not technically horses," Nate called out from one of the zebras, hanging off its ear. "Though horses and zebras *do* both belong to the Equidae family, and to the *Equus* genus. Despite this, they are different species, with horses being *E. ferus caballus*, and zebras *E. quagga*. The difference is—"

"Not pertinent, Nate!" I said, pulling my leg from the car door. A group of toads, patiently waiting for me, immediately jumped back onto my leg. I scrambled to my feet, eager to get back in the fight, but I still wasn't accustomed to my new strength and basically shot myself off the sidewalk like a cannon, smashing backward into a mailbox and wrenching it from the sidewalk.

"Bzzz?" Melville asked, flying closer.

"I'm fine!" I said as all the toads hopped back to me, sticking to me like glue. It was the strangest definition of "fine" I've ever spoken.

Picking up the crushed mailbox, I hurled it at Maculte. My aim, as expected, was perfect. There's a section of my obstacle course where I stand on an unsteady platform and throw various things (baseballs, shoes, etc.) through a tire that's hanging from our most climbable oak tree. At first I was not particularly talented, although the broken window wasn't really my fault, owing to how it shattered so easily. After a few days of practice, though, my aim was better, and so it was no great chore to toss a mailbox at the leader of the Red Death Tea Society.

"Hah!" I said, watching the mailbox zoom closer to Maculte.

"Don't be absurd," Maculte said, disintegrating the mailbox with a blast from his pistol.

"I'm wearing a coat made of toads!" I said. "How can I *not* be absurd?" Using my new tremendous strength, I leaped to the attack, looking like a comet, except instead of trailing glowing gas and dust I was trailing a stream of perplexed amphibians. It was all very dramatic, especially with my red hair, and it would've been even more sensational if I hadn't misjudged my jump and landed on Kip Luppert and knocked him out.

"Oh," he said, in a resigned sort of way as he fell. I suppose if he'd been watching me for the past few months then he would've known that, sooner or later, I'd be accidentally knocking him out. It's sort of my thing.

"*Piffle!*" I said, sprawling, with toads popping off me like popcorn.

"Bzzz!" Melville said, hurrying past me to attack Maculte and Luria, because she knew I was vulnerable. But my bee was still twenty feet away from the leaders of the Red Death Tea Society, and I could see Luria raising her weapon to fire, and I could see what was going to happen.

I was going to lose Melville.

It's true that my bee is incredibly good at dodging. Insects see time at different speeds. To them, humans seem slow and plodding, which is why they're so good at dodging us. But . . . the disintegrator ray moved at the speed of light, and there's no dodging *that*, no matter *how* talented you are.

Luria's finger was tightening on the trigger.

Melville was still nineteen feet away from her.

Speeding to her doom.

Luria's finger was squeezing.

Melville was eighteen feet away from her.

I yelled, "Melville! Look out!"

She stopped and looked back to me, saying, "Bzzz?"

Yelling at her was the worst thing I could've done. Now she was hovering in one spot, looking back to me, wondering what I was worried about.

Luria's gun was making the "**WZWZWZWZ**" noise they make at the instant they're about to fire.

"No," I whispered, knowing what was about to happen, but cursing that I didn't know more. Why couldn't I be as smart as Nate? He would have calculated a solution. He would have saved the day. He would have saved *Melville*. It would've been an *odd* solution, of course, because Nate's mind is odd, which is why he'd taught a mouse to sword fight, and it was why I was wearing a coat made of . . .

. . . toads.

"Sorry!" I told a toad. Then I grabbed it off my arm and tossed it, needing it to be not only the best throw I'd ever accomplished, but also the most perfectly timed.

The toad said, "Roaak?" as it left my hand, arcing away from me, staring back in wonder. Toads are not accustomed to flying, of course, and I'd positively *launched* this one.

The toad whooshed through the air, rocketing toward Melville, and then *past* my confused bee, so that for some few moments both the bee and the toad were staring at each other with a shared expression of bewilderment, obviously wondering what I thought I was doing.

Luria's finger tightened on the trigger.

She fired.

The disintegrator ray flickered out from her weapon, washing over the exact spot where Melville was hovering.

There was a whiplike **zakkt** noise and the smell of burnt hair. There was a burst of light. A tremble in the air. The smallest of concussions.

But I'd done it.

The toad, immune to the disintegrator ray, had shielded Melville, passing in front of her at just the right moment. "Bzzz," my bee companion said in comprehension, finally understanding what I'd been warning her about.

"Kee-roak?" the toad said, still perplexed. It was continuing to zoom through the air, because I'd thrown it with a good deal of muscle, thanks to the "Power" pill I'd swallowed. With all the strength I'd put into the throw, the baffled toad could've kept going for miles and miles, except for one little obstacle in the way.

Luria's face.

Impact sent the toad rebounding into the air, and Luria tumbling over backward. I used the distraction to race closer, using my newfound power to run at twice my normal speed, but I was still too slow. Maculte took out a small pellet from his pocket and tossed it to the sidewalk. There was a sharp cracking noise, and then thick blue smoke began billowing from the pellet. With a touch to one of the buttons on his vest, Maculte started the helicopter's rotor moving again, spreading the blue smoke all over the street like a fog.

The toads began falling from my arms and legs, peeling off my stomach and back, tumbling to the street.

"What's happening?" I asked.

"Simple," Maculte said. "Nathan's charmingly

titled 'Toad Finder' pill works on the principle of stimulating the amphibian nose into thinking a target smells like a spider, thereby attracting the toad's attention, as spiders are a source of food."

"I smell like a spider?" I said, sniffing at my armpits. The odor was that of a sweaty Delphine Cooper. I hoped that wasn't the same thing.

"You *did*," Maculte said. "But my smoke obscures that scent."

"Should Bosper be biting?" the terrier asked, looking back and forth between me and Maculte.

"Sure," I said, because I was worried that Maculte would start ranting, and nobody wanted that. I'd heard enough of his opinions in the past few months, none of which were interesting. They were all about how he deserved to rule the world, or how most people were no more than cattle. He never had interesting opinions, such as how Liz thinks Bigfoot actually does exist, but he grew tired of hanging out in the woods, so he shaves his entire body three times a day and works at Popples, the hamburger place.

"Bosper is biting!" the terrier said, and he bounded forward, but when he was just about to snap his teeth shut on Maculte's leg, he ran into a force field. There was a sharp burst of light and a tinfoil rattle, and it was as if the terrier had been kicked backward. Bosper rolled and tumbled along the sidewalk, his impacts luckily dampened by all the toads, acting like little airbags. Squeaky ones, in this case.

"Bosper has found a difficulty," he said, once he'd come to a stop.

"An impassable one," Maculte said. "My force fields cannot be breached." His voice sounded like a storm cloud. Like the rumble of thunder. Like cannon fire. It sounded like . . .

. . . wait a minute.

That *wasn't* his voice. It was the winds picking up again. It was the flappings of the awnings all along the strect. It was the way the buildings were shivering and shaking, as if several tornadoes were suddenly fighting one another, with forces so powerful that there were sparks in the air, concussions of sound and fury.

There was a blur of yellow and blue and red.

It was Chester.

"I," he said. He was blocks away.

"Can't," he said. He was right next to me, and the force of his speed sent Maculte and Luria tumbling, unconscious, caught up in the slipstream, with Maculte's force field spraying electrical discharges in all directions, with Luria bombarded by the bursts of electricity, gasping in pain as the winds tossed the two leaders of the Red Death Tea Society into the air, the winds so forceful that they destroyed the helicopter, shredding it to tiny bits.

"Stop!" Chester yelled. He was disappearing into the distance.

There was a moment of calm . . .

. . . and then the storm closed in.

Chester's relentless and incredible speed was creating an epic storm. I'd barely regained my feet when the lightning began hitting all around, and there was tremendous rain, with raindrops the size of my fist. There were hailstones hurtling down to the streets, plunging through cars and ripping trees apart. There were screams from all around. Everyone was running for cover. Melville buzzed in the air next to me, urging me to find safety, but there didn't seem to be any place I could reach, no cover to be found. The hail and the rain were battering me as I reached out and grabbed Melville in my hand, providing some shelter for her, at least.

"We have to get out of this storm!" I yelled to Bosper.

"But Bosper is biting!" he said. His statement was most decidedly true. He'd taken advantage of how Chester's speed had destroyed Maculte's force field and was now biting at the unconscious man's legs. Luria, nearby, was dazed, crawling on her hands and knees to the relative safety of an oak tree, though the hail was beginning to strip the tree of its leaves and even its branches, whittling it down.

"Save the biting for later!" I told Bosper. He whined, but did as I asked, releasing Maculte after one final chomp. Then the terrier came scampering back to me, bounding left and right, sometimes stopping, sometimes darting forward. It was an intricate dance of mathematics, as Bosper plotted the courses of all the hailstones plunging down from above, then dodged them.

"The dog has done good biting," he proclaimed when he reached me, and then I heard a moan from behind.

"Kip!" I yelled. He was still unconscious, and entirely helpless in the ferocious hailstorm. I couldn't just leave him there, crumpled against the side of an ice-cream truck, where the winds from Chester's passing had hurled him. There was an ongoing river of rain washing through the streets, with countless hailstones bobbing in the water, swept along, thumping off Kip. I had to save him, even if he *was* a spy, because there were those who would argue that *I* was to blame for knocking Kip unconscious, merely because I was the one who had done it.

"Remind me to add weather elements to my obstacle course!" I told Bosper.

"There is peanut butter!" he yelled back.

"What?" He'd lost me. Was there peanut butter on my obstacle course?

"The butter of peanuts!" Bosper yelled. "It has been discovered!"

"Seriously," I said. "What are you talking about?" But then I noticed how a jar of peanut butter had rolled out onto the sidewalk when the wall of the Chandler grocery store had collapsed the earlier time Chester had run past. Unfortunately for the poor terrier, the peanut butter jar was partially under the collapsed wall, a chunk of bricks twice the size of a door. Bosper was pawing at the pinned jar, whining, looking back to me, wanting help, as if I, at ninety-three pounds, was strong enough to lift a brick wall and uncover . . .

Oh.

Wait a minute.

"Here!" I yelled, reaching over and picking up the wall, because I was still charged full of power from the pill I'd swallowed. I held the wall above my head, protecting us from the damaging hail, nudging Kip beneath my makeshift shelter with my foot. I had to hurry, because I could see Maculte was waking up, and we'd only stopped him by pure luck the first time, and I was in no way confident that we could do it again.

And so it was that I hurried off down the block as best I could, our escape hidden by the tremendous rains and the cannon-fire hailstones, holding a brick wall above my head, listening to the sounds of the roaring winds, the buzz of Melville at the end of my nose, the grunts of an unconscious spy as I continuously nudged him along the sidewalk with my soggy shoes, and the slurping joy of a terrier with a jar of peanut butter stuck to his face.

Chapter 5

Thirty minutes later I'd taken a shower and was just about to use the blow-dryer that Nate gave me. It's an excellent blow-dryer, so efficient that I only have to blow-dry my hair for about two seconds before it's dry, and there's some sort of atomic moisturizer that makes my hair silkier than normal, which is great because my hair usually feels like it's made out of a combination of uncooked spaghetti and arcs of electricity. That's one of the disadvantages of being a redhead. Of course, one of the advantages of being a redhead is that I'm a redhead, so it's worth it.

The only real problem with my blow-dryer is that Nate made the handle from an old robot toy of his, so that whenever I turn it on the robot says, "To space, brave captain!"

I'd just turned it on when my phone beeped. I turned off the blow-dryer and looked at my phone. It was a text from Liz.

It said, **Can't wait for tonight. I'm coming over.** I grimaced, because I had a pet bee perched atop the bathroom mirror, and there was a talking terrier in my living room, and an unconscious spy in my room, and somewhere in Polt my brother Steve was being a zebra. Plus, Chester needed to be rescued somehow, and the Red Death Tea Society was on one of its exasperating binges of trying to wipe Nate and me off the face of the planet. Furthermore, I had no idea where Nate was (he wasn't answering my calls or texts) and Mom and Dad were going to be home in an hour (they'd gone to a soccer game) and it did not seem like an excellent time to finally explain to Liz all that had been happening in my life, because even a short version would take nearly all of infinity to explain.

Now is not a good time, I texted back, then turned on my blow-dryer again (*To space, brave captain!*) but had barely pointed it at my hair when my phone beeped with another message from Liz.

Guess where I'm at! it said.

"I do not need to guess," I said to my phone, because Liz had attached a picture of her standing right in front of my house.

There was a knock on the door.

Melville, buzzing, took to the air. I waved her back down.

The knockings continued.

"There is knocking on the house!" I heard from the living room. "Bosper will chew on the door!"

"No you will not!" I yelled, loud enough that poor Melville tumbled in the gust of my breath.

"Bosper will not!" the terrier called back. "He is a good boy who will chew on the spy!"

"Ahhh! Don't do that, either! At least not yet." There was silence for a bit, then the bathroom door squeaked open a few inches, and Bosper peeked in through the opening.

"Bosper will save his chewing," he whispered, then slowly pulled back out of sight.

There was more insistent knocking on the front door, and equally demanding beeps from my phone. Melville took to the air again, but I waved her back down, saying, "I don't have time for Liz right now. So, be quiet, and hopefully she'll go away." I picked up the blow-dryer and turned it on (*To space, brave captain!*) but hadn't even managed to start it on my hair before Liz was knocking on the bathroom window.

"Delphine!" she said. "Are you in there?" The curtains were closed. She was only guessing where I was. If I stayed quiet, she would probably go away, and though I felt like a snake I really didn't have time just then. I needed to save Chester and question Kip and retrieve all the science potions and the pills from all over Polt, and I needed to find Nate and—

"Nate!" Liz said.

"Huh?" I said. Had she read my mind?

"Hello, Liz," I heard Nate's voice say.

He was outside.

With Liz.

"Oh no," I whispered.

Cautiously moving the curtain aside no more than an inch, I peered outside to see what new complications were developing.

Nate was outside with five zebras.

Talking with Liz.

"What's up with the zebras?" she asked.

"They're not truly zebras," Nate answered. "This one is Delphine's brother, Steve." He put his hand on the flank of one of the zebras. I couldn't tell that it was any different from the others.

"What?" Liz said. She had the kind of expression you might expect from someone being told that a zebra was my brother. It must have been doubly unexpected for Liz, because she and I usually consider Steve to be a baboon.

"I don't believe Delphine has ever told you that I'm the smartest person on earth," Nate said.

"Nope," she said. There were, like, nine syllables in the word.

"Well, I am. And that brings certain problems. For instance, the Red Death Tea Society, which occasionally tries to assassinate Delphine and me."

"Okay," Liz said. Slowly.

"Oh, there's my dog!" Nate said. Bosper had gone outside and was bounding around the corner of the house. I was holding on to the window curtains for support.

"Bosper can talk," Nate said. I was *clutching* the curtains.

"Hello, Liz Morris!" Bosper said, jumping up and down. "Bosper has been told that farting is okay!" He farted. I was positively clawing at the curtains.

Liz was turning an amazing shade of red, and then she went pale. One of the zebras was nudging at her. It might well have been Steve.

"Anyway," Nate said. "Because my brain works at such high levels, it's sometimes necessary for me to create a little chaos, just to keep things amusing."

"Wwwagf," Liz said. It was an admirable try at a word, considering the circumstances. "Whagg . . . where's D-Delphine?"

"I'm calculating a 99.87 percent chance that she's

watching us through that window," Nate said, pointing to the bathroom window, and to me, without even looking in my direction. Liz's eyes turned my way. And narrowed. I trembled.

"Every Friday the thirteenth, I specifically do three dumb things," Nate said. "This time, circumstances have led to Steve Cooper turning into a zebra. Also, I'm suffering from the effects of a truth serum, so I can't help but tell you all of these things, no matter how angry I make Delphine."

"The dog is a good jumper," Bosper said. "Watch Bosper do some jumping!" He did some jumping. Liz watched him for a couple of seconds, then stared back to the window, where I was still trying to hide. I planned on trying to hide forever. I planned on becoming the world's best hider.

"Bzzz?" Melville said. She was right next to my ear, peering out the opening alongside me, and I guess I hadn't noticed her, and I guess I might have been a little tense, and I guess I screamed, and then I guess I tried to climb the curtains in order to escape, and it's for certain that they came tumbling down, taking me with them.

Liz peered in the window, looking at me, tangled in the curtains.

"Hey, Delphine," she said.

"Hi, Liz!"

"So . . . it sounds like we have a few things to talk about."

"Meet you at the door?" I asked.

This time, she only nodded. No more words needed to be said. At least not *yet*.

And so it was that I left my bathroom and began the slow walk to my front door, where the smartest boy on earth was waiting alongside my best friend in the whole world, along with five zebras, one of which was my brother, Steve.

"To space, brave captain," I whispered, reaching for the door.

It turns out that the extra zebras were a mailman, a grad student in Mexican American history, a burger chef who'd been on her way to Popples, and, lastly, Susan Heller, our classmate and Nate's dream girl, who I thought looked better as a zebra.

"I'd been hanging from Steve's ear," Nate said, gesturing to one of the five zebras in my living room, where neither Mom nor Dad have ever *expressly* said I couldn't have any large ungulates. "And then Luria noticed me and correctly deduced the identity of this zebra." He tapped on one of the zebra's necks. I still didn't know how Nate was telling them apart, or how anyone else could have possibly noticed that Steve was . . . Steve.

"How could you tell?" Kip asked. He was looking through Dad's bookshelf, the one that's full of history books, and books on cartography, and on the days of vaudeville.

"His DNA is still identical," Nate said. "It's merely a matter of noticing the match on your atomic structure display scanners." Nate held up his phone, which *is* a phone, but it's also a lot of other things, apparently including an atomic structure display scanner.

"Most people don't have atomic scanners handy," Liz said. I wanted to high-five her, since I'd been saying similar things to Nate for months now. Ever since I met him, actually. But, high-fiving Liz was currently out of the question. She was miffed at me. She was discovering the monumental number of secrets I'd been hiding from her.

"Bosper," I said. "Give Liz a high five for me." Since Liz wasn't talking to me, we were using the terrier as a means of communicating.

"Five is the only odd untouchable number," Bosper whispered. He often whispers when he's talking about math. "It is a Fermat prime number!"

"I have no idea what this dog is talking about," Liz said, talking to Kip and Nate, *not* me. Kip had moved to our green couch, sitting all the way to one side, because it put him against the wall, where it was harder for the zebras to nibble on his hair, which it seemed they were fond of doing.

"I have no idea how this dog can *talk*!" Liz added. Kip gave her a sympathetic smile. Only a couple of minutes after I'd let Liz and Nate and all the zebras in through the door, Kip had come wandering out of my room, rubbing the bump on his head where some unnamed person had landed on him in a completely understandable accident. While introductions were being made, and while Kip was admitting to Nate that he was a spy, and while the two boys were explaining everything to Liz, I'd put a bunch of cookies in a bowl, and then absentmindedly poured potato chips on top of them. I was as terrible as Nate at providing snacks, although at least *he's* never had to serve snacks to five zebras.

I take that back. He probably has.

"So, what's up with these extra zebras?" I asked Nate.

"Oh. Well, once Luria knew about Steve, I was worried she'd try to kidnap him. I needed to disguise him in some way, so I used a spray can of 'Make Any Animal a Zebra' on the nearby crowd, making more zebras so that Steve could blend in."

"Brilliant," Kip said, because it was becoming clear that Kip idolized Nate.

"Weird," I said, because "making more zebras" and "making more chaos" were not . . . I'll just go ahead and admit . . . the ways I would've thought to solve the problems of too much chaos and too many zebras.

"Super-weird!" Liz said, because of absolutely everything she was hearing.

Liz has short brown hair, the color of driftwood when it's wet. Her ears stick out from her hair and also from beneath any hats she's ever worn. She jokes that they make it hard for her to walk through doorways. I think her ears are adorable. Her eyes are a strange near-purple and she's five feet three inches, an inch taller than me. She was wearing a light blue dress with stick-figure drawings of wolves. Her fingers were twitching. She grabbed her phone from her purse and tapped on the keys.

My phone beeped.

There was a text. From Liz.

It said, I'm too mad to talk to you, but we can still text, right?

I looked up to Liz and nodded. Her eyes narrowed.

"Oh," I said. Then I texted, Yes.

Liz's phone beeped.

She read it. Then typed for a moment.

My phone beeped.

The text read, Am I dreaming all this?

I typed back, No. Would you like some pie?

"Yes!" Liz said, speaking to me again. The smile on her face looked like sunshine and flowers and bunnies.

"Nate," I said. "Order some pie. Several different kinds."

"Okay," he said, grabbing his phone. One of the many things I like about Nate is that he doesn't question oddities. If you tell him to order some pie, he will order some pie. If you tell him that you're considering how to plant flowers on the moon, he will devise a way to plant flowers on the moon. It's just who he is.

"And get some bales of hay," I said. "The zebras look hungry." They were again nibbling on Kip's hair. Nate tapped on his phone for a bit, and then nodded, putting it back in his pocket. Liz came over and sat next to me on the blue couch, the one where Dad likes to stretch out and watch soccer.

"Sorry about getting mad," she said.

"Sorry about giving you a reason to get mad."

"It must have been tough, all these secrets?" She gestured to Nate, who was talking to Kip about the Red Death Tea Society, asking him to spill the beans about some of the inner workings, meaning that Kip wouldn't only be a spy, but a double agent. Liz's gesture also included the zebras, which were milling around, looking confused, for which I could not blame them. And of course Liz's gesture also included Melville (who was busily stinging any zebra that came too close to any particularly breakable objects, herding them toward the center of the room) and Bosper, who was repeatedly telling Liz that he knew how to dig holes and if she wanted to come outside he would show her.

"Yeah," I said. "I've been wanting to tell you, but it's all so . . . so crazy."

"Is this 'tea' thing, the Red Death Tea Society, is *that* why you've been telling me not to drink tea?"

"Yes. I'm worried they might try to poison my friends. Or mind-control them. Or turn them into zebras." I gestured to the zebras, in case Liz didn't know what I was talking about.

"Oh. I'd just been thinking you came across some

146

article about how tea might be bad for you, the way the Internet makes *everything* sound bad for you."

"Nope," I told Liz. "It's because of a murderous league of assassins."

"Hmm," she said.

"Yeah," I agreed. "Hmm."

I heard a car pull up outside.

"That'll be our pie!" I said, jumping up. "What kinds of pie did you order, Nate?"

"Pumpkin and cherry and apple and strawberry and rhubarb for us," he said.

"Wow," Liz gasped.

"And a peanut butter pie for Bosper," Nate added.

"The dog is making drools," Bosper said. He was, indeed, making drools.

"And then grass pies for the zebras," Nate added. The zebras all looked up at this, bewildered, as if they'd never before heard of grass pies. I haven't, either, but I still wasn't too surprised, because when you're friends with Nate you learn to adjust.

"Sounds like a lot of pies," I said. "Anybody want to help me carry them inside?"

"Me!" Liz yelled, doing a somersault off the couch.

"The dog can also be carrying pies!" Bosper said. "Good boy, Bosper!" The terrier was quite pleased with himself, jumping off the back of the couch to launch himself into space, tumbling to a momentary stop, then scrabbling on the wooden floor and scurrying for the front door. Liz wasn't too far behind him, because of the great love she has for pies. She was so quick that I'd barely made it to the hallway before Liz flung the door open and then froze in place, staring outside.

"Oh," she said.

And then she said, "Hello, Mr. and Mrs. Cooper."

My parents were at the door.

"Oh," I said.

From behind me in the living room, I could hear my brother Steve snorting, along with all the other zebras.

There are various ways to avoid getting into trouble with your parents. If, for instance, you've done poorly on a test, merely promise that you'll study harder and improve your grades. It's important that you then actually *do* this, because if you *don't*, they will catch you in the lie, and lying is another way of getting into trouble with your parents. If you *have* lied to your parents, I'd advise volunteering your own punishment, such as mowing the lawn, doing the dishes, or even going so far as to ground yourself for a day. The point is, the most important thing to remember about getting into trouble with your parents is not to panic, and to remember that they love you, and that you are not doomed.

"I'm so doomed," I whispered.

I forgot to mention another important thing about getting into trouble with your parents. Similar to dogs, parents can smell fear, so do not panic.

"Ahhh!" I said, entirely panicked. "You were supposed to be at a *soccer game*! Why are you *here*? What are you doing *home*? Ahhhh!"

"The soccer game was canceled," Mom said. "Haven't you noticed all the horrible weather we're having? And, why are you so panicked? What's going on here?"

"Nothing about zebras," I said. Liz glared at me.

"What have you been up to, Delphine?" Dad said, all but floating in a sea of suspicion, stalking past us into the living room. I felt like I was shrinking. I closed my eyes and waited for the terrible tolling of my Bell of Doom. How many dishes would I have to wash for having zebras in the house? *Infinite* dishes? How many times would I have to take out the garbage when Dad found out that I've been fighting a secret society of assassins? Also . . . infinite? Did I have *time* for two different infinite chores?

"Nothing wrong in there," Dad said, coming out of the living room. "She's just having some friends over." Two zebras came ambling out behind him. Mom didn't react. It was like she didn't even see them. Melville quickly stung the zebras, herding them back with the others.

"Oh? We have guests?" Mom asked. "Who?" She walked right past the zebras. I followed her into the living room.

"Oh, it's Nate," Mom said. "Good to see you." Nate looked up from his phone and nodded, furiously tapping on the keys, typing so fast that it almost looked like there was smoke coming from his phone.

"This is Kip," Nate said, gesturing to Kip, who was sitting sedately on the couch, with half of his hair in a zebra's mouth.

"Oh," Mom said. "I remember you. Weren't you the lead in some of Delphine's plays? Like, the alien wizard in *A Midsummer Night's Spaceship*?"

"Yeah!" Kip said, with the joy of a semi-celebrity finally being recognized. "That was me!"

A zebra ambled across the living room and began to nibble on Mom's hair, but Melville stung it away from her. The zebra neighed in displeasure, but *clip-clop-clomped* back to the rest of the herd.

Bosper told Mom, "The dog will not be talking, because it is a secret." I felt like my heart was going to collapse into a black hole.

"Is this Nate's dog?" Mom asked, kneeling down to scratch Bosper behind his ears. "Who's a cutie?" she asked him. "Who's a good boy?"

"Bosper is the good boy!" the terrier said, bouncing all over, with the joy of a good boy finally being recognized.

"Yeah," I said. "That's . . . Nate's dog." It was like Mom didn't even notice Bosper was talking, despite how he was currently explaining how butterflies are liars because they are *not* made of butter, and that 88,813 is his favorite prime number. Mom just scratched behind his ears, and Dad watched her as if nothing was wrong, as if neither of them could hear the dog talking, or see the zebras, or—

Hmm.

There really *was* smoke coming from Nate's phone.

"Nate," I said. "What are you doing?"

"Releasing a series of mind-altering nano-bots so that your parents won't notice anything out of the ordinary. Incidentally, pie at the door."

"What?" I said.

"Pie at the door!" Bosper said. Just then, there was a knocking at the door.

"I'll get it!" Liz said.

"Uh, okay," I said, watching her run for the door, and watching as my parents left the living room while talking about the day's strange weather patterns, and Mom was talking about maybe getting a little work done (one of her clients was having a gallery show in less than a week, and most of the paintings still needed to be framed, and there was lighting to be strung), and Dad said he was going to grab some lemonade and watch some television. I remembered how Algie and Maryrose, Nate's parents, had acted when we were fighting the Red Death Tea Society in their house, how they'd been completely unaware of anything that was going on. I felt a little guilty about my own parents acting so oblivious, but there was only a little bit of guilt, and a towering amount of relief.

"Anyone need lemonade?" Dad said, poking his head back in through the doorway.

"I could use one," Nate said.

Kip said, "That would be great."

"Me too," I said. "And one for Liz." Liz was struggling back into the living room, carrying pies stacked up past her ears in a delicious and somewhat unstable tower. I nabbed three pies from the top before any pie-related tragedies could occur. Bosper, meanwhile, was tugging several more pies along with him, pie plates with little bales of grass on them, complete with chocolate filling.

"Here," Dad said, stepping over Bosper and the pies. "I just brought the whole lemonade pitcher and some glasses. You kids can help yourselves." He put the lemonade on the coffee table, not taking any notice of how two zebras, one of which was possibly his son, were nibbling on a stack of video game magazines.

"Thanks, Dad," I said. He ruffled my hair and left. It embarrassed me for some reason.

"Bzzz," Melville said. She'd landed on an apple pie.

"That one's hers," I told the others.

"The whole pie?" Kip said, grabbing one of the plates.

"Bzzz," Melville said.

"Unless you want to get stung," I translated. Melville was all but dancing in the middle of the apple pie. I reached out and poked a hole down through the crust, giving my bee better access to the riches.

"Bzzz," she said.

Kip stepped back.

Quickly.

The first order of business was the pie.

While it is true that I'm well known for my feelings on cake (it is simply the greatest thing ever), I *do* enjoy pie, and so I'm not afraid to admit that I had three slices. I *am* afraid to admit, however, how many slices of pie I ate *after* I'd had those three slices. Let's just say I ate less pie than Liz, and that she stopped before she exploded. Nate and Kip both ate three slices apiece, and Mom and Dad snuck away two slices for each of them, which they richly deserved, owing to how half of their children were currently zebras.

Speaking of the zebras, they seemed to enjoy their grass pies, eating them with a gusto unmatched by anything past that of a terrier eating a peanut butter pie, because Bosper was devouring his pie in great gulping heaves, chomping, smacking, and growling in pleasure.

"Bosper is being a good eater!" he yelled at one point, referring . . . I can only assume . . . to how he was managing to eat a huge *amount* of pie, and not at all referring to how *tidy* he was being, because he was spraying peanut butter and pie crust in all directions.

Melville, meanwhile, had eaten a thumbnail-size portion of her apple pie, which is a fair amount of apple pie for a thumbnail-size insect.

"Bzzz," she said.

Or maybe it was a burp.

The second order of business was asking Nate what the Red Death Tea Society was doing in town.

"Maculte can't just have come to Polt for *revenge*, can he?"

"He definitely *could* have," Nate said. "He really hates us since we stopped his bumblebee invasion plan."

"That was the Red Death Tea Society?" Liz said. "Those bees were everywhere! They were *so* mean!" Melville zoomed over and tried to hide in my hair, buzzing in apology. I've long since forgiven her, but she still feels bad.

"That was them," Nate said. He was working out an equation on his pants, writing with an ink pen the way he does. Liz was staring at him, and I could almost see her changing the way she thought about Nate. Before, with all the inked equations on his pants, all the numbers and the weird little drawings he does, Liz had considered Nate to be weird. Now, she was considering him to be a weird genius. Totally different.

"**Uh-oh**," he said.

"Something up?" Liz asked, pouring lemonade.

"What is it?" Kip said, with a mouthful of pie.

"I believe I know what the Red Death Tea Society is doing in Polt," Nate said.

"Of course," I said. "They're trying to steal the inventions you idiotically hid all over town. That's obvious."

"*Too* obvious," Nate said, raising an eyebrow in a manner I will graciously call dramatic, because he is a friend and I want to support him. "Maculte works on too many levels for that to be the entirety of it. But, look at this." He handed me his phone. I looked at it. There was a picture of Susan Heller.

"Why's there a picture of Susan Heller?" I asked. I looked to the zebras, which were all warily watching as Melville circled above them, giving them the evil eye. I wasn't sure which of the zebras was Susan Heller, but I was certain that the stinkiest one had to be Steve.

"Oog," Nate said. His face went red. "That was a mistake. I meant to show you a calculation, not the picture of Susan I have on my phone so that I can look at her whenever I want, because her smile makes me feel funny, and right now I wish I hadn't programmed myself for honesty because this is very embarrassing please give back my phone and I will show you the calculations and maybe I should have my nano-bots wipe away everyone's memories of the last few minutes because that way Delphine wouldn't give me too much grief about oh no . . . oh no . . . I'm talking out loud, aren't I?"

"You're talking out loud," I said.

"Wait," Liz said. "I thought *you two* were together?" Her finger waggled between Nate and me, back and forth, while her eyes narrowed in "best friend defense" mode.

"No!" I said. The puff of my breath sent Melville spinning through the air.

"No!" Nate said. "Although to be honest I *do* have a picture of Delphine on my phone as well, because she's much more intelligent and adventurous than Susan, who frankly is a bit rude and pretentious and I very much enjoy looking at the image of Delphine from time to time and oh no I hate this honesty thing."

"Whoa," Liz said, sitting back on the couch.

"Gosh," Kip said.

"*Piffle*," I whispered, because I was blushing much harder than Nate had blushed. I was blushing as hard as if I'd had a seven-hour training session on my adventure course, including the part where I have to hang upside down for as long as possible, in case the Red Death Tea Society attacks us with *bats* next time, and I have to infiltrate them in disguise. I like to be prepared for all eventualities.

"So, maybe we should see that thing you were *supposed* to show us on your phone?" Liz told Nate, meanwhile handing Kip several paper towels, because an unnamed someone had accidentally done a lemonade spit-take all over him right before she started blushing.

"Yes!" Nate said. "Move on from the embarrassing parts! Good call!" Nate handed me his phone, this time showing me rows and rows of . . . numbers. *Lots* of numbers. They meant nothing to me. I looked around for Bosper, because he's good with math and I was hoping he'd translate what Nate was trying to tell us, but the terrier had vanished.

"These are just numbers," Liz said, taking the phone from me and looking at it. Kip slid closer to her and we all looked at the phone. Then, all together, we looked up to Nate, shook our heads, and shrugged.

"Oh," Nate said. "I forget that not everyone speaks Math." Nate considers math to be a language.

"What that means," Nate said, "is that the Red

Death Tea Society has finally realized I'll never join them."

"That's good news!" I said.

"So they've decided to trigger an earthquake that will destroy Polt, obliterating the entire city and annihilating every living creature, including myself, thereby eliminating my threat to their continued plans."

"That's . . . bad news," I said.

So, the next thing on our agenda was to sit around and stare at one another in horror. We each tried to think of something to say.

Kip managed to say, "Wh-wh-what?"

Melville landed on my shoulder and said, "Bzzz?" which translated into exactly what Kip had said.

Liz told me, "I'm starting to wish you *wouldn't* have told me all these secrets."

I just said, "**Piffle**," but I said it enough times that I was the most vocal of us all.

Nate just sat on the couch, writing equations on his pants.

"Okay!" I finally said. "We can only deal with one problem at a time, and right now there's a zebra standing on my foot." Melville swooped through the air and gave it a sting on its rump, which made the zebra buck a bit, but by then my bee had it fairly well trained (except for the "don't stand on Delphine's feet" part) and the zebra quickly rejoined the others.

"That's one problem solved," I said. "But we still *have* zebras and we should *not* have zebras. Raise your hand if you can solve this." Liz did not raise her hand. Kip put his hands in his pocket. We all looked to Nate.

"Okay," he said. "But we can't let them know they've *been* zebras, either. So, before I cure them, we'll need to use this." He reached into his shirt and brought out a dart gun.

"Ooo!" Liz said. "Me! I will shoot the dart gun!" She snatched the dart gun away from Nate, bounding as excitedly as Bosper so often does. I looked around for the terrier again. Where *was* that dog?

"Okay, ready?" Nate said. He had a bright pink pill in his hand.

"Yes!" Liz said, excitedly waving the dart gun. Then, only a moment later, she said, "Oops!" . . . because she'd accidentally triggered a shot. A tiny dart whooshed across the room, bounced off the lemonade pitcher, and then hit the ceiling fan, from where it ricocheted off and sank into Kip's arm.

"**Guhh?**" he said, already leaning to one side,

starting to go unconscious. Liz hurried over and propped him up as his eyes flickered, and then closed.

"No problem here!" Liz said. She was struggling to keep Kip from toppling onto the floor, and also to keep a zebra from eating his hair. "Totally ready!" she said.

"Okay," Nate said, because he nearly always takes people at their word. "Here goes!" He held out the bright pink pill for one of the zebras. It looked at the pill with interest, then licked it off Nate's hand and swallowed.

The zebra's eyes went wide.

It trembled.

Steam started billowing off the zebra and then there was a strange *blorrrrrrk* popping noise, and suddenly there was a grad student in Mexican American history in my living room. He was a bit over six feet tall, wearing black jeans and a jealousy-inducing T-shirt depicting Moby Dick jousting against Godzilla. The grad student had blue eyes, blond hair, and an impressive mustache.

"Where am I?" he said. His mustache twitched.

"You're in the firing line!" Liz said, enthusiastically dramatic. She did a somersault and fired a shot from the dart gun. The dart whooshed past the grad student and stuck into one of the zebras, which shivered and then slumped to the floor.

"Hmm," Liz said. "It turns out you were a little to the *left* of the firing line. But now . . . *hahh*!" She fired another shot. The dart embedded in Moby Dick. Meaning the grad student's chest.

"Hahh?" he said. Then his eyes rolled up and he started to topple.

"Ooo!" Nate said. "Catch him!"

"Got him!" I said, because if Liz was going to be on the dart gun, I had to do *something*. So I reached out and tried to catch the grad student, which did not go very well in either the "planning" or "execution" stages.

Basically he fell on me.

"There!" I said. "I cushioned his fall. Exactly as I planned." I was crawling out from underneath the grad student, who was heavier than he looked. Maybe it's because he had a whale on his shirt?

"Well done!" Liz applauded. She clapped her hands together, which is an admirable thing to do when your best friend could use an ego boost, but not so smart if you happen to be holding a dart gun in your hands. Which Liz was.

So she triggered another shot.

Luckily, it only sank into the wall.

Unluckily, it hit less than an inch from Melville, who'd been taking a rest from an exhausting regimen of zebra-stinging.

"Bzzz!" she said, because Melville has a hair-trigger temper and had decided she'd been attacked.

"Grgargh!" Liz yelped, as my bee stung her left arm.

"Stop!" I told Melville, leaping to my best friend's defense, tossing my entire body in front of Liz just as my bee struck again, getting *me* this time.

"Huh?" I said, confused. Because the bee sting hadn't hurt.

"The nano-bots in your system should have nullified the pain," Nate said. "Did it work?"

"Yeah! It didn't hurt at all. I barely felt it."

Liz was apologizing to Melville and Melville was buzzing her embarrassment over being so hotheaded. Nate had that smug look he has when one of his experiments turns out the way he expected.

"Fantastic!" Nate said. "To be honest, I wasn't sure if that was going to work. It actually had a thirty-seven percent chance of making the pain a lot worse."

"Really?" I said, wearing a smile. I wasn't smiling. I was *wearing* a smile. There's a difference.

I said, "As it turns out, it *did* make the pain worse."

"Huh?" Nate said. And then I said, "*Your* pain!"

And then he said, "Unghh!" This was because I'd punched his arm, which is something of a hobby of mine. I am getting to be very good at it, because of an old tire I've roped to an oak tree in the middle of my adventure training course. The tire is labeled "Nate's arm," and I practice punching it every day, building up my muscles and my accuracy.

It's important to be prepared.

The grad student wandered out of my house, completely oblivious to all that had happened. I knew this was because of the way Nate had erased part of his memory, but at the same time I've met quite a few college students and I have to say that "completely oblivious" is really their natural state.

Kip was still asleep.

"How long will he be out?" I asked.

"A few hours, likely," Nate said. "I configured these sleeping darts for zebras, so it will take longer for it to wear off with Kip. He's smaller."

We put the slumbering spy on the recliner against the wall, and we covered his head with a blanket, so that the zebras wouldn't eat his apparently delicious hair.

The zebra in the dart-induced slumber was the mailman. I had to push one of the bright pink pills through the zebra's teeth, where it was Slobber Central. A few seconds later the transformation was complete, and Nate touched his cell phone to the back of the man's neck. There was an arc of electricity, and the man quickly stood, his eyes bright and alert.

"Time to get back to my mail route," he said. "Meanwhile, I should keep in mind that nothing out of the ordinary has happened." He quickly walked out of the living room and then down the short hall to the front door, passing Dad, who was on his way upstairs. Neither of them noticed the other.

"This is what your life's been like?" Liz asked me.

"This is what my life's been like," I said.

"Ready?" Nate asked Liz, with one of the pink pills in his hand.

"Super-ready," Liz said. She was in the shooting stance we'd learned back when we were cowriting

Detective Cat-Fist, our play about a feline detective who uses guns that shoots fists instead of bullets.

"Here goes," Nate said. He fed the pill to one of the three remaining zebras. Five seconds later, a burger chef from Popples was standing in the middle of my living room, looking as bewildered as she had when she was a zebra.

"How did I get here?" she said.

"Detective Cat-Fist *strikes*!" Liz yelled, and fired a dart. It made a little *thoook* sound when it stuck in the woman's arm. She was in her late twenties. Tall. Her nose had big fat freckles and her hair was in a bun. Her Popples uniform had a few grease stains that no laundry detergent would ever defeat. She had rings on each of her fingers.

Her whole body twitched.

I didn't try to catch her. I'd learned. Instead, I just pushed her toward the couch.

"Excellent," Nate said, looking at the slumbering chef. "My 'Mind-Reorganizer' pill works much better when people are sleeping." He was touching his phone to the back of the woman's neck.

"And have you done . . . *extensive* tests of this mind reorganizer on sleeping people?" Liz asked. Melville flew closer and buzzed in curiosity.

"Wait!" I yelled. "Nate, I know you're forced to

tell the truth right now, so . . . before you answer Liz's question, I want to ask one of my own. Do you think it would be for the best if you *didn't* answer her question? If you *didn't* tell us about how many times you've 'reorganized' the minds of Polt's slumbering citizens?"

"Yes," he immediately said, leaving Liz and me in our beautiful ignorance, as a burger chef wandered out of my house.

"Only two zebras left," Liz said. "Which one's next?"

"This one," Nate said, giving a bright pink pill to one of the zebras. It chomped up the pill in a single gulp, meaning it was far more likely the zebra was Steve rather than Susan, because Steve eats like a garbage truck.

"What the heck?" Steve was soon saying, looking all around the living room. "How'd I get home? Is that . . . is that a zebra?" My brother is sixteen years old. His light brown hair is full of waves, swooping all around. He thinks it makes him look enigmatic. I say "*piffle*" to that, and he knows what I mean. He has a roundish face and he's compulsively checking for zits, for underarm odors, for stains on his clothes, and for ketchup on his nose, the last one because of an incident where he got ketchup on his nose at the Ballyhoo Burger Joint and then tried to flirt with three college girls . . . *without* knowing about said ketchup on his nose . . . despite how his sister (whose name I will not mention) could've told him about it at any time, and didn't.

"Delphine," Steve said. "Is this *your* doing?" He was pointing to the last of the zebras as if he'd always suspected me of harboring zebras and he'd finally caught me in the very act. "You are in so much trouble!" he said.

"Give me that," I told Liz, holding out my hand.

"Of course," she said, slapping the dart gun into my open palm.

It made a *thook* sound when I shot Steve with a sleeping dart.

All five times.

"Oh, you're that weird guy," Susan Heller said when she was no longer a zebra, having been returned to her usual far more annoying self.

Nate was stricken.

"That . . . weird guy?" he said. Melville buzzed in sympathy.

"He's an *awesome* weird guy!" I said in his defense.

"Who are *you*?" Susan asked me, even though we've been in the same classes for several years.

"I'm the daughter of this house," I said, using the same dramatic voice I'd used when playing the lead in Liz's production of *Lady Kickface*, the play that was never actually staged because of a strange outbreak of broken noses that were not my fault. "I am Delphine Gabriella Cooper. You will fear me, Susan Heller. You will know the true horror of . . . of . . . hmmm. Oh geez, Nate, will you stop acting so dreamy-eyed?" I'd stopped because Nate had recovered from his momentary understanding of how unpleasant Susan could be, and was again staring at her with his usual idiocy.

"Seriously, Nate. Count of three . . . and then I'll have Melville sting you." I pointed at Nate and said, "One. Two. Thr—"

"What are you weirdos *talking about*?" Susan said. "This isn't making any sense! How did I get here? I'm supposed to be *shopping*!"

"Want me to dart her?" Liz asked.

"In a second," I said. Then, "Susan, I was only having some fun being extra dramatic because you won't remember any of this."

"Are you some idiot?" she said.

"And . . . *three*!" I said to Melville, but instead of

pointing at Nate, I changed over to Susan. Melville stung her on the butt. At the same time, I pointed to Susan with my other hand, and Liz did an amazingly dramatic roll and fired a shot. The move was exactly like one that I'd practiced on my adventure training course, and I have to say that it appeared as though Liz should probably start training with me, because she certainly could've used the practice.

She shot herself in the back of the leg with a dart.

"Oh *piffle*," she said.

"Hey! That's *my* word!" I said, catching her. Luckily, she was much lighter than a grad student, so I was not crushed for a second time. She just slumped in my arms, the dart gun falling to the floor and triggering a shot just as Snarls, my mom's cat, came slinking into the room, finally having heard enough noise to consider it of interest.

"**Thook**." That was the sound of the dart striking home in Snarls's chest.

"**Hssst!**" That was Snarls.

"**Fwwwww**." Snarls, again, now toppling to one side.

So now I had an unconscious best friend in my arms and an unconscious cat in the doorway and an unconscious spy on the recliner and an unconscious brother on the floor. Everything was going grand. I wondered how many darts were left in the dart gun and how many people lived in Polt. Given time, I was fairly certain we could get them all. By accident, of course.

"You people are crazy," Susan whispered. It was difficult to argue her point. Luckily, I enjoy a little craziness in my life. It keeps things from getting boring.

"Catch!" I told Nate.

"Okay!" he said, and he put out his hands to catch the dart gun, because he knew we needed to dart Susan before she left, and she was already turning in a huff (which is really the only way she ever turns) and racing for the door. Unfortunately for Nate, I was not throwing a dart gun, I was throwing a Liz Morris, which took him entirely by surprise and sent him tumbling to the floor and sliding for a bit, sending Snarls (still unconscious) skidding along the floor like a hockey puck and tripping up Susan in turn.

She fell with a satisfying *kerplunk*.

"Oh no!" she said, scrambling to all fours.

"Oh *yes*," I said, looking at her crawling away from me, meaning her stupid butt was the biggest target in the world.

As it turns out, the dart gun had four shots left.

I counted.

Chapter 6

I crossed my arms.

Nate grimaced.

He knows what it means when I cross my arms, just as he knows what it means when I'm scowling, or nodding meaningfully, or judgmentally toe-tapping, as these are skills that I've been forced to develop when dealing with Nathan Bannister.

"Umm," Nate said. We were in my room, where I'd agreed that we could stash Kip in the closet. We'd sprawled Steve in his own bedroom and arranged Snarls on the living room windowsill where the cat usually sleeps for hours anyway, so nobody would notice any difference.

As for Susan, we'd sent her stumbling on her way, totally brainwashed, which I'm just going to mention didn't make any difference in her overall intelligence.

But now Nate wanted to leave *Liz* behind as well.

I crossed my arms a bit more, raised my left eyebrow, and scowled.

"Umm," Nate said again. I was making him nervous. Or even nervouser than that.

"Nathan Bannister," I said, taking a step closer. He took two steps back and thumped against my dresser, toppling a standing picture frame that displayed an image of Liz and me wearing bikinis and jumping off from Don't Jump Off from Here Rock, the huge boulder that juts out a good thirty feet over the lake outside town, and which is basically named like a dare.

"Umm," Nate said.

"How many important things do we still need to do?" I asked him. It was a discussion we'd been having for the last few minutes.

"Three," he said. "Including stopping the Red Death Tea Society from triggering an earthquake that would destroy the city."

"Which is important," I said.

"It is. And we also have to find a way to save Chester Humes from basically running himself to death."

"Also important," I said. Nate swallowed heavily, because he was about to mention the third thing that we *very much needed to do*, and since there were only *two* of us, and there were *three* things that needed to be done, it only made sense . . . *mathematical* sense . . . that we wake Liz and ask her for help.

"Saving Chester is also important," Nate agreed. "And, uhh, thirdly, we need to recover all the science vials I stashed around town."

"That we do," I said. "So wake up Liz, because we need help."

"Umm," he said.

A word about Nate Bannister.

Before we met he really didn't have any friends. Not in school. Not anywhere. It's true he had Bosper, and I suppose he had Betsy, his car, but all our class-mates just thought he was weird. Nobody talked to him in the halls. Nobody sat with him at lunch. Nobody ever picked him for their teams during gym, they just picked *on* him. They'd call him "Egghead."

So Nate had been largely alone.

Because of this, because of the way people barely noticed he was alive, he wasn't good with friends. I've built up my muscles and endurance thanks to my adventure training course, but Nate never had an opportunity to build up his *friendship* muscles. That's one of the reasons he serves such snacks as mixed bowls of gum when I come over, because he's simply not accustomed to guests. He doesn't know how to act.

And he doesn't know how to *trust*.

It's tough for Nate. I do understand.

Nate is . . . who he is. And to a mind like his, friends don't always fit. They don't always do what you'll expect.

Friends aren't math.

"Do you trust me?" I asked Nate. It was a dangerous question, I knew, because Nate was currently unable to tell anything but the truth.

"Yes," he said. Nothing else. I breathed a sigh of relief and sat back on my bed, where Liz was sleeping on her side, snoring a bit, and drooling on my pillow.

I told Nate, "Well, if you trust me, then trust Liz. Because I trust her." I gazed meaningfully to Liz, trying to convey how much I trusted her, cleverly using my pillowcase to cover up how much she was drooling.

"Okay." Nate sighed. "Let's wake her up. But not Kip."

"Agreed," I said. Kip had been a spy, after all, and there was nothing to say he wasn't *still* a spy, and that he'd only confessed so he could get closer to Nate in order to spy more efficiently. I felt a little bad about leaving Kip curled up in the closet, though. He did, after all, save the day during last year's sixth grade theater production of *Goose-zilla*, where Liz and I built a scale model of Polt out of cardboard, which the goose was *supposed* to rampage upon, but it had instead chosen to rampage through the audience until Kip managed to wrestle the goose to the ground and bring an end to what I still consider one of my most successful plays. In gratitude, I made sure that Kip was comfortable in the closet, giving him my extra blankets to sleep on, and a pile of comic books in case he woke up.

Nate brought out a small device from inside his shirt. It looked like a bracelet made out of electricity, which was strange enough, but it was *silent*, which made it even weirder. Electricity is supposed to make noises like *zzakkk* or *crack-crakkle* or something, but in this case it was completely silent.

"What's that?" I asked.

"A neuro-massager. It stimulates the synapses that the sleeping dart deadened. It also has some side effects." He was putting it on Liz's head, stretching it out to fit. Her hair began sticking straight out. Her eyes flickered.

"Side effects?" I said. "Maybe . . . you should have told me about the side effects before putting it on Liz's head?" I put a *lot* of meaning into my words. Liz's eyes were opening. Who knew what strange side effects Nate's device might trigger? Would Liz turn into a giant tortoise? Would her skin glow bright blue? Would she start liking cake more than pie, which is in fact the *only* reasonable way to think, but then she wouldn't be *Liz*.

"I smell licorice," Liz said, sitting up.

"That's the side effect," Nate said.

Hmmm, well, that wasn't too bad. If the only side effect was that Liz smelled licorice, then—

"I'm floating?" Liz said.

"Oh, that's the other side effect," Nate said. "But don't worry, it won't last long."

"What do I do?" Liz asked, with just a very minimum of anxiety in her voice, despite how she was now a few inches above the bed. One of the reasons Liz and I are friends is because she adjusts very quickly to new experiences, such as the time we tied several bottle rockets into our hair during camp, because our common sense wasn't really working very well after we'd stayed up too late and eaten too much chocolate, and, anyway, it hadn't gone *quite* like we'd planned, and Liz and I had both adjusted very quickly from being two sleepy girls to two very awake girls who were running across the campgrounds with sparks shooting everywhere around our heads until we dove into the lake.

"Hold on to my hand," I told Liz, so she wouldn't float any higher. She was already halfway up to the ceiling.

"It's like I'm your balloon!" Liz said. "Nice! But, umm, seriously . . . how long will this last?"

Nate said, "Only a couple of minutes."

"Oh good," Liz said.

"And then it might trigger sporadically for the next few days."

"Oh bad," Liz said.

"Sorry," I told her. "But we needed you awake. Nate and I need to stop the Red Death Tea Society from triggering the earthquake, and we also have to stop Chester Humes from running so fast. That means you, my balloon friend, need to gather up all the science vials that Nate stashed around the city."

"Okay," she said. I was walking her down the hall, toward the living room. "But, how am I going to do that?"

"Nate can give you a list of where they're at," I said. I could feel Nate squirming beside me. "And then you team up with Stine and Ventura and Wendy, and get those vials."

"Okay!" Liz said.

"What?" Nate gasped, squirming worse. "*More* people? But—"

"No buts, Nate. You caused the problem, and now we have to deal with it. My friends can handle it." I said this with all the confidence in the world, but in truth I was worried. After all, Liz was the only one who had even attempted my adventure training course, and even she'd been too chicken to swing over the spiked pit trap (which is only a foot deep, and the spikes are made of cardboard) because a squirrel had been scolding her for climbing into its tree. If she couldn't stand up to an irritated squirrel, I worried about what might happen if she had to fight the Red Death Tea Society, as they are not anywhere near as adorable as squirrels.

"Hi, Dad," I said, walking through the living room.

"Hi, Mr. Cooper," Liz said, holding on to my hand and floating behind me.

"Hi, girls," Dad said. He was stretched out on the couch, watching soccer. "You heading off somewhere?"

"Gotta fight assassins," I said.

"Have fun!" he told us with a jaunty little wave. I'm not sure if it was because Nate's nano-bots were changing the way Dad perceived things, or if he thought we were just joking.

Either way . . . time to go.

When we walked outside, Nate kept stumbling, because he was too absorbed with scribbling another of his equations on his pants. Even *I*, a girl who's mastered such skills as doing one-handed cartwheels while texting Liz with my other hand, would find it difficult to walk while writing equations on my pants.

So Nate tripped when he was going down the steps.

And then he stumbled when he was going across the lawn, hopping as he tried to maintain his balance, too intent on the equation.

And finally he tripped when he was walking across the sidewalk, this time so off balance that I had to reach out and keep him from flopping onto his face, meaning that Liz almost floated away. Luckily, she grabbed my hair at the last moment, doing so in a move that was slightly more than uncomfortable, and I let out what could be considered a groan of agony, and in fact *should* be considered as one.

Nate made a terrible frown.

"No. I'm okay," I told him.

"I'm glad," he said. "But I was frowning at this equation." He pointed to his pants, to where a herd of numbers was all but snickering at me, because they knew I would never understand them.

"What's wrong with it?" I asked.

"It didn't turn out the way I hoped."

"Math problems often don't turn out the way I hope," I told Nate. "They're rather stinky that way. Remember that time I yelled '*piffle*' in math class?"

"Which time?"

"Exactly," I agreed. "What I mean is, sometimes the numbers don't add up, not even for a genius. Don't worry about it. Life goes on."

"Yeah, I guess," Nate said, as Liz gracefully floated down to the sidewalk.

"Take the car," Nate told Liz.

"Huh? I can't drive."

"You won't have to," I said. "The car can do all that. Her name is Betsy."

"Hello, driver Liz Morris," Betsy said. Her blinkers went on and off, I suppose in greeting. Liz's hand tightened on mine. It was a gesture of friendship, like our usual one, as the side effects of Nate's neuro-massager had dissipated and it was no longer necessary to hold on to Liz's hand to keep her from floating away, unless you count that her sanity might float away when she heard Betsy talking.

"That car just talked to me!" Liz said. She went a bit weak and leaned against me for support.

"Betsy's really nice!" I told Liz, which is often true, though Betsy does have her mood swings.

"Thank you, friend Delphine," Betsy said.

"Betsy projects holograms on her windows," I told Liz as she got inside. "It will look like an adult is doing all the driving, instead of a twelve-year-old."

"How old is Betsy?" Liz asked, buckling herself into the driver's seat.

Nate said, "Two years."

Liz said, "So, to anyone watching, it will look like an adult is doing the driving, rather than me at twelve years old, but in reality it's a two-year-old driving?"

"Essentially correct, and welcome to my world," I said. Nate had been fiddling with his watch, summoning Sir William, his robot gull, which came gliding down to a stop on the sidewalk.

"Oh, a gull," Liz said as I picked him up. We were going to need him for scouting the current locations of Chester and the Red Death Tea Society, although of course it wasn't too hard to tell where Chester was at, on account of the violent storm clouds that were following him around.

"He's not really a gull," I told Liz. "His name is Sir William, and he's a robot."

"Oh," she said, in a small voice.

"Screech!" Sir William said, in my voice, because we recorded my voice for Sir William to use whenever he's trying to communicate. So now the gull could say "*screech*" and "chuk chuk chuk" and "*piffle*," the last of which Nate still didn't know about, because I'd recorded it when he was in the bathroom.

"Oh," Liz said again, looking at the gull. Her voice was even softer this time.

"You going to be okay?" I asked.

"Let me get this straight: all this time I thought you were a completely normal though awe-inspiringly wonderful friend, you've actually been utterly *un-normal* and *un-sane*, and you've been fighting the Red Death Tea Society and riding around in a talking car with a talking dog and a pet bee and a robot gull?"

"Basically accurate," I said.

"Oh," Liz said, which was apparently her new mantra. Her eyes were half closed, and I was afraid she was going to zone out completely, but then she got that grin of hers and she reached out and clamped a hand onto my forearm, yanking me closer.

"Have you been to the moon?" she asked. Liz's nearly purple eyes were sparkling, and her whole expression was one of delight.

"Huh?" I said. "The moon?"

"I WANT TO GO TO THE MOON!" Liz roared. "That's my completely fair price for helping you! You have to take me to the moon!"

"Huh?" I said. "Liz, that's impossible. We can't take you to—"

"Deal," Nate said. "Shouldn't be too much trouble." And then he reached past me and closed the car door, and I watched as Liz and Betsy drove away.

"Wait," I said. "We can go to the *moon*?" Then, before Nate answered, I said, "Hey, *double wait*. Forget the moon, how are we going to get around *Polt* now? Liz just drove away in our only available car."

"Improved jetbelts!" Nate said, holding out a belt for me. It looked like a regular belt, but with diamond patterns around the length.

"Ooo! Pretty!" I said, taking the belt. It had a slightly buzzing feel, like when you're touching an electrical cord and can feel the electricity whizzing around inside.

"More than pretty," Nate said. "These diamond

shapes are miniaturized deuterium-powered variable specific impulse magnetoplasma rockets." He tapped one of the diamond shapes on his own belt as I put mine on.

"I'm going to stick with calling them pretty," I told Nate.

"No! Listen, this is really cool. The rockets will—"

"Ahhh!" I interrupted, because I was suddenly zooming up into the air.

"My fault!" Nate said. "I should have calculated that would happen." I was whooshing all over my lawn, zooming here and there at a speed far faster than my old jetbelt, although all I really wanted to do was hover in place and . . .

. . . and . . .

I was hovering in place.

"There!" Nate said. "Now you're seeing how it works. My new jetbelts sync with the nano-bots in our systems, so all you have to do is think about where and how fast you want to fly, and the belt will respond."

"Will we be fast enough to catch Chester with these?"

"No," Nate said, rising up off the ground to join me in the air. "Chester's *minimum* speed is still two thousand miles per hour *above* our maximum speed."

"Really?"

"It's the truth," Nate said.

"Oh yeah. I guess it would be."

"You should practice with your jetbelt," Nate said. "Let's meet up at Polt Pond, outside of town, in twenty minutes." He was starting to fly backward, leaving me behind to practice, which made sense, I guess.

"Why Polt Pond?" I asked.

"I have an idea of how to stop Chester, and I'm also calculating that Maculte and the Red Death Tea Society will be there."

"Because . . . ?"

"Oh. The lake. It's much deeper than most people suspect. In fact, it's over a mile deep in some parts, way down to where a fault line is in place. If Maculte could activate the fault line, it would rip open the earth and destroy all of Polt. You see, tectonic forces are—"

"*Go*, Nate!" I told him. "I'll practice and see you in a few minutes!" If I let Nate start talking about science, we'd be standing in the city's ruins before he finished. He gave me a nod, and then zoomed off and away, toward the waiting storm clouds.

Chapter 7

I practiced with the belt.

I went high into the sky. I zoomed along the ground. I waved hello to Dad as he began mowing the lawn. I was almost thirty feet up in the air when he saw me, but he waved as if I was standing on the lawn, so I knew that Nate's scientific gadgets were still cloaking Dad's mind, rearranging the way he saw the world. Nate has told me that *nobody* sees the world as it really is. Our senses can't comprehend all the true colors, for one thing, so . . . *everything* is different than we think it is. That's scary. But exciting, too.

Another exciting thing was to zoom along through the air with one of my best friends, Melville. It was easy to keep up with her. The new jetbelt was amazing. I hardly needed to practice at all.

"This isn't so hard," I told Melville. "Not sure why Nate thought it would take twenty minutes for me to get the hang of this."

It was then that I saw the note.

One of Nate's notes.

With

"Delphine"

written on it, in Nate's distinctively florid handwriting.

"Bzzz?" Melville said. She was circling the note, which was dangling above my backyard obstacle course, hanging from the oak tree on a string.

"Hmm," I said. "Why would Nate leave me a note, here, when he could have just *told* me whatever he wanted to say?" I thought of zooming closer to the note, and the jetbelt responded, but suddenly it was jerkier than before, so that I was bobbing up and down in the air. I realized it was because I was nervous and the jetbelt was responding to my thoughts. Something didn't feel right.

Melville was circling my hands as I unfolded the note, buzzing with the same sort of apprehension I was feeling.

It was then, just as I was unfolding the note, that I heard Bosper's voice.

"Red Death Tea Society," he whispered. I stiffened, startled, and because of this the jetbelt responded to my thoughts and whooshed me through the air, incorrectly translating "I am startled" into "I sure would like to zoom through all the branches of this oak tree, and then scrape along the roof of my house until I smack into the chimney."

Moments later, dazed, slumped against the chimney, assuring Melville that I was okay, I could still hear Bosper whispering.

I peered over the edge of the house, down to the hedges.

There was Bosper.

He was bouncing up and down with the nervous excitement of all terriers, and he had a jar of peanut butter with him, with a bright pink ribbon tied around it.

The jar was open.

And it was full.

But Bosper wasn't eating it.

"Bzzz?" Melville said, puzzled.

"I know," I told her. "Bosper *not* eating peanut butter? That's totally weird."

I couldn't see who he was talking to, so I hovered off the roof, sneaking closer, making sure to stay out of Bosper's line of sight, and thankful that my jetbelt was entirely silent. Whoever Bosper was talking to was hidden by the hedges, even hidden *in* the hedges, so the mystery person *had* to be small. I could hear them moving the branches aside, with the hedges rustling, and I *really* wanted to see who it was.

So . . . I accidentally flew full speed into the hedges.

You see, this is one of the problems with having a thought-controlled jetbelt. The moment I thought about *really* wanting to see who Bosper was talking to, my jetbelt happily kicked into full speed and flew me into the hedges.

My impact was uncomfortable.

The hedge-dive left me covered in considerable scratches and even more considerable pain, with leaves stuffed into my mouth and ears. I had a momentary awareness of something white racing away from the hedges, and then Bosper was barking at me and all I wanted was to be far away from the painful hedges.

So of course the jetbelt decided I wanted to be about eighty feet in the air, and it tore me out of the hedges and soared me upward, bouncing me off the side of the house again and again in the manner of a fly repeatedly thumping against a window, although flies do not repeatedly yell "*piffle*," at least to the best of my knowledge.

"Quit flying me everywhere!" I told my jetbelt, which faithfully decided to cut out completely, like a dog slinking away when it knows it's in trouble. Speaking of dogs slinking away, Bosper was slinking across the yard, dashing beneath the oak tree and heading toward the hole in our fence, looking guiltily back at me as I plummeted from high above, thanks to a jetbelt that clearly didn't understand me as a person.

"Bosper!" I yelled. But he kept running and I kept falling and it was irritating to once again fail to discover who Bosper was talking to, and I wanted to catch up to him and ask, so of course my jetbelt kicked back into life, overly eager in the manner of a dog that's decided not only that she's been *forgiven*, but that it must mean she's never been in trouble in the first place.

My jetbelt insisted the shortest path to catching Bosper was through the branches of the oak tree (which felt like getting hit by a multitude of baseball bats) and then through the hole in our wooden fence, the diameter of which is approximately one-third that of a Delphine Cooper, or at least it *was* before I hit the hole at about two hundred miles per hour. The fence made a noise like "*B-CRAKKK!*" and I made a noise like "*Seriously?*" and then there were pieces of the wooden fence flying this way and that, pinwheeling through the air much in the same manner as I was doing, because I'd closed my eyes during impact and was literally flying blind.

"Up!" I thought, because I was bouncing off the street like a rock skipping across a lake, and I was worried about slamming into houses or trees or cars or a wide variety of other things that generally stick to the ground. If I went *up*, then all I had to worry about was clouds (not generally considered impact threats) and an occasional bird (all of which have learned to stay out of my way when I'm in the air), and that meant that flying upward was by far the safest—

Okay, so I almost ran into a helicopter.

It was a bright red helicopter with an image of a teacup painted on the side, and there were three men in suits inside, and one woman dangling from a cable almost fifty feet below the helicopter. She had some weird machine in her hands, something that resembled a crystal ball with a handle, pointing it in all directions while the helicopter went zooming over Polt, heading toward the storm clouds in the distance.

"Oops," I said, accidentally flying into her.

"Ahhh!" she said, as if she was surprised that I would run into her, merely because she was flying a thousand feet over the streets of Polt, which proves that the Red Death Tea Society doesn't really understand how talented I am at accidentally running into people.

"Bzzz?" Melville asked, having caught up to me.

"Sure," I answered. "Sting her."

Melville whooshed forward in an instant, because she never needs much encouragement to sting someone.

"Don't you dare!" the woman told me, as if I could still stop my incoming bee. It was much too late for that, and also much too *fun* for that. Instead, I flew up to the open door of the helicopter and landed inside.

"Surprise!" I told the three men, who did indeed seem surprised. The nearest spat out the tea he'd been drinking.

"Delphine?" he said. "You're Delphine Cooper!"

I nodded, because it is impolite to lie. Then I said, "Mind if I break this?"

With that, I grabbed a handy crowbar and smashed the instrument panel, which reacted in the wholly gratifying manner of sparking and fizzing, spraying electricity like a water fountain and shocking the copilot unconscious. Meanwhile, I could hear the shrieks and gasps of bee-sting agony from the woman who was dangling beneath the helicopter, doing whatever it was that she was doing.

"What's that woman doing?" I asked one of the men as he tried to punch me. He had one of those strange glass guns, the disintegrator pistols, clipped to his waist, but he'd obviously decided against using it, which is an intelligent decision if you're having a scuffle inside a helicopter that it would be inconvenient to disintegrate.

I dodged his punch by the simple expedient of stepping entirely outside of the helicopter, using my jetbelt to keep me aloft. Then I whooshed back inside and punched him in the face with the full force of my jetbelt behind me.

He toppled.

"Ouchies," I said, looking at my fist, because I'd skinned my knuckles.

"Oww, you guys," I told the other two. "Why are your faces so hard?" It's possible they had a perfectly reasonable explanation, such as force fields or just plain blockheadedness, but the helicopter was starting to spin out of control and it was making me dizzy. Luckily, I had the option of leaving.

"We'll talk about this later," I told them, and then stepped out of the helicopter and dropped below, to where Melville was still chastising the dangling woman for being a member of an unpleasant assassin society.

"Bzzz?" Melville said.

I looked at the woman, who had bee stings all over her face and arms, and said, "Yes. I think that's enough." Melville stung her three more times just to be sure, and then landed on my hand, which was *still* holding the note I'd found in my yard. It'd become a bit battered during my adventures with the roof, with the chimney, the oak tree, the fence, and the helicopter that was now wobbling off, spitting sparks and the tiniest amount of black smoke.

"Bzzz?" Melville asked. I nodded. She was right. It was indeed time to read the note.

Hovering in midair, I read,

"Delphine. Hopefully my timing will work out. I calculated that it would only take you five minutes to master the thought-controlled jetbelt. They can be a little tricky, though. For instance, zoom to the left."

"Zoom to the left?" I said. Why had Nate written—

I zoomed to the left.

And frowned.

Then returned to the note.

It said,

"See? There's a 98.6 percent chance that merely looking at those words made you zoom to the left, simply because you were thinking about it. Oh, but now I'm the one who's being distracted; I meant to tell you that I do not expect to live through this day."

"What?" I said. My voice was thick. I could barely swallow. "Did I . . . did I just read that right?"

"Yes,"

the note said.

"You did indeed read that correctly. This is the reason why I went alone to the lake, telling you to stay behind to practice. It was almost a lie, but it came close enough to the truth... since you DID need to practice with the jetbelt. It's just that... I've been doing some calculations... and I think I've found a way to stop the Red Death Tea Society and save Chester, but I've calculated a 92.768 percent chance that I will not survive what needs to be done."

"What?" I gasped. Melville buzzed in dismay, picking up on my distress.

"Nate, you are being *so* stupid," I said to the note. It didn't answer back. I was already beginning to trigger my jetbelt, flying toward the distant lake.

And I was still reading.

"Anyway, Delphine, I just wanted you to know you're the best thing that's ever happened to me. I've always had fun making inventions, solving math problems, trying to understand how the world works, but... you're the one who made life fun, and I never truly understood how the world works, not until I met you. If you look at the back of this paper, you'll see a handprint, and it will tell you what to do. Oh, and please tell Bosper that I've solved the Erdős-Turán conjecture on additive bases. The solution is written on one of my socks. He'll be interested to know."

I was flying ever faster, heading toward the faraway lake and the storm.

I turned the paper over, and at first there wasn't a handprint, and I was wondering what Nate was talking about. Then, the paper turned almost blindingly white, and a handprint began to form.

It was entirely black, centered on the white paper.

In the middle of the handprint it said, "Put your hand here."

I did, but nothing happened. The handprint felt oddly warm, but that was all. My own hand was slightly smaller than the one on the paper, just like my hand is somewhat smaller than Nate's. I moved my hand outside the handprint to see if the surrounding paper was as warm as the handprint, but it wasn't, and, and . . .

"Oh no," I said.

The words on the handprint had changed.

Now it just said, "Goodbye."

I slammed my hand back into place, as if that would change anything, and I kept flying through the air, zooming far above the city of Polt, the city where I'd lived all my life, and where my life had truly begun on the day that I'd met Nathan Bannister, the smartest boy on earth.

Five blocks later, with me flying along via my jet-belt, a thousand pigeons and a multitude of other birds suddenly took to the air from below, flapping desperately.

"*Why did they*—" I started to think, but then the ground began to shake and the buildings began to quiver. A few windows broke, then the trembling quit, and the birds went back to their perches.

A few blocks later, a much stronger tremor cracked a big line across the middle of Rathbun Street. A broken water main sent water bursting into the air. More windows were shattering. A wall collapsed. The neon sign for the Laurelhurst Theater wrenched free of its moorings and toppled toward a group of people standing in line. I put on a burst of speed and swooped lower, grabbing people as fast as I could, moving them aside, a blur in the air as the huge sign cracked free of the building, ripping free from the bricks and the mortar, with people screaming and panicking, but everyone was moving so slowly, frozen in place by confusion, which is why I train all the time, because you have to be *ready* when the unexpected happens, when the buildings are shaking, when you *have* to save people like I was doing, straining my muscles to take two or even three people at a time as the huge sign came crashing down, with me dropping them safely away and hurtling back for more, yelling for everyone to run, with Melville stinging them so they'd move faster, so they'd snap out of the daze of horror they were in, with me moving so fast that I was an unrecognizable blur in the air, rushing people out of the path of the oncoming sign until it was barely above the sidewalk and there was only one person left and I could feel the broken steel of the plummeting sign grazing my back as I grabbed up the last person and then there was a tug on my legs as the sign slammed into the sidewalk, nipping at my feet, but I pulled him away just in time, although we went into a spin as the two of us flew onward, the panicked move unbalancing me so that I lost control and we clipped the top of a parked car and went tumbling to the sidewalk.

But we made it.

We were safe.

"Delphine?" I heard.

"Huh?" I looked to the last person I'd saved, the one I was still holding, the both of us tangled in our crash positions, with his legs up against a car and one of my hands having slid through a sewer grating to encounter an assortment of Things I Very Much Wished I Was Not Touching.

"Delphine?" the boy said again. And it *was* a boy who I was still holding. It was . . .

"Tommy?" I said. It was Tommy Brilp, my classmate and the leader (and current sole member) of Captain Underworld's Circus of Breakfast Hellfire, a band that even on its best days sounds like a robotic cow in extreme distress.

Tommy has a huge crush on me.

And now I'd saved his life.

Again.

"I thought that sign was going to crush me!" he said. He was still holding me, but I was no longer holding him, having pushed him away only moments after pulling my other hand out of the sewer grating and wiping some unthinkable green stuff on Tommy's shirt, which I do think was a fair exchange for saving his life, though with the way that goo smelled we were probably even now.

"Oh, I could just kiss you!" Tommy said.

"No you couldn't!" I said, and then flew up and away, just as the streets began to shake yet again.

Two blocks of flight later, my phone rang.

It was Liz.

"Is it earthquaking?" she asked.

"Yes! So be careful. Any luck with the science vials?"

"Absolutely! We found a 'Gravity Dispersal' vial, and Stine drank it."

"She did *what*?" My voice was possibly a shriek.

"Ouch," Liz said. "You trigger many earthquakes with that yell of yours? Oh, hold on, here's Stine."

"Delphine?" It was Stine's voice. "I *had* to drink the 'Gravity Dispersal' vial. You don't understand. Liz has been floating."

"Liz has been floating?" I was nearing the edge of the city. A few more miles and I'd be at the lake, where there was a tremendous storm over the waters. There was lightning everywhere. And rain. And hailstones so large and so pounding that I could hear the roar of their impact even from miles away.

"Delphine?" It was Wendy's voice. "You've been

hiding lots of secrets from us. What else don't we know about?"

"I—"

"Ventura, here," I heard on the phone. "Liz and Stine are *both* floating, bouncing on the roof of the car, like balloons, or bubbles, or frogs. You should see them. Oh, and, *wow*! This car is neat. Her name is Betsy."

"Hello, friend Delphine," I heard Betsy say. "Your friends are nice. They don't know Nate very well and are not trying to steal him from me."

"I don't know why I said 'frogs,'" Ventura said. "I was thinking of something else."

"Me again," Liz said. "I had to let Stine drink the 'Gravity Dispersal' vial because she was jealous of my floating. Oh, I'm floating again. This won't last forever, right?"

"Umm, I don't think so." Nate was the only one who would know, but I was trying not to think about Nate, because whenever I *did* then I started to sweat, and my throat would choke up, and there was a growing pit of *nothing* that felt like it was hollowing me out from the inside. I was flying over the Grabachs' farm, the one with the ostriches. The birds were staring up at me, their heads swaying like grass in the winds.

"Hey, Delphine! This is Wendy. What does 'Crayon Summoning' do? We found it just where Nate said it would be, tucked into an old pair of shoes hanging from a telephone wire. Liz floated right on up there to get it, and then Betsy brought her down with a grappling hook. Anyway . . . this 'Crayon Summoning' potion-thingy? Should I drink it?"

"No!"

"Hey, Delphine! It's Ventura. Wendy just drank that 'Crayon Summoning' vial. Should she have done that? Was your brother really a zebra?"

"Yes. I mean, no. I mean, Wendy *shouldn't* have drunk that potion, and, *yes*, Steve was a zebra, but he's better now."

"Delphine!" It was Liz's voice. "I *totally* under-stand your adventure training course now! All the obstacles! We should all train together. We could do it every Saturday right after our Cake vs. Pie meetings."

"No way!" This time it was Ventura. "If we train after the meetings then we'll be too sluggish from all the cake we'll be eating."

"*You'll* be eating cake, not me!" I heard Wendy say. "Because pie is better. Anyway, Delphine, are you still there? Because I have a question for you. Are these Red Death Tea Society people *nice*?"

"I would say . . . *no*," I told Wendy. "Not considering how these earthquakes are their fault, and that 'death' thing in their name is real."

"Okay, then," Wendy said. "I'm officially building my own obstacle course. I need to train. Also, pie has a lot of calories and I could use the exercise."

"What are all these crayons doing?" I heard Liz ask. "Delphine, there's seriously, like, a hundred crayons on the car. Make that a thousand. They're just coming from nowhere, landing on our car like bugs."

"Like frogs!" Ventura yelled out.

"Frogs?" I said.

"Not frogs," Ventura said. "Sorry, got messed up again. And, *oh*, we keep forgetting to ask . . . is there any way we can help with the earthsqueaks?"

"The whats?"

"Earthsqueaks. You know, like earthquakes, but smaller."

"Oh," I said. "No."

"No? That's it?" It was Liz again. "Is something wrong? You're not talking very much. Did Nate make a 'Delphine Doesn't Talk Very Much' potion? Why would he *do* that? Oh, we just found the 'Speed Reading' potion. At the Hergé Café. Right in the display cabinet. Stuck inside a blueberry muffin. Does anybody have three dollars? We have to buy it. Delphine, you're not answering. Is everything okay?"

By then I was entering the edges of the storm, flying faster with every moment, desperate to find Nate. The rains were slashing down on me, soaking me, hitting my arms, my head, my back, and my legs, everywhere, including on the note I was clutching against my chest, holding it with my right hand pressed against the black handprint, where the ink was starting to run, with the rains washing it away.

The rain felt so cold.

"Yes," I lied to Liz. "Everything's fine."

"Go home," I told Melville. It was too dangerous for her with all the rain, with the hailstones that could smash into her, and the winds that would blow her around like no more than a leaf struggling in the storm, or . . . quite frankly . . . as no more than a *Delphine Cooper* in the wind, because I felt like I was in an aerial ocean, being tossed about by the waves and swept away by the currents.

"Bzzz," Melville argued.

"Oh, don't be like that! It's just too dangerous for you!" As if to illustrate my point, a huge burst of lightning came crashing down only a few yards away from us, slicing through the air like a dagger. There were *hundreds* of lightning strikes, crashing down all around.

"Bzzz," Melville said.

"I *know* it's dangerous for me, too! But I have to help Nate! I have to save Polt! I have to stop the Red Death Tea Society!"

"Bzzz! Bzzz! Bzzz! Bzzz!"

"I know you want to do all those things, too, but you're too small to survive the storm! Please! Go back home."

Melville hovered in place for a time. I could see that she was thinking, and I knew she wanted to help, but she's awfully intelligent for a bee, and she knew I was right.

"Bzzz," she said, turning around and flying off.

I watched her zoom away.

Wondering what she was doing.

Because I couldn't understand what she'd said.

I landed at the edge of the lake.

Nate was nowhere to be seen. There were a few dozen people who'd taken shelter when the storm began, huddled beneath the protection of picnic tables or the open pavilions, where at least there was *some* shelter, but the storm was so intense that it was a constant barrage of danger. Even the birds had taken refuge, abandoning the skies and their trees and squeezing into the same spaces as the humans and the other animals, so that all of the people in their bright bathing suits were grouped together with pigeons and squirrels, with dogs and cats and seagulls and even an owl, all of them shifting uneasily, much like happens at our school dances, where everyone huddles against the walls with their closest friends and avoids the dance floor at all costs.

One of the gulls came wobbling out from beneath a picnic table. It trembled and squawked with the efforts of pushing onward through the storm, waddling closer and closer, barely visible in the driving rain. The hail plummeted down, rough pellets the size of marbles or golf balls thumping off the gull, making a constant *clang clang clang* noise.

"Wait," I said. "Clang clang clang?" I tried to shield my eyes from the horrible rain so that I could see the bird better, but the downpour was too thick and the constant flashes of lightning too bright, so I didn't recognize the seagull until it had hopped and flopped all the way to my feet, where it stopped and gazed up at me with a unmistakable expression of distaste for the storm.

"**Piffle**," it said.

"Sir William!" I said. Then, "Where's Nate? He's doing something stupid! I need to find him!" I shoved the note I was carrying at the robot seagull, as if to prove what I was saying, but of course Sir William has known Nate longer than I have, and there's no way he still required any proof that Nate could do some intensely and immensely foolish things, such as going off all by himself and trying to be a hero.

The rain all but dissolved the note, and the hailstones battered it away. I was getting bruised by the fierce weather, and even though I wasn't using the jet-belt the wind was picking me up, gusting me around.

The earth shook.

Again.

Worse this time.

The ground jerked upward and I was slapped into the shallow water at the edge of the lake. I'd barely stood up before I was tossed again, this time by an enormous wave that washed me almost fifty feet onto the shore, where a group of pigeons were staring at me from beneath the shelter of a picnic table that was luckily bolted down to a section of concrete. Several of the pigeons and I made eye contact, and I could tell they were judging me, which is probably the only time in my life that I've felt mentally inferior to a pigeon, because pigeons are, as my dad once explained, whimsically brained.

"Don't you have something better to do?" I asked the pigeons, fully aware that they never have anything better to do, which is why we should teach them to play checkers or perhaps how to read a book, or at least teach them some common courtesy, because walking under phone lines where pigeons are perched is the bravest act in most people's lives.

My phone rang.

It was Liz.

"Delphine," she said. "This is not fun anymore. Where are you?"

"The lake. Don't come here. It's too dangerous."

"See you in a bit," she said. Then hung up.

"Ahh! You pigeon-brain!" I told my phone. Then I looked to the pigeons and said, "I'm sorry. That was rude."

The rains and the wind were still blowing me around, and I still couldn't find Nate. Maybe he'd lied about where he was going? I didn't want to believe that the last words he'd ever spoken to me were lies. I didn't want to believe that he'd spoken any last words *at all*. But where was he? What was I supposed—

"Delphine!" I heard. The lake waters erupted in a straight line.

"Help!" This time the voice came from a blur of blue, yellow, and red that zoomed across the beach.

"Me!" Another blur from a different direction, cutting across the picnic area. It was Chester, running so fast that when he rushed past the bolted-down picnic table, it was ripped up in the wake of his speed, shattering into wooden shards, ripping chunks of concrete from the ground, with pigeons scattering in all directions and immediately buffeted by the winds and the hailstones, in deadly danger of being torn apart in the same manner as the picnic table. Then, the pigeons started disappearing from midair, plucked out of their windswept flight by Chester as he rushed the poor birds to the safety of another pavilion, much as I'd saved the moviegoers from the falling sign.

"Chester!" I yelled, but by then he was gone again, running so fast that he dashed across the lake itself, sending violent sprays of water out in both directions, as if a giant knife had sliced down through the lake to . . .

. . . to . . .

"Hey," I said.

For the briefest of seconds, before the water had filled the trench caused by Chester's speed, I could see the top of a building.

Then the lake settled back into place and the building was gone. But . . . I'd seen it. Out in the middle of the lake, far off shore and far below the surface, there was a submerged building with a bright red teacup painted on its side.

"Hey," I said again, and dove into the waters.

Chapter 8

The first time I'd ever gone to Polt Pond, I'd been with my family. Back then I was maybe four years old and probably as smart as a cheese sandwich.

I'd been snorkeling with my brother Steve, who even in today's world is mostly the kind of brother who . . . when he gets transformed into a zebra . . . you shrug and say, "Well, it was going to happen eventually."

Snorkeling was a lot of fun, because I was wearing flippers and a mask and I could sneak into someone else's world, where the fish would stare at me like I was some unfathomable creature, which of course I was, to them. The fish would swim right up to my face and just stare, even if I reached out and touched them. One small fish tried to hide in my hair.

Because I was very naive and only cheese-sandwich smart, I'd tried to swim to the bottom of the lake, which, considering the depths, was very much Something I Should Not Do. Luckily, Dad was there and he touched my shoulder and shook his head before I'd gone very far, and so I'd kept to the shallows, diving no more than five or six feet, all with Dad watching, and with the colorful fish investigating us, occasionally nibbling at our fingers.

It was magical.

It was a whole other world, beneath the surface.

Beneath the surface, it was still a whole other world, even more so than the last time, because this time there were SO many fish. They were coming from the deep water, scared up to the shallows by something happening down in the dark depths that made it too dangerous even for the fish, with them now circling around me in vast schools of all shapes and sizes, many of them looking to me as if in hope that I could solve whatever problem was bothering them.

I gave them a thumbs-up, which was perhaps more confident than I felt, and also it struck me that fish do not have thumbs, so it's likely they found my gesture to be confusing.

I swam toward the center of the lake, where I'd seen the building.

The water went deeper, first a little more than ten

feet, and then maybe twenty, and then a vast black hole where I couldn't see the bottom. Swimming was very easy, because as luck would have it my jetbelt worked underwater, meaning I was swimming much faster than any of the fish that were following me, which quite likely annoyed them. It would be like a visiting goldfish beating my best time on my adventure training course.

When I reached the edge of the seemingly bottomless pit, I stopped for a bit. I wasn't hesitating; there was *no way* I was going to chicken out, not with Nate's life at stake and all of Polt depending on me. It's just that, one talent where a goldfish *definitely* has me beat is that of breathing underwater. It's not so much a lack of training; it's more a lack of gills.

So . . . I stared at that watery void and wondered how far I could swim, how deep I could make it, before my breath ran out.

"About four hours," one of the fish said.

"**Gahh!**" I gasped, exploding bubbles out of my mouth.

The fish said, "What I mean is, you can breathe and even talk underwater, thanks to the nano-bots in your system. I took a quick moment to upgrade them after the flooding in the school."

"**Gahh!**" I said again, and tried to swim past the

fish and escape, because I was seriously *not* in the mood to deal with a talking fish. I have not, in fact, *ever* been in that mood.

"Sorry, Delphine," the fish said. It was about the length of my forearm and had a bit of a pancake shape, the way some fish do, so they look chubby from the side but thin from straight on. It was vibrantly colored, with bright reds and glowing oranges. Basically, it was a Dazzling Pancake Fish, if such things exist.

The fish's voice sounded a lot like . . . Nate's.

I reached out and tapped on the fish. It went *clang clang clang*, which is not a fish noise. It is a robot noise.

"You are a robot fish," I said, the first time I'd ever made such an accusation.

"If you're wondering what I am," the fish said, "I'm a robot fish. But also I'm a note that's been left for you. I would like to point out that I am only responding to your probable statements, as I've calculated your likely responses."

"I doubt that," I said.

"If you need to punch me, I have installed a punching pad." The fish twisted in the water, and on its opposite side it had a somewhat fatter area, like a cushion.

"I no longer doubt you," I said, punching the fish,

which . . . on impact . . . whooshed a couple of feet back in the water. I hadn't punched it very hard, because while the topic had never before come up in my life, I honestly do think it's rude to punch fish, even when they're robots.

The fish said, "So, if you're here, that means you've probably come to rescue me. It's too late for that. Go back."

"I'm not going back," I told the fish. I was hovering twenty feet below the surface of the water. Several schools of fish were swimming around, like flocks of birds in the air. They were investigating me, and they were investigating the Nate-fish, and also examining the hailstones that were plunging into the water before bobbing back up to the surface.

"I calculate that you will refuse my request to go back," the fish said. "So I will now pose this as a request. Delphine, as a favor, please go back."

"No," I said, beginning to swim toward the dark void of the bottomless pit. The robot fish followed, whirling in circles around me, then even swam in front of me and began pushing back . . . trying to stop me.

"In all probability, you're not listening to what I'm saying," the fish said.

"I never listen to what talking fish tell me to do," I mentioned, which is a rule that I think more people should live by, or at least those people who encounter talking fish, which, I'll admit, is probably uncommon.

"Six," the fish said. I was pushing forward, moving it back, diving deeper into the darkest parts of the water.

I said, "What? Six?"

"Five," the fish said. If I wasn't wearing my jetbelt, I wouldn't have been able to make any progress pushing against the fish, but . . . as it was . . . we were already a good forty feet under the surface, and going down, and down.

"Four," the fish said.

I said, "Nate-fish, I know you're only a pre-programmed series of messages, but even so I'd think you'd be smart enough to understand when you're beat. I'm not backing down, not if you think you're going to sacrifice yourself, not without me at least *trying* to help." The fish clamped its mouth onto the hem of my shirt and tried to tug me back, but I wouldn't let it stop me.

I *wouldn't*.

"Three," the fish said. It was difficult to see anything, because the light from the surface couldn't reach this far down. I was at least a hundred feet under the water.

"Two," the fish said.

"Just stop it! I'm not sure why you're counting down, but we're friends and I'm not stopping! So if you think you're going to spray me with some knockout gas, you'd better think again, and if you think you're going to do that thing where you play with my mind, you'd *better not*, or I'll *triple* all my shoulder-punches from now on, and if you think you're going to—"

"One," the fish said, circling back to my front and pushing against me even harder than before. It was starting to be *much* more difficult to make any progress, because I wasn't only fighting against the robot fish, I was fighting against the intensifying water pressure, and I'd swum so far down that it was pitch black, so I was catching only the slightest glimpses of the fish, chance metallic gleams in an otherwise black void, but I was *sure* I'd seen that building, and I *was* going to find it, and I *wouldn't* let some stupid robot fish keep me from Nate, not when he was *stupidly* going to sacrifice his life to stop the Red Death Tea Society, not when Nate and I had never had a chance to—

"Zero," the fish said.

And the lights came on.

They were so bright against the blackness.

The lights were streaming from the robot fish's

eyes, powerful searchlights that were probing the water's depths, illuminating the vastness as if I were floating in the middle of some gigantic cathedral, sinking lower and lower. The robot fish was no longer pushing against me, but instead leading the way.

"I may as well just give up and let you help," the fish said. "Index level one has been reached."

"What? Index level one? What's that mean?"

"In all likelihood, you have inquired about index level one. While I would normally avoid the question, perhaps by talking about cake in order to distract you, I find that—"

"Talking about cake *would* distract me," I admitted. "What's all this about cake? Wait. Did you just admit that . . . whenever you don't want to answer one of my questions . . . you fool me into talking about cake?"

"Yes," the fish said, then pivoted to the side with the punching bag.

I punched it.

"Okay . . . get back to talking about level one," I ordered. The fish began swimming deeper into the depths. If you're wondering if it was creepy following the glowing eyes of a talking fish into a bottomless void, then the answer is *yes*, and I was wishing I could distract myself with cake.

The fish said, "Because I'm currently programming this robot fish on a day when I have to tell the truth, the truth is that I keep a chart of stubbornness."

"Okaaaaay," I said. I already didn't like where this was going. And I also didn't like where *we* were going, because the eerie fish-face lights were no longer the only illumination in the watery depths. There was a strange red glow coming from below, and at no point in the entirety of human existence has a strange red glow in the darkness meant anything nice.

"Level Six stubbornness is not wanting to go to bed when you're supposed to," the fish said. "And Level Five is not wanting to quit playing video games. Level Four is not wanting to quit studying the atomic interplay at the center of black holes, although maybe that's just me. Level Three is not wanting to do your homework, although that one's *not* me. Level Two, the second most stubborn thing in the entire world, is wanting cake more than pie, although that one's just *you*."

We were getting closer to the pulsing red light. It was about the size of a beach ball, hanging in the depths of the blackness.

"And what's Level One stubbornness?" I asked. "What's the most stubborn thing in the entire world?"

The robot fish said, "The most stubborn thing in the world is . . . Delphine Cooper." It swiveled to show the punching pad again, with the red lights of the strange floating object illuminating it from below, making the fish look almost too scary to punch, but I was able to do it anyway, because I am stubborn that way.

My phone rang.

It was Liz.

"Bad weather we're having," she said. "Rain. Hail. There's a couple of those one things. What do they call them? Umm, oh yeah. Tornadoes."

"Plus the earthsqueaks!" I heard. It was Ventura's voice.

"Right," Liz said. "Those, too. Where are you?"

"Nearing the bottom of the lake," I said.

"Cool."

A pause.

"Seriously?" she asked.

"Yep."

A pause, and then, "How do you even get cell phone reception down there?"

"Probably because my phone is super-charged. Nate worked on it. He said I can get reception anywhere. Even in space. Listen, Liz . . . get somewhere safe. It's too dangerous there."

A pause, and then I could hear Stine and Ventura and Wendy and Liz talking back and forth, wondering if *anywhere* was safe, and there was a discussion that I couldn't catch because it was hard to hear my friends over the roar of the winds coming through the phone, plus the sounds of the lightning flashes and the **crakk-crakk-crakking** of hailstones hitting all around them.

Then Liz was on the phone again.

"Bottom of the lake, huh?" she said. "See you in a bit."

The red light turned out to be, as these things do, a bomb.

"**Piffle**," I said.

"I'm going to predict that you are disturbed by the bomb," the Nate-fish said, circling the bomb in question, which was shaped like a large translucent beach ball, glowing from the inside with weird symbols all over it.

"That can't have been your hardest prediction," I told the robot fish. "Pretty much anyone is disturbed by bombs. The calculations must have had me at one hundred percent disturbed. Well, I mean . . . disturbed by the bomb, although Liz would probably predict me at one hundred percent disturbed in general, because of me liking cake more than pie, or because of the time I dressed like a ghost and hid in her closet. Okay, the *five times* I did that, or the time that—"

"I predict you are now babbling, because of your anxieties about bombs, but you don't have to worry. I'll have disabled all of them by now."

"All of them?" My voice was squeaky. Bombs are bad enough, but it's when they travel in packs that things really go wrong.

"Maculte and the Red Death Tea Society have surrounded their underwater headquarters with defenses, such as the bombs, or the poison-water, or the Annoyed Octopus."

I said, "The Annoyed Octopus? What's that?" Then, before the Nate-fish could answer, I said, "Hold on. That's pretty self-explanatory, isn't it?"

The fish didn't answer. It just swam ahead, with the searchlights of its eyes scanning the depths. As we descended, we went past other beach ball–size bombs, all of them glowing red, suspended in the depths. I made sure not to touch any of them; just because they were disabled, didn't mean they were friendly.

After two minutes of silence that were far more silent than silence has ever before been, we reached the bottom of the lake. It was a thick murky silt, like most lake bottoms, with occasional rocks and some weird plants and a huge pile of inert robots. I suppose most lake bottoms don't actually have huge piles of inert robots, but this one did. There were *hundreds* of them strewn out over the lake bottom. They were shaped like men, but their heads were entirely smooth, and they had flippers for feet and an extra set of arms.

The robots all had a soft, red glow.

I said, "Did you disable those, too? Like the bombs?"

"I predict you will ask about the robots. They are called 'Tea-bots,' and I easily disabled them by using quantum entanglement to subtract resonance from their anti-matter engines. Hah! Can you believe Maculte didn't protect them from fifth-dimensional quantum entanglement? Ha ha ha!"

"That's ridiculous!" I said, laughing along, pretending to be someone who knew what the robot fish was talking about.

It was at that point that the ground beneath us shook. It was a small tremor, though one that sent the murky silt swishing and swirling, like we were in a heavy fog made of dirt.

"**Piffle**," I said. "We really need to stop these *earth-squeaks* before they become *earthquakes*. How much farther is it?"

"We're here," the Nate-fish said.

I looked around.

But there wasn't anything to be seen.

I mean, it's true there was a murky dirt-fog, and it's true there were hundreds of inert Tea-bots, and occasional rocks and some weird plants, and a confused seventh grade girl named Delphine Cooper, and a robotic Nate-fish with searchlights for eyes, but none of that really counted as being "here."

"Where is *here*?" I asked, but the fish didn't answer. Instead, it began burrowing in the dirt, spraying silt upward in what amounted to a miniature mud tornado. The Nate-fish burrowed until I could no longer see it, and then I couldn't see *anything*, because without the searchlights there were no lights at all.

"**Piffle**," I said, into the vast darkness.

The darkness just . . . kept being darkness.

It was hard to breathe, because of being nervous,

and because of the crushing depths of the water, and because I couldn't ever remember feeling more alone.

"So . . . it's pretty dark down here," I mentioned.

Nothing.

"Seriously," I said. "**Piffle**."

And then the lights came back, with the Nate-fish swimming back up out of the silt holding a cord in its mouth, a length of rope that stretched down into the soft sandy dirt.

"Pull this, would you?" the fish said.

"Okay!" I said, so happy to have someone to talk to that it didn't matter if it was a robot fish asking me to do weird things.

I pulled on the rope.

"Nothing's happening," I told the fish, on account of the nothing that was happening.

"Wait for it," the fish said, which made me run through my mental repertoire of glares, but before I could choose the best one . . .

. . . the bottom of the lake fell away.

The rush of the waters whooshing down into the sudden void swept me along in a miasma of silt and churning waters. I was flailing and struggling, but even with my jetbelt the current was too strong.

"I probably should have warned you about this," the robot fish said, swept along beside me.

"You think?" I said.

And then everything went black.

My phone rang. I opened my eyes. And struggled to my feet.

I was in a huge room, at least three hundred feet square, and almost as tall. The walls were made of crystal, though they were dull, barely shining at all. There were three hovering globes of light, swaying somewhat, so that shadows were shifting on the walls.

"Delphine?" my phone said. It was Liz's voice.

There were several unconscious members of the Red Death Tea Society against one wall, along with more of the Tea-bots. There were scorch marks on the wall next to them, and various cracks in the crystals.

"You there?" I heard from my phone.

There was an eerie ringing hum in the room, like music from someone else's earphones.

"Seriously," my phone said. "Delphine?"

The robotic Nate-fish was flopping at my feet. There was no water in the room, though I couldn't see where it had all drained. The robot fish flopped, flapped, shuddered, and then went still.

"If you're there," Liz said on my phone, "then *say* something. In fact, unless I hear you speak in the next five seconds, I'm going to assume you like pie more than cake. Ready? Three, two, one, zero. I know I said you had *five* seconds, but I was nervous and impatient. I still am."

In the far corner of the room there was a strange . . . robot? It was at least ten feet tall, with no features at all. It looked to be made of rubber, with thick arms and legs, an even thicker torso, and tentacles for fingers. A thin band of light circled its entire head.

The robot straightened when it saw me.

And began to move closer.

"Delphine," my phone said. "I'm really starting to get nervous."

The big rubber robot came charging toward me in gravity-defying leaps. Ten, twenty, or even thirty feet with each jump, accompanied by a sound like "*thoomb*" from the robot and an "*eek*" from me as I triggered my jetbelt and soared out of the reach of even the tallest of robots.

Or at least the tallest of robots that couldn't *fly*. However, this was a *cheater*-bot, meaning that it zoomed into the air after me, so that we were in an aerial chase scene, but the cheater-bot was faster and seemingly able to predict my every move. If I went up, it was already cutting off my path, and the same for down, and for left and right, meaning that no matter which way I went . . . *boom* . . . there it was, closing in on me.

"**Piffle**," I said, because running was no good. There was nothing to do but abandon my escape attempts and move to Plan B.

Attack.

Luckily, my adventure training course has taught me to be excellent at hand-to-hand combat. There's a section of my course with padded wooden boards that I jump kick, and there's a punching bag where Liz painted a picture of a penguin, on account of a traumatic incident at the zoo. Also, my training course is next to the back door of our house, so I can quickly run inside and watch a wide variety of kung-fu movies, such as *Meteor Mustache Vs. Yeti Warriors*, or my current favorite, *Adorable Queen's Martial Arts Adoption Agency*. There is no better way to learn how to fight than by studying the moves of these masters, although it's true that I have yet to encounter any yetis, or proven able to grow a mustache.

"Attack mode!" I yelled, deciding on a flying kick as my best option, since I was currently flying. The huge robot didn't try to avoid me or even ward off my incoming blow, obviously too awed by my incredible battle capabilities to do anything but hover in place.

"Hah!" I said, as my foot struck home.

"Huh?" I said, as my foot then sunk *into* that home. In fact, my foot sank all the way past my ankle, and then *stuck* there, so that I was dangling from the robot. Trapped.

"**Piffle**," I said.

"Why did you do that?" the robot asked. It was Nate's voice.

"Nate?" I said, trying to look up, which is difficult when hanging upside down from a robot's stomach.

The robot turned see-through, revealing Nate and Bosper inside.

"Oddly enough," I told Nate, "I attacked because I didn't recognize you, and thought *you* were attacking *me*."

"How could you not recognize me?" Nate asked. "My atomic structure is consistent."

"This is going to sound weird, but I don't recognize my friends by their atomic structure. Mostly I go by . . . do they look like my friends? So if my friends were to . . . and this is just a whimsical example . . . dress themselves with a giant rubber robot, I might not *immediately* recognize them, especially if I was terrified."

Nate said, "Oh, I suppose that makes sense," in a tone of voice making it clear that he also supposed that it did *not* make sense.

The robot's hand plucked me from its stomach. Then, holding me, it whooshed to the floor and set me on my feet, at which point the robot's stomach opened and Nate flew out, using his jetbelt. Bosper then appeared in the opening and sprang outward, yelling, "Bosper has a jetbelt!"

He fell to the floor.

"Bosper does not have a jetbelt!" he said, getting back to his feet. "The dog has forgotten."

Nate and I were just looking at each other.

Just . . . looking.

Finally, I said, "You went off without me."

"Yeah," he said.

"I was worried."

"I'm sorry," he said. It sounded like he meant it, and I suppose he *had* to, on account of the honesty thing, where he was forced to tell the truth at all times.

We went silent again.

Just looking at each other.

Then I stepped forward and hugged him, and he hugged back, and he said, "Delphine, I—"

"DOUBLE PUNCH!" I yelled, hitting him with

both fists, in a move I'd learned from *Double Punch Pirates*, a kung-fu movie about pirates who spent an incredible amount of their time punching.

"Oww," Nate said. "In fact . . . double oww."

"You big stupid!" I yelled. "Who said you could go off like that? Don't you know how worried I was? Did you think I would just go, 'Oh, sounds like Nate is doomed, I guess I'll go eat cake' or something stupid like that? That's stupid, you stupid. Don't be so stupid! You left me alone! I was scared!" I was pushing him in the chest, poking at him, and he wasn't fighting back at all, because he's so stupid, and he kept tripping over the fallen members of the Red Death Tea Society, the ones he'd apparently been smart enough to defeat, which was *amazing* because he was so *stupid*, and I felt like my stomach was flipping over and over, and I felt like my chest was breaking, and I felt like I couldn't breathe at all, and I also felt like I was breathing too fast, and Bosper was barking and Nate was so . . . so . . . *stupid*!

"Stupid!" I roared.

He reached out and took my hand.

And just held it.

Bosper quit barking.

I went red in the face.

It wasn't because of how Nate was holding my

232

hand. Or how warm he felt after it had been so cold in the dark waters of the lake. It was the look in his eyes. Nate is . . . Nate is different. He always has equations in his head. Inventions in the making. Thoughts of atomic structures and the very fabric of the universe. Things like that. Because of all this, his amazing mind is amazingly distracted, so whenever he looks at me he's also partially looking inside his own mind, caught up in mathematical concepts far past anyone else's ability to understand, distracted by technological epiphanies and the secrets of the cosmos. His attention is always scattered. It's always in a hundred different places, mulling over a thousand different concepts.

Except right then.

His eyes, his thoughts . . . I could tell they were only on one thing.

Me.

"Sorry," he said again.

I was blushing *so hard*.

"Don't do it again," I whispered.

"I won't," he whispered back. I wasn't sure why we were whispering. Nate's eyes were so focused on me, and the room was so warm and so . . . so full of *something*. I couldn't tell what. It felt like the weird hum was getting louder and louder.

"Should the dog be whispering?" Bosper asked. We ignored him. Nate took my other hand in his. His stupid hands felt stupid warm.

"Bosper could make barkings," the terrier said. We ignored him.

The room seemed to be vibrating. It was the slightest tremble, the merest quiver. The crystal walls now had a soft green glow, reflecting off Nate's glasses. He looked like he was glowing, too.

"Rarr-rarrf," Bosper said. And then, "Bosper has done a barking. The dog does a good job and is a good boy."

"What's he talking about?" I asked Nate. For some reason I couldn't look away from him. The way the soft green glow of the crystals was reflecting off his glasses, off his eyes . . . it was fascinating.

"Oh," Nate said, with his eyes locked on mine, not looking to the terrier at all. "I told Bosper that if another earthquake was going to be triggered, he should warn me. Bosper is very sensitive to the tectonic vibrations that are the warning signs of an earthquake, so he's probably sensing that a big one is about to hit."

"Oh," I said, looking at Nate.

"Yeah," he said. A stray breeze caught a bit of his hair and made it tremble, which was odd, because there weren't any breezes, not down here in the weird crystal room hundreds of feet below the surface of the lake, the room that was getting brighter and brighter, the green glow intensifying, a strange hum being emitted by the walls, so the attractive fluttering of Nate's hair couldn't have been a breeze, it had to have been caused by the way the walls and the floor were starting to shake.

Wait.

What?

"*PIFFLE!*" I said, looking to Bosper.

"OH!" Nate yelled, looking to his dog. "Did you mean there's about to be an earthquake?"

"Here comes big shivers!" Bosper said, and the walls suddenly flashed a bright green, so that for one moment it was like the three of us were in a giant X-ray machine and I could see right through to Nate's bones, and also to the incredible array of machines and devices he was storing in his shirt, and then the ground lurched this way and that way, and finally in all directions at once. There was rumbling and a roaring, and then Nate was picking me up and stuffing me inside a giant rubber robot, which is the first time that's ever happened.

It felt like he was pushing me into a giant blob of bread dough. Inside, it was hollow, and much roomier than I would've expected.

"Here's the dog!" Bosper yelled as he came through. Then, Nate's hand appeared, and I grabbed it and pulled, and we were all inside.

"Just in time," Nate said. "The Earthquake Cavern was activating."

"Earthquake Cavern?"

"A precisely shaped underground chamber lined with lonsdaleite crystals, each of them calibrated to a very specific vibration, with the accumulated vibration spreading through the surrounding geo-structure and activating tectonic faults, causing earthquakes."

"Bosper chews the wall!" the terrier said, clenching a part of the robot's doughy interior in his teeth.

"I think I get it," I told Nate. "It's like when you see those videos of tuning forks that shatter wine glasses, right?"

"Right! Nice example. Luckily, I designed this exoskeleton out of rubber, so the vibrations will be nullified. We're safe in here."

"But what can we do? I mean, how do we stop the earthquakes?" Together, we were crawling up the robot's interior to a chair in the chest. The chair (also made of rubber, with racing stripes) was surrounded by odd bits of tech, with a wide variety of devices modified from cell phones, wristwatches, and microwave ovens and a video game console.

"I was about to destroy the walls," Nate said, pulling himself toward the chair. He hesitated and looked back to me. "Unless . . . *you* want to do it?"

"Are you asking me if I want to sit in a giant robot's control center and use its massive power for untold destruction?"

"Well . . . *yes*."

"That's the most romantic thing anyone's ever said to me," I told him, leaping into the chair and buckling myself in. Nate took out his phone and his fingers went to work, tapping commands, and the robot became partially transparent, so that we could see right through it.

"It's like one-way glass," Nate said. "We can see out, but nobody can see in."

"Privacy is important when you're hiding inside a giant robot," I agreed. Then I gestured to one of the modified cell phones and asked, "What's this do?"

"Laser beam."

"Ooo. How about this one?" I tapped on another customized cell phone, this one with glowing wires running into it.

"Force blast."

"Nice! And . . . this?" I pointed to one of the wristwatches, which was simply hovering in place, with silver and gold needles circling it, the way gnats fly around a rotten piece of fruit.

"That interrupts the flow of time by adhering anti-matter hooks to the subatomic—"

"Too complicated," I said, waving him off. "How about these?" I nodded to the weirdly modified microwave ovens and the video game console.

"One of the microwave ovens is for a radiation spray that sends quantumly attuned nano-bots on . . . uh . . . oh. You're making the face you make when I get too complicated." Nate was absolutely correct. I was indeed making that face.

"The other microwave is for making popcorn," he said. "Would you like some?" I began making a different face. It was my well-known "I Would Like Some Popcorn" face.

"Bosper is the corn popper!" Bosper yelled, grabbing a big packet of microwave popcorn, leaping atop the microwave, pawing the door open, and then putting the bag inside. In the brief time Bosper held the bag in his mouth, he'd managed to soak it in drool. I customarily prefer butter and salt on my popcorn, as opposed to dog drool, but decided it would make Bosper feel bad if I said anything, and we all make sacrifices for the sake of our friends.

"We better get to work," Nate said as we waited for the popcorn.

"How do I run this thing?" I asked. There didn't

seem to be any control system. No steering wheel. No gloves to put my hands into, so that the robot would mimic my movements. There was no gas pedal, and no giant button labeled "Destroy All Enemies." Just . . . nothing. I wasn't sure how to make the robot step forward, for instance, and—

The robot stepped forward.

"Oh," I said.

I thought about moving my arm, and the robot moved its arm.

"Neat," I said.

I thought about jumping.

The robot jumped.

I thought about running in place.

The robot ran in place.

I thought about flying into the air and firing laser beams and shooting a flurry of concussive explosions and pounding my chest the way gorillas do . . . and all of the time I was thinking these things, the robot was doing exactly what I was envisioning, so that there were simply lasers and force blasts *everywhere*, with me swooping around like a fighter jet firing all of its rockets and . . .

. . . it . . .

. . . was . . .

. . . awesome.

"Whoa!" Nate was yelling. "Delphine! Calm down!"

"Poppity pop corn popping," Bosper whispered, staring into the microwave, watching the bag of popcorn spinning around.

"Why should I calm down?" I asked Nate.

"Hmm. Good question. Maybe you shouldn't, but the first thing we need to do is open the door and get the Red Death Tea Society members out of this room. Once the crystals really start vibrating, they won't be able to survive."

"Where do we put them?" I asked, scooping up the unconscious assassins in my giant robot hands, trying to be gentle, but not trying to be *too* gentle, because we were in a hurry, and I think they probably deserved a few bruises anyway, on account of how they were trying to destroy an entire city.

I spun around, looking for any doorway I could go through, or a closet where I could stash them. There wasn't anything.

"We need the code," Nate said. "Or else we can't escape the room."

"Fine. Get the code. Do you have the code? We need that code." My sudden barrage of code-related questions was linked to how the crystals were now

240

glowing suddenly brighter, and the weird hum in the room was now a weird *roar*.

"Check their wallets," Nate said, gesturing to the men I was holding in my rubber robot hands.

"Seriously? You're the world's smartest genius and 'checking their wallets' is the best you can do?"

"I believe it's the best of our two options," Nate said.

"What's the other option?" I asked. It had to be better than rifling through wallets when the fate of the entire city was at stake.

Nate said, "Well, since these assassins are normally stationed in this room, the scanners must be set to read them whenever they come or go, meaning that the codes need to be tattooed on them somewhere, and I calculate a 99.43 percent chance that the tattoos will be partnered with their Red Death Tea Society tea-leaf tattoos."

"You mean the ones on their butts?"

"I mean the ones on their butts."

"So you're saying that I either check through these guys' wallets, or else I pants them?"

"Yeah."

"I vote on the wallets."

"I predicted that," Nate said.

So . . . in case anybody is wondering, using giant robot hands is not the best way to search through somebody's wallet. The robot was made for awesome destruction, not intricate work, so I dropped the wallets a few times, and dropped the people a few more times, which might normally be categorized as rude, but I think the intricacies of social etiquette are put on hold when giant robots and Earthquake Caverns come into play.

"Nothing here," I told Nate, searching the first wallet.

"Check the next one," he said.

I did.

"Still nothing," I said. The walls were vibrating so hard that the floor was jiggling. Even through the rubber robot body, it was starting to make me feel weird.

"Keep checking!" Nate said. "And hurry!"

I did.

"There's nothing in these wallets!" I said. "No codes!"

Nate just looked at me.

I sighed.

"I really have to do this?" I asked.

He shrugged.

So that's how I found myself inside a giant robot,

in an Earthquake Cavern, clutching a half-pantsed assassin in my big rubber hands, holding him up to the scanners, with Nate trying not to laugh.

"Popcorn's ready!" Bosper yelled.

The popcorn was one of Nate's recipes.

It was entirely delicious.

I tried not to think about the dog drool.

After we activated the security scanner, a door opened at the base of the nearest wall. I pushed the unconscious assassins out through it, using my giant robot leg to nudge them along, feeling like I was sweeping them beneath the rug.

"There," I said. "Now what?"

In answer, Nate pointed to the crystal walls with their eerily unsettling glow.

"Destroy," he said. Then, "I'll get us some lemonade."

I did, indeed, destroy.

I punched at the crystals with my giant robot fists, and the crystals cracked and broke and shattered.

I used a laser beam that melted the crystals into goop.

I used a force blast that brought a rain of crystals bursting out from the walls with explosive power.

I used a disintegrator ray on the ceiling above us, causing a barreling rush of water to come crashing into the cavern, an enormous torrent of lake water surging inward with unimaginable force. The laser-heated crystals were screeching and shattering on contact with the water, the burning crystals so hot that they were still on fire even beneath the water, with the water and flames fighting against each other. The boiling water was billowing steam throughout the room, a sizzling cauldron of ongoing destruction, and I was still firing force blasts, and the room was vibrating not only with the hum of the crystals but also with the inconceivable power I was unleashing, the sheer magnitude of Nate's genius being unleashed, the chaos and the destruction raining everywhere, with electrical bolts far more destructive than any crack of lightning, with the raw power I was releasing causing the very air to explode, to burst into flames, the roar of science and nature colliding, as if the very atoms from which all matter is formed were being ripped apart in an awe-inspiring display of nearly cosmic-level devastation.

Also . . . the lemonade was *so* good.

Leaving the annihilated Earthquake Cavern, we ventured out into a hallway sinking ever deeper into the earth. There were rows of lights and a series of speakers blasting propaganda about Maculte's supremacy, making me glad for the roar of the rushing water drowning out most of what was being said about Maculte's supposedly impressive accomplishments, which I might add were not at all impressive to me, because if you're not nice to other people then you're not accomplishing much in your life.

Oh, forgot to mention something. That "rushing water" was because we were flooding the Red Death Tea Society's headquarters.

It was easy enough to do. We'd left the door to the Earthquake Cavern open, and water was *bursting* outward, and whenever I passed a door I would use my robot force blasts to make a hole, or my robot laser beam to cut openings, or my robot microwave oven to make more popcorn, because it really was quite tasty.

Bosper floated by.

"The dog is surfing?" he asked. He'd ventured outside the robot because there were no "poo facilities" inside, and was now being washed down the hallway, standing atop a serving tray from the Red Death Tea Society cafeteria.

"Bosper," I said. "Quit surfing."

"The dog will bite the water," he said. He leaned over and bit the water.

"This has not helped," he said.

I went sloshing along after him, hurrying to catch up before he was washed away, but he was moving too fast. The current was too strong, and the hallway was too small for me to move efficiently.

"Do we have a tractor beam?" I asked Nate.

"Like, in *science fiction movies*?" Nate scoffed. "The ones where *spaceships* grab objects with *beams of light*?"

"Don't make it sound weird," I said. "It was a perfectly reasonable question."

"Well, I guess I *have* been experimenting with biaxial birefringent media," Nate admitted, or at least I *think* he was admitting something, but as so often I was not quite sure what he was talking about. I had no time to ask, either, because the flood was washing Bosper around a corner. So I leaped forward and started to fly, but I went too fast and slammed through the wall at the end of the hallway, scattering cement blocks everywhere and tumbling into a barracks where row after row of Red Death Tea Society assassins were sleeping in their suits, which was a bit gross. Didn't they have pajamas?

Anyway, they all woke up for some reason that was probably related to having a giant robot crash through their wall, or possibly the immediate flooding.

"Sorry!" I said, giving a cheerful wave. "Go back to sleep!"

They did not go back to sleep.

What they did instead was arm themselves with a wide variety of weapons and begin firing at us, which was rude, although I suppose that since I'd crashed through their bedroom wall when they were sleeping I was hardly in a position to talk. I *was*, however, in a giant robot.

"We safe in here?" I asked Nate.

"Pretty much," he said.

"Meaning?" I asked, kicking a couple of beds to send them sliding along the floor, knocking down a few assassins like bowling pins, but the room was huge and there were hundreds more of them swarming around.

Nate said, "Most of their weapons can't hurt us, but if they use an atomic rearranger, we could be in trouble."

"What's an atomic rearranger, and what's the chance of them having one?"

The intercom system clicked on.

"Attention," Maculte's voice said. "Use the atomic rearranger."

"Oh," I said.

"Hmm," Nate said.

The nearest woman held up a weapon that looked like a combination of a laptop computer and a sniper rifle.

"Hmm," Nate said.

"Preparing to fire!" the woman yelled to the other members of the Red Death Tea Society, all of whom immediately took cover, which did not bode well.

"Un-prepare to fire!" I told the woman, but she did not take my suggestion. Her finger was tightening on the trigger.

"Hmm," Nate said.

"Quit saying that!" I told him, and I rushed forward to try to grab the weapon from the woman's hands, but, just before I could reach her . . . she fired.

There was a sudden burst of light.

Nate and I were bathed in it.

And then our big rubber robot was atomically rearranged into a pile of sand.

"*Piffle*," I said, because standing in a pile of sand

in front of hundreds of well-armed minions of the Red Death Tea Society is the sort of thing that can really make you nostalgic for your giant robot. Everyone in the room was getting back to their feet, and also getting back to pointing weapons at us. Meanwhile, the rushing flood was carrying all of the sand away, so that Nate and I didn't have any cover at all, unless you count "frantically making a time-out signal" as cover.

"Do you have a section on your training course where you practice running?" Nate asked.

"Yes."

"Good. Start running. I'll inflate their clothes."

"What?" I asked, because it sounded like he'd said he was going to inflate their clothes, which is absurd.

"They're wearing synthetic suits," Nate said, tapping on his phone again. "I have the atomic structures for all synthetic materials on file, and all I have to do is encourage quarks."

"Are they difficult to encourage?" I asked.

"Not when you know how. Quarks are elementary particles that make up composite particles, like protons and neutrons."

"That's nice of them," I said, noticing that a large number of assassins were about to open fire on us, which Nate seemed to be prioritizing *after* explaining about quarks.

"They *are* nice!" he said. "And they're also applicable to our current purposes, because they make up atomic nuclei, which means that if I can encourage the quarks to relax a bit, then they'll spread out, take up more space, and—"

It was at that moment that there was a collective booming noise, like, *guh-GLORK*, and every suit in the room abruptly expanded into huge balloon shapes. This proved to be wholly unexpected to the members of the Red Death Tea Society, who said things like "What?" and "Hey!" and "I truly did not expect our suits to inflate!" . . . with all of these things spoken as the raging current washed the now bubble-shaped assassins along with the flood, with several of them bunching up near the door, accumulating like leaves and soda cans at a sewer grate during a heavy rain.

"C'mon!" Nate said, grabbing my hand. "We have to find Bosper!"

So we went wading out into the hall, and then we waded through a fair number of rooms and a few more hallways, and I have to say that the wading was tiring and getting more difficult all the time . . . because the water level was rising, and rising, and *seriously* rising, and while that had seemed keen when I was inside a giant rubber robot, it was no longer entirely wonderful that the headquarters were filling up with water.

But . . . we kept going.

We saw shooting ranges. We saw weight rooms. We saw swimming pools, which we had to swim across so that we could get back to wading. We saw a computer room filled with monitors displaying live feeds from all over the world. We saw an amazing number of rooms, but we didn't see Bosper.

"Uh-oh," Nate said.

I punched him.

"Oww!" he said, stepping back as if he was afraid I was going to punch him again, even though we've long since established that I'm not supposed to punch him more than once every five minutes, a rule we negotiated after Nate suggested that I not punch him *at all*, which was ludicrous.

"I punched you because—" I said, beginning to explain that I'd punched him because it makes me nervous when he says "uh-oh," but I was interrupted by how . . . when Nate took a step back . . . he slipped and fell under the water, with the current carrying him away from me.

He surged along with the water, smacked into a wall, and was knocked entirely unconscious.

Of course.

Chapter 9

The churning waters swept Nate away. I was hurrying after, careful not to be swept away myself, because I wasn't just struggling against the current; I was also fighting against everything *else* that was being washed along in the rush of the waters. There was furniture, disintegrator pistols, and a toaster. There was an amazing number of teacups, an occasional member of the Red Death Tea Society, and a wide range of fish that had been sucked down from the lake and swept inside the rapidly flooding headquarters.

The water in the halls was already up to my waist, and steadily rising.

"Nate!" I yelled out. Nobody answered.

"Bosper!" I shouted. Nobody answered.

I was getting ready to call out again, but . . .

"Delphine!" I heard, which is my name, but it was called out by *Maculte's* voice, so I didn't answer, because a man who tries to destroy all your friends

and your entire city is not the best of company in trying times, or during any times at all.

I ducked beneath the water.

Luckily, the upgraded nano-bots in my system
could still provide a couple more hours of underwater breathing, and hopefully in two hours I would
no longer *need* to be breathing underwater, and
would instead be eating celebratory cake after defeating the Red Death Tea Society. And all I had to do to
earn that cake was stay out of sight of Maculte, find
Nate, find Bosper, defeat a few hundred members of a
nefarious gang of genius-level assassins, put an end to
the ongoing earthquakes, and find some way to stop
Chester Humes from running himself into the grave,
because he was presumably up there . . . above the
water . . . still dashing around.

First things first. I needed to find Nate, so I kept
moving below the surface of the water, searching for
him, hoping to see him, and occasionally swearing.
The fish all gave me curious looks, because even a
reasonably intelligent fish could look at me and correctly deduce, "That creature is *not* aquatic."

But I *had* to be aquatic for a while, and I had to
do it quietly, because I could hear Maculte calling my
name, and I could hear Luria calling my name, and I
could hear a wide range of people who sounded very

much like assassins for the Red Death Tea Society calling out my name. Their voices sounded as greasy as oil and as sharp as broken glass, and they felt wrong . . . just *wrong* . . . in that way you feel when you find a spider crawling on your arm, and for hours afterward you can just *feel* other spiders crawling all over you.

So I swam below the water's surface, occasionally poking up my head in the hopes of finding either Nate or Bosper, but not having any luck finding either of them, and barely having any luck staying out of the sight of Maculte, who I could hear wading through the halls, searching for me, calling out my name.

I kept peeking up my head, making sure I wasn't being spotted.

"She has to be around here somewhere," I heard Luria say.

I ducked back down and kept swimming.

There was still no Bosper. Still no Nate.

I peeked above water, again, then almost gasped when I discovered I was no more than ten feet from Maculte. Luckily, he was faced the other direction. Unluckily, just before I sank back beneath the waters, I heard him say, "She won't be too hard to find. Release the robot octopus."

Now, I have to be honest about something: having

heard what Maculte said, I was of conflicting emotions. First, I immediately decided that "Release the robot octopus" was something I would very much like to say at some point in my life. It's a far more enjoyable sentence to say than, "Hey, what's on television?" or, "I suppose I should do my homework," or, "Yes, I know it's on fire, but here's why it's not my fault," which is something I've had to say on several different occasions, none of which need to be explained just now.

I swam fast, which was easy enough, since I was still wearing the jetbelt, meaning I was basically a torpedo whooshing through the hallway waters, which might *sound* awesome, but it's *much* less awesome to be a torpedo in water that's filled with debris. I had to avoid the furniture, the various teapots, and the cans of beans from the cafeteria, all of which seemed to be intent on colliding with my head.

I popped up out of the water, trying to gauge my position and make sure I was moving away from Maculte. I'd made progress, because now he was at least fifty feet down a long hallway, so that was good and all I had to do was—

My phone rang.

"What's that noise?" Maculte said. His eyes snapped in my direction.

"Sounded like a phone," Luria answered.

"Not one of ours," Maculte said, which he would have known because the Red Death Tea Society all use a teapot's whistle for their ringtone.

I ducked back beneath the water and sped off in the opposite direction, eventually reaching a hallway where the flood tapered off, with the water going from four feet deep, to three feet, and so on, so that soon enough I was on dry land. Or, dry *hallway*, I guess.

I looked to my phone and saw that I'd missed a call from Liz. I called her back.

"What's up, Liz?" I asked.

"We're docked," she said.

"Docked?"

"We're in some sort of hanger. We drove Betsy down under the lake. Did you know she's a submarine?"

"I didn't, but I'm not surprised. I *am* surprised you're here, though. It's not safe. You should go back."

"Nope," she said. And then, "Look at *that*! I think we found the reason for all the flooding. Somebody punched a hole in the roof."

"That was me."

"You? You're strong enough to punch a hole in a ceiling? Seriously? What else aren't you telling me?"

"I'm *not* strong enough to punch through ceilings. I was wearing a robot."

"Huh?" Liz said. Then I could hear her telling Wendy and Ventura and Stine that I'd been wearing a robot, and I could hear a discussion of what that could possibly mean, and also how *they* wanted to wear robots, but there was a weird clicking noise that was making their words difficult to understand. Then, Stine's voice came on the phone.

"We all want robots," she said. "I want a pink one. But dark pink. Are you the one making the water go away?"

It was getting harder to hear what my friends were saying, because that strange clicking noise was getting much louder.

"Huh?" I said. "What did you say about the water going away?"

"It's like, evaporating. Disappearing. We were having to wade at first, but now the water's gone."

"Really?" I said, looking back over my shoulder to where I'd crawled out of the water. And Stine was right; the water was simply disappearing. Vanishing. Like it had never been there in the first place.

Also, I'd been wrong about something. The weird clicking noise was not, as I'd believed, caused by any interference on my phone, but was instead the noise of a robotic octopus charging down the hall.

Toward *me*.

The robot octopus had a central body the size of a small car, and then eight tentacles with razor-sharp points clicking against the walls and the floor as it scurried closer. The central body had a display screen showing Maculte's face, with his maniacal eyes all but bursting into flame, focused on me with intense hatred.

"*Piffle*," I whispered.

"Delphine," the octopus hissed, with steam billowing from numerous vents. The robot crawled over an office chair that'd been washed into the hallway by the force of the vanished flood. Then, with an evil grin on Maculte's face, the robot reached back with two of its tentacles and sliced the chair apart, chopping with its razor-sharp tentacles until it was nothing but a heap of confetti.

"Delphine," the octopus said again. A panel slid open and a tube came out, hissing as it sprayed a vapor that dissolved the nearest wall.

"This is *seriously piffle*," I said, summing up the entire situation. It'd only been two or three seconds since I'd seen the robot, and I'd spent my time doing nothing but hovering in place with my jetbelt, wondering what to do.

"Delphine?" I heard, but it wasn't the robot this time; it was Liz, from my phone.

"Have to go," I told her. "I'm being attacked by a giant robot octopus."

"Oh," she said. "You really should concentrate on that." She disconnected.

The roboctopus was coming closer, charging forward, and I was realizing that I didn't have very much experience with fighting a robot octopus. I was honestly pretty okay with that, feeling no great desire to add to my total.

So I decided to fly away.

Which is when the octopus grabbed me.

One of the tentacles whipped out, wrapping around me in a crushing grip and then smacking me against the side of the hallway. I fell, stunned, as the tentacle released me and then poised for a brief moment above me, before thrusting its razor-sharp point downward.

"Eek," I said, or possibly it was some other scream, because I wasn't keeping track of my screams at the moment, deeming it far more important to keep track of razor-sharp octopus tentacles.

I tried to dodge.

This worked out better than I'd hoped, but also much worse. Better, because I did in fact dodge the incoming tentacle, so *yay* for that and let's have a round of applause for my jetbelt, which had, in my panic, whooshed into life, sending me sledding along the hallway floor, away from the roboctopus. But also, *boo*, because I slid right into a washing machine that the floodwaters had washed into the hall, a washing machine that thunked wide open with my impact and covered me with the Red Death Tea Society's laundry.

Boxer shorts.

It was mostly boxer shorts.

"Really?" I chastised the washing machine and the boxer shorts, which did not look contrite, because of course they were inanimate objects and had no brains at all, but if they *did* have brains they'd have been saying, "Delphine, you should pay more attention to the roboctopus."

skrikktt!

That was the sound of the knife-point of a robot tentacle slicing into the floor only a few inches away from my toes, which is about a mile too close.

Thump thump sssfff WHOMPP!

That was the sound of a seventh grade girl trying to run away, but getting her feet tangled in a pair of boxer shorts and falling face-first onto a hallway floor.

skrk skrk skrk, etc., etc.

Those were the sounds of robotic tentacles moving quickly down the hallway, scratching against the walls and floor and ceiling as the roboctopus scrambled forward, and there were many other noises as well, like the bursts of electricity exploding away from three crackling rods that had extended from the robot, and there was a continuous hissing as the acidic cloud dissolved everything it touched, and there was a horrendous scraping noise as the robot pulled itself through the hall, like a titan's fingernails scraping against a chalkboard, and there were some of the world's choicest curses as I summed up my feelings on the situation. Also, there was a horrendous wrenching sound as the robot reached the washing machine and simply ripped it in half, pulling it apart like the world's noisiest taffy, and lastly there was the soft *thupp thupp thupp* of a terrier bounding to my rescue.

"Here's a good time for dogs!" Bosper said, charging past me, his head held low as he dashed straight for the incredibly dangerous robot octopus, which was at least a hundred times his size.

"Bosper, no!" I yelled, thinking of what I'd seen the robot do to the washing machine and the chair, neither of which were as lovable as Bosper . . . but were certainly much more durable.

"Big fight!" Bosper said, dodging one tentacle by leaping over it, landing on another tentacle that was slashing for him, running along it for a couple of steps before ducking under a burst of electricity, jumping back to the floor to avoid a cloud of acid, leaping quickly to one side as a spear-pointed tentacle came hurtling down from above to slam inches deep in the hallway floor. With that, Bosper hopped from one flailing tentacle to another until he was standing on top of the robot.

"Find chewy!" he said. He bent down and started biting, plunging his teeth into the control box.

The tentacles all went crazy, slashing for the terrier, cutting at him, firing bursts of electricity, but each and every time he was attacked, Bosper would coolly step to one side at the last millisecond, then yell, "Find chewy!" and resume biting.

The robot shivered . . .

. . . and shook . . .

. . . and then the tentacles went limp. Maculte's face on the display screen shorted out. A huge burst of steam, long and slow, billowed out from behind the robot as it crumpled to the hallway floor.

"Robot has farted?" Bosper asked, poised atop the inert robot, looking back to the steam vent.

And then I scooped up the terrier into a truly monstrous hug, because I'd been terrified he was lost for all time, which is an entirely understandable fear when you've seen a friend helplessly surfing down a hallway in the flooding headquarters of a gang of super-assassins, only to reappear in a fight with a deadly roboctopus.

"The dog is squished," Bosper said.

"Don't care," I said, continuing to squish him, because of all the relief I was feeling, and also because I was still wet and Bosper was reasonably absorbent, so I was basically toweling off.

It was at that point that my phone activated and I heard Liz's voice say, "Delphine? How's things going with that octopus? I'm asking because we're in an exceptionally large amount of trouble."

It was at that moment that I heard footsteps.

And turned around.

To see Maculte.

I pride myself on how calm I can remain in scary situations. Dad has always taught me that you can work yourself out of any difficult situation . . . as long as you keep your composure.

"Ahhh!" I yelled, completely panicking and tossing the nearest weapons I could find at Maculte. In this case, "the nearest weapons" happened to be several pairs of soggy boxer shorts, most of which wrapped around his face so that he looked like a mummy with boxer shorts instead of bandages.

"Yuck," Maculte said.

And then he said "Ooof!" because I ran at him and delivered one of my all-time very best double-twisting flying kicks, and in fact the *only* double-twisting flying kick I've *ever* accomplished, because although I *do* practice these kicks on a store mannequin I have on my adventure training course, I invariably miss (the spinning part makes me too dizzy to be accurate) and end up falling into what I've named the Volcano's Caldera, which is more accurately a mud pit.

"The girl . . . attacks the best friend?" Bosper said. His voice was utterly confused, totally heartbroken, and had many other nuances best summed up by being the exact tone of voice I would use if someone stole my birthday cake. This was notably odd coming from Bosper, but I couldn't let it bother me during a fight with the deadliest man in all existence.

"Shin kick!" I yelled, kicking Maculte in the shin.

"**Gahh**," he said.

"Cannonball!" I shouted, driving my head into Maculte's stomach. He made a noise like that of a giraffe trying to cough up a soccer ball, although in this case the noise was somewhat muffled, since his head was still covered by a thick layer of soggy boxer shorts.

"Do not be attackings!" Bosper pleaded. He was talking to me, not to Maculte, even though Maculte was the head of the Red Death Tea Society and therefore very much in need of attackings.

"Shrieking Vulture Foot Stomp!" I yelled, stomping on Maculte's foot, having decided that just calling it a foot stomp sounded far too commonplace. Maculte moaned in agony. Strangely, Bosper moaned in sympathy and then . . . as Maculte fell to the floor holding his foot in pain . . . Bosper very reluctantly turned to me.

And growled.

What was going on? Why was Bosper mad at *me*? And why had he called Maculte his *best friend*? Had something happened to Bosper after he'd disappeared? Had he turned . . . traitor? Had Maculte brainwashed the terrier's mind?

"Give back Bosper's mind!" I yelled at Maculte, nudging him. And by "nudging him" I mean kicking him five times in the rump when he was trying to stand up.

"Delphine," he said. "Hold on for a—"

"Tornado Punch!" I yelled, punching him in the jaw. And then Maculte made a noise I've come to recognize. It was a familiar noise, one I've heard time and time again, and in fact there are some who would argue that I've heard it *too* often, but that would be overly judgmental and also make me feel bad, so enough of all that.

Anyway, the noise was that of Nathan Bannister being knocked unconscious.

In specific, it was the noise he makes when I, Delphine Cooper, knock him out.

"Huh?" I said, as Maculte crumpled to the hallway floor, falling right on top of Bosper, who was trying to catch him. This was unfortunate for Bosper, because while terriers can catch sticks and Frisbees and a few other objects, their talents are restricted to catching *small* things.

"Bosper is catching!" the terrier said.

This was followed by an impact.

"Bosper has *not* been catching and is now trapped," the terrier said, from somewhere beneath Maculte. There was a moment of struggle, and then a sharp little noise.

"The dog has farted," Bosper said from beneath Maculte. "But this is okay."

There was more struggle, and then the sounds of Bosper sniffing.

"The dog has done wrong with the farting," he

said, after his sensitive nose had come into play. But I was no longer paying attention to him, because while Bosper had been struggling to crawl out from under Maculte, he'd caused a folded note to fall out of Maculte's pocket.

It had my name on it.

I picked it up.

It said . . .

"Delphine, in case you've knocked me out again (78.6 percent chance), I'm leaving this note so that you'll know I've disguised myself as Maculte."

"Oops," I said, speaking this in an apologetic manner to Nate, who was apparently disguised as Maculte. I leaned over and peeled several pairs of boxer shorts (*ick*) off his face and chest, hoping he would look like Nate again, but he still looked exactly like Maculte, so much so that I wanted to kick him again. I looked back to the note instead.

It said . . .

"Please do not kick me (I calculate a 65.4 percent chance of you wanting to kick me) no matter how much I look like Maculte. Hopefully Bosper will be there with you (82.7 percent chance) and he'll be able to confirm that I'm Nate, because my disguise can't fool his sense of smell, and he'll know it's me."

"Is this Nate?" I asked Bosper, pulling the terrier

out from beneath the unconscious person who was almost assuredly Nate, based on the scientific premise of how I'd knocked him out, which is something I do.

"Yes," Bosper said.

"Oh," I said. This was putting a damper on my first official defeat of Maculte, and even on my first ever successful double-twisting flying kick. Still, I could hardly be blamed for this unfortunate incident because Nate looked so much like Maculte that I *still* wanted to kick him.

The note said . . .

"There is a small can of Knock Out Knockout Gas in my shirt. Could you spray it in my face, please?"

I reached inside his shirt and grabbed the first thing I could find, which turned out to be a mechanical beetle.

"**Gahh!**" I said, tossing it aside. It made a *thakk thakk thakk* sound as it bounced to a stop, then Bosper sniffed at it, accidentally flicking a switch, and the beetle came to life and scurried away, disappearing down the hall.

Still resisting the overwhelming urge to kick my disguised friend, I tried again to find the can of Knock Out Knockout Gas, reaching inside Nate's shirt and pulling out a small metal cube that hummed when I touched it. I put it aside and reached into Nate's shirt again, pulling out a glass vial full of tiny swirling robots, and then a remote control device labeled "French Toast and/or Kraken," and then a pencil-length mass of entwined wires that were making a clicking noise, and some sort of display device with four different screens showing blinking dots, and then a spray can labeled "Toe Stub" and a ray gun with "The Bat's Bell" written on the handle in glowing green ink.

"What *is* all this stuff?" I asked, tossing aside a few more items, accidentally bonking a glass globe (full of swirling numbers) off Bosper's head, but not *quite* knocking him out, for which I was mildly proud.

"You have found the dog's head," the terrier said. He moved back a couple of steps.

"Ah-HAH!" I yelled, pulling out the spray can of Knock Out Knockout Gas from Nate's shirt, imme-diately spraying it at his face, but aiming it a bit hastily, so that I whooshed most of the gas in my eyes, my mouth, and my nose. Instantly, I became super-alert. I could smell the scent of the vanished water, the cologne that Nate sometimes wears (it's called Essence of Eureka), and all of the pairs of soggy boxer shorts, and so many other things. I could actually *taste* the air, which had the flavor of electricity and wheat crackers. I could hear the rustle of Bosper's fur and the echoing clicks of a robotic beetle dashing away down the hall. I could see the individual threads of fabric on Nate's shirt, and even the countless tiny robots crawling between the threads, each of them far smaller than the head of a pin. I could see colors I'd never experienced, and even the currents of air in the hallway. I could hear the real Maculte several hallways away, separated by several walls. And, above everything else, I could smell the scent of tea. Hundreds of different flavors scattered all throughout the underwater headquarters, with their scents wafting through the halls.

"Weird," I said, properly aiming the spray can, sending a cloud billowing around Nate's face.

His eyes flew open.

"Delphine," he said. His voice, to my hyperaware senses, felt warm. I can't explain exactly *how* it felt warm, but it *did*. I leaned over and hugged him, hyperaware of the feel of his shirt and even the tremble of his blush.

"Sorry about knocking you out all the time," I said.

"It's exciting!" he told me, sitting up. "It injects an unknown variable into the day, forcing me to recalculate at a moment's notice."

"Recalculation is joy!" Bosper said, bouncing up and down. That dog truly loves math. His brow suddenly furrowed and he stopped bouncing, and in a solemn voice he uttered, "The girl knocks out the best friend based on an escalating scale of rational Diophantine m-tuples."

"Really?" Nate said. His eyes closed for a moment, then snapped open. He gasped and said, "You're right! Good boy!" while patting Bosper. The terrier resumed his normal bouncing around. My hyper senses did *nothing* to help me understand the math being discussed (at least I *think* they were discussing math), but I could hear each individual pad of Bosper's paws hitting the hallway floor, and the soft "*g-glork*" of his drool splattering to the floor.

"Catch me up to date," Nate told me in his warm voice. "What happened since the first time you knocked me out?"

"The first time ever?" I asked.

"The first time down *here*," Nate said, gesturing to the Red Death Tea Society headquarters, reducing the number of accidental knockouts to *two*, rather than . . . well . . . a lot *more* than two.

"Oh," I said. "Let's see. Severe flooding. Liz and my other friends are here now. There was a robot octopus, which I decided to call a 'roboctopus.' "

"Clever," Nate said.

"Right? Luckily, I was able to defeat it. Well,

mostly Bosper did. Okay, it was *entirely* Bosper." I gestured to the terrier.

"I did a good chewing!" Bosper said. He bounced and wiggled with delight.

"That's about it," I told Nate. "Other than how I accidentally sprayed some of that Knock Out Knockout Gas into my face, and now my senses are so acute that I can even hear the gas roiling in Bosper's stomach." I again gestured to Bosper, but this time he didn't bounce and wiggle: he just stood still and puckered up, looking guilty.

"The dog is having some problems," he whispered.

"What's this gas do, anyway?" I asked Nate, holding up the spray can.

"It stimulates the senses, working on the same principles as my knockout gas, but while the knockout gas *deadens* the senses until you fall unconscious, *this* gas"—he tapped on the can—"*heightens* senses, activates them even if you're unconscious, effectively waking you up. That is to say that it . . . *knocks out* being *knocked out*, which is why I called it Knock Out Knockout Gas." He did the anticipatory smile of someone waiting to be told his joke is hilarious.

I just looked to him.

Nate's smile faded a bit.

He looked to Bosper.

"**Pfft**," Bosper said. Well, he didn't actually *say* it, he just . . . made a noise. He was still having his tummy troubles.

It was at that moment that my phone beeped.

There was a text from Liz.

It said, Help?

My phone beeped again even as I was reading. It was a second message from Liz.

It said, Help

"This way!" I told Nate, taking him by the hand and charging off down the hall.

"How do you know?" he asked.

"Because I can hear Liz!" My hyper senses were still in full effect, meaning that I could hear the pounding of my own heart, the thumping of my shoes against the hallway floor, and I could most definitely hear the buzz of Melville, my pet bee, several rooms away, attacking a squad of Red Death Tea Society assassins who were trying to reach Liz and the others, all while Liz was explaining in great detail (and at great volume) why everyone should quit shooting at her.

So we ran as fast as we could, and as directly as we could, because Nate scooped up one of the Red

Death Tea Society disintegrator pistols that had been carried along with all the other debris in the now-vanished flood. He kept firing at walls, disintegrating them so that we could run through the gaping holes. Even as we ran, Nate was studying the ray gun, working on it, modifying it, murmuring about the shoddy workmanship.

Finally, Nate dissolved a wall and we ran through it to find Liz, and Stine, and Wendy and Ventura, all of them backed up against a wall in a vast room *filled* with octopus robots like the one that had attacked me. *Seriously*, there were rows of them on the floor, and scores more of them on giant shelves anchored to the walls, and hundreds of them hanging from hooks, dangling like Christmas tree ornaments, except with tentacles and blades and acidic spray nozzles, which would make for a very bad Christmas.

Most of the robots were inert, lifeless, but about twenty of them were helping five members of the Red Death Tea Society back my friends against the wall. There were four women and one man, a huge seven-foot-tall man covered in tattoos. I could remember seeing him several times before, and I think Melville remembered him, too, because my bee was doing her very best to concentrate her stings on him, trying to land on his face and his hands, which were the only parts of him that were exposed.

"Hi, Delphine!" Liz yelled. She was waving at me.

"Hi, Liz!" I said, charging forward, noticing how the huge man had a remote control device in his hands and . . . as Melville stung him . . . the roboctopi jerked and twitched exactly the way *he* did, reacting as if *they* were being stung along with him.

"They're synchronized to his brain waves," Nate told me. "We have to make sure he doesn't get a chance to switch the robots over to full auto, because then they would be dangerous."

"They actually look dangerous right now," I mentioned, because of all the weapons and the blades and the bursts of acid, none of these things being normally categorized as "friendly."

It was very strange to watch the fight with my hyper senses, because everything was happening in slow motion. I could even see Melville buzzing around, the way she was easily dodging the swatting hands of the members of the Red Death Tea Society, always staying close to someone so that they couldn't fire on her without hitting one of their friends. I could see the red welts where Melville's aim had been true, where she'd stung someone, but her actions were increasingly frantic and I could hear the strain in her buzzing, because the assassins were learning to cover their faces and their hands and Melville couldn't penetrate through their suits, meaning that she wasn't very effective. Also, she didn't dare stay in one place for too long, or else she'd get swatted. If anyone pointed a disintegrator pistol at Liz or the others, she would sting their hands and interrupt the shot, but she was growing exhausted, and my friends were trapped, and it was looking bad. *Horribly* bad.

"No!" I yelled as three members of the Red Death Tea Society raised their pistols at the same time, like a firing squad aiming at my friends. Even with my jet-belt, there was no way I was going to be able to reach them in time. Bosper was charging past me, much faster than I could run or fly, but even he wasn't fast enough to do anything in time.

Melville was doing her best, of course. She stung one of the assassins, and the assassin's hand jerked back, with the pistol flying from her grasp, but my bee wasn't speedy enough to stop the other two.

We were going to be too late.

"No!" I yelled. "Liz!"

She was going to be shot.

Disintegrated.

"Only one thing to do," Nate said, and he raised the disintegrator pistol he'd found, aimed it in a wide swath that included all five members of the Red Death Tea Society, and pulled the trigger.

It had to be done, I suppose.

It was either the members of the Red Death Tea Society, or it was my friends, and that was no decision at all.

Still, as the disintegrator ray washed over not only the attacking roboctopi, but the five human assassins as well, I felt a little bump in my heart, a big kick in my gut, and my eyes started to water.

"**Gahh!**" the tall man yelled in horror.

"**Eeee!**" one of the women screamed.

"**Ahhh!**" another of the women choked out.

And then, and then . . . I just couldn't look.

Seriously, I just couldn't look . . . because while we'd been running toward the fight, Nate had taken the opportunity to modify the disintegrator pistol, changing it so that it could no longer dissolve organic matter. This left the five members of the Red Death Tea Society completely unharmed.

But, you know . . . *naked*.

With all their clothes disintegrated.

"Oh no," the tall man said, looking to Melville.

My bee was staring in wonder at the incredible bounty of exposed skin.

"Bzzz," she said.

It did not take my hyper senses to detect the glee in her voice.

I would now like to describe the elated hugs that Liz and my other friends gave me, the looks of admiration they gave Nate now that they truly understood how smart he was, the round of high fives we all gave one another, and the immense difficulties of high-fiving a bee no matter how much she deserved it. I would like to describe the small piles of dust that had once been the disintegrator pistols that the Red Death Tea Society had been using, the slightly larger piles that had been their clothes, and the much larger piles that had been the attacking roboctopi. I would also like to describe the way we all laughed at how the members of the Red Death Tea Society, covered in welts, had run out of the room (Stine laughs like a duck being squeezed), and of course there was the further confirmation of how all the members of the Red Death Tea Society have tea leaves tattooed on their butts. I'd like to speak about how Ventura and Wendy and Stine had never heard Bosper talk before, so when he was jumping up and down and asking if anyone had brought any peanut butter (no one had thought to do so, which proves we're no good in a crisis), their eyes were huge and twitching, and in fact we were all so focused on listening to Bosper that we almost missed it when Liz began to float into the air (she was still having her troubles), and I had to fly up with my jetbelt in order to pull Liz back down to the floor.

I really *would* like to talk about these things, but there was the little problem of how all of the remaining robots, meaning the ones Nate hadn't disintegrated . . . meaning the *hundreds* of lethal roboctopi that were arranged in immense rows on the floor, and the ones that covered the walls like big warts and the scores of them hanging from the ceiling on hooks . . . all began to shimmer and glow. Their tentacles began to writhe and their blades began to slash. Bursts of super-heated steam began to vent, hissing violently, as if the room was filled with giant snakes.

Then it got even worse.

The door to the room opened and Maculte and Luria Pevermore walked inside.

"Full auto," Maculte told his robot army.

"Kill them all," Luria said.

The robots on the floor rose up on their tentacles to tower above us.

The robots on the walls scurried down from their shelves, their knives plunging into the walls to anchor their descent.

The robots hanging from hooks simply reached up and slashed through the massive chains, easily severing several inches of metal. The roboctopi then dropped to the floor, joining the others, with the remnants of their chains dragging behind them as they advanced.

"Hmm," Nate said. "I predicted this."

"Then why come here?" Maculte called out from across the room. "If you *knew* you were doomed, why are you here?"

"Because it was the only way to stop you," Nate said. "It's worth the sacrifice." Maculte's eyes narrowed, not in hatred or spite or even with the evil that normally narrows his eyes. This time it was confusion. Despite his vast intelligence, he simply couldn't comprehend how someone would sacrifice their own life in order to save others.

"Then why bring *her*?" Luria asked, sipping from a cup a tea, then pointing to me. "And . . . *them*?" she added, gesturing to our friends.

"I didn't mean to," Nate said. "I actually told Delphine *not* to come."

"It's true," I said, adding a shrug. "I'm not very good at following directions."

"Me neither," Liz said. "And, while I have the chance to speak up, I'd like to add that pie is better than cake."

"What?" I shrieked. "It is not!" But our lifelong debate was interrupted by the roboctopi charging closer, closing a circle around us. All of their display monitors were now showing images of Maculte drinking his tea, exactly as he was doing in the doorway, with the same look of triumph, the same glint in his eye, the same drop of tea on his lips that he soon wiped away with a finger, licking it clean, unwilling to miss a single drop of his tea, savoring both the taste of his drink and also his moment of revenge.

"I calculate your chances of survival at . . . *zero*," he said.

"Agreed," Nate said. There was a catch in his voice.

Maculte laughed, a gritty "sand in his throat" chortle, then he and Luria turned and walked out of the room, leaving us to fight an enormous army of unstoppable robots.

The door closed behind.

Chapter 10

"Zero?" I asked Nate. "As in . . . *zero* chance of survival?" It was hard to hear even my own voice through the clashing tentacles coming closer and closer. My hyper senses were fading, but even with my normal hearing, the robots were overwhelming. There was the scrape of the knives against the floor, the hissing of the vents, the echo of Maculte's laughter coming through the display monitors, and the shotgun-like clicking of their joints as the robot horde took tiny steps forward, small feints, as if playing with us in the manner of cats with terrified mice.

"Zero," Nate agreed.

"Oh," I said.

Here's the thing. I've taken considerable math tests through the years. I actually enjoy them. Math is like a vast puzzle, and it's fun when the numbers line up. And while it's true that my numbers don't *always* line up, it's not because *math* is wrong, it's because

I'm wrong. When I answer a math problem incorrectly, it's because I didn't understand the equation. It's not math's fault. It's mine. Math is never wrong.

Also, *Nate* is never wrong. This is because he understands all the equations. That's his thing. If Nate said our chances of survival were zero . . . then . . .

Zero it was.

Here's the *other* thing. An equation is only as good as the numbers you put into it. *Two* plus *two* is *always* four. That's just basic math. If you want to come up with any other answer, if you desperately *need* to come up with any other answer, then what you have to do is change the input. *Don't* add two plus two.

Change things.

"Unacceptable," I told Nate. "And further, *no way*. Also, **piffle**. Let's fight!"

"But the odds—" he said, just before the robots reached us, nabbing up Liz with a tentacle. Melville immediately began stinging the tentacle, but robots don't care about that. Robots care about very few things, to be honest, except for those things they're specifically programmed to care about . . . such as eliminating pests and being entirely wrong about Liz being a pest.

So I had to save her. But, how? I confess that I hadn't thought to put any robot-fighting obstacles on my adventure training course. A clear failure on my part.

"What should I do?" I asked Nate, but he was busy running from robots, which was an excellent plan and in fact the plan I'd been ready to put into action before the door had closed and Liz had been grabbed by a killer robot. A tentacle slashed at Nate, the blade coming so close that it sliced away his jetbelt. It fell to the floor, spitting out sparks as the electronics short-circuited, smelling like my brother's armpit (distinguishable from a range of twenty-three feet) and flailing like a tentacle, of which I had plenty of examples for comparison.

Nate dodged another robot, and then another, and then he dodged so many robots that he was lost in the crowd.

He was gone.

I had to save Liz all by myself.

Okay, I could do this. I remembered how Bosper had beaten the earlier robot, so all I needed to do was jump past a series of writhing tentacles to reach the top of the robot, and then wreck all the exposed wires. That was my new plan.

"*Piffle!*" I said, as my new plan went awry, because the first tentacle I encountered smacked me so hard that it totally flipped me up into the air.

"Hooray!" I said, landing atop the robot by the merest chance and taking the opportunity to strike a dramatic pose so that I could later claim it was exactly what I'd meant to do.

"Gurff!" Liz said, squeezed by the tentacle and menaced by some razor-sharp blades. Something needed to be done. There was a gaping hole atop the robot, like an open manhole full of wires and buttons. Balancing myself as best I could, I started pulling all the wires and clicking all of the buttons. Meanwhile, I had to dodge razor-sharp tentacles and also acidic sprays, because the robot was not delighted to have me on its back, bucking far worse than any rodeo bull. One slash went through my shirt, but caught only the barest hint of my skin. Another slash cut through my jetbelt, and then a tentacle tore it away. Then a slash took off several locks of my hair, the strands falling in front of my face before dissolving in an acidic mist I had to desperately leap in order to avoid, holding on to one of the tentacles and twirling around it, landing where I'd started and once more plunging my hands into the hole, flipping switches and unplugging wires. Then . . . the robot shivered. The robot shook. The robot sparked and it hissed and I leaped to safety just as the robot exploded.

The noise of the explosion was like "SKRANNNG," which was great, but what was *not* great was the following noise of, "**Gahhhh!**" . . . that being the sound of my best friend Liz Morris being flung high into the air.

My heart almost stopped.

"Catch her!" I yelled to . . . well, no one. I couldn't find any of my friends. Nate had disappeared into the horde. Stine and Wendy and Ventura were gone. Melville had vanished. I could hear Bosper barking somewhere far off, but the terrier was nowhere in sight. I was on my own and I *needed* to catch Liz. My calculations were that she was going to fall smack dab in the center of a huge horde of robots, and I was utterly positive that my calculations were correct, because no matter *where* Liz fell, there was a huge horde of robots.

I started dodging more tentacles, more bursts of acid, more slashes from knives, and even tried to dodge Maculte's laughter, which was coming from each and every one of the robots like a physical force. I was squeezing between robots, and they . . . I have to be honest . . . were being rude. Mostly it was that "trying to kill me" thing, but there was no time to instruct the Red Death Tea Society's robots in proper murder etiquette, owing to how I had to reach the spot where I predicted Liz was going to fall. Then, once I got there, I would have to figure out a way to *catch* her, and I'd have to do that *immediately*, because, glancing up, my best guess for where Liz was going to fall was . . .

. . . was . . .

Hmmm.

She wasn't falling anymore.

"I'm floating again!" she said, floating high above the fight, giving me a thumbs-up.

"Excellent timing!" I yelled back. And then, even in the midst of fighting an endless horde of robots, I felt a wave of relief wash over me. And it was also at that moment that I felt something touch my shoulder.

I turned around.

It was Nate.

He said, "You're right."

"Of course," I said. "About what?"

"We *should* fight. Even though there's no way we can win."

"There's always a way we can win," I said. "Nothing in life, *nothing*, is ever truly a zero percent chance." I said all this while grabbing him up in a hug, because Nate was willing to overlook our mathematically zero percent chance of winning, willing to overlook *math*, in order to fight with *me*. Nate would never be like Maculte, a cold, calculating man who believed in nothing but numbers. Nate believed in people. He believed in me. That's why I was hugging him. I *wasn't* hugging him because it makes me feel better when I do, because that would be ridiculous, owing to how Nate and I are not dating and would never even *think* about it, not in a million years.

There's just a zero percent chance of it.

"Can't you disintegrate the robots?" I said, pointing to his pistol while doing a backward flip to dodge a tentacle, accidentally thumping my butt off a robot and sprawling to the floor, almost getting stomped on by another robot but being pulled to safety at the last second as Bosper came charging through the horde, chomping down on my collar and yanking me back. You know, the usual conversational problems when I'm talking with Nate.

"Tried," Nate said, aiming his disintegrator pistol at one of the robots and pulling the trigger. The ray flickered over the robot, but . . . nothing happened. "Maculte adjusted their molecular structure. This pistol's useless now."

"No it's not," I argued. "Dissolve a wall so we can escape!"

"The walls are immune now, too," Nate said, shooting one of the walls. It briefly glowed red, but the color faded and the wall was otherwise unmarked.

"Okay, here's my *last* idea," I said, but as I spoke, two of the nearest robots spewed an acidic mist into the air. Luckily, it was going to miss me.

Until, that is, Nate grabbed me by the shoulders and plunged me right into the worst of it.

"Nate!" I yelled, in what could easily be considered an admonitory tone, or even a chastising voice, or possibly even a shriek of outraged shock and horror.

"Don't worry!" Nate said, which is an interesting thing to say to someone you're holding in the middle of an acidic cloud.

"You're safe!" he added. "The nano-bots in our systems will counteract the chemical changes. Sorry I didn't have a chance to warn you, but I needed something to block the oncoming spray or else your friends would have been . . . umm . . . well, it was for the best that they didn't get any mist on them." I looked behind me and saw that Stine, and Ventura, and Wendy had joined us, all of them still alive, which is the way friends should be, even if the only way to keep them that way is to stand in front of a cloud of highly concentrated acid that smells like a heavily perspiring rat.

"**Guhh**," I told my friends. "Don't smell this."

"Actually," Nate said, "don't let it touch you at all."

"That, too," I said. "But seriously, don't smell it."

Bosper came bounding across the tops of several robots, bouncing and leaping from one to another, using his incredible mind to calculate the various roboctopi attacks, avoiding them with ease since he could predict every last one. He bounded atop the nearest robot and was about to jump down next to us, but then he skidded to a frantic stop. His nose wrinkled.

"Has someone been doing the farting?" he asked.

"It's the acid gas," I said, dodging a tentacle by leaping up and over it like it was a jump rope, with Wendy, Stine, and Ventura doing the same. Liz was still floating in midair.

"The dog's nose is going away," Bosper said, repeatedly sneezing. He jumped from robot to robot, farther away, then stopped to chew on some wires, causing one of the robots to fall to the floor. One down, millions to go.

"Six hundred and seventeen," Nate said.

"Huh?"

"I predicted you'd be counting how many robots there are. There are six hundred and seventeen."

"Six hundred *sixteen!*" I heard Bosper call out

from nearby, accompanied by the sound of another robot crashing to the floor.

"We're winning!" I said, but then I heard a yelp from Bosper and looked to see him being smacked like a home-run ball, hurled into the air, his legs limp. Unconscious, he arced high above us, crashing against several of the chains hanging from the ceiling, causing them to jingle like wind chimes. And then he started to fall. He was helpless. Unconscious. And plummeting toward certain doom.

Liz caught him.

"Got him!" she yelled, floating far above.

"*Keep* him!" I said. "It's not safe down here!"

"It's not safe *anywhere*, Delphine," the roboctopi said, all of them speaking with one voice, the sort of voice that might come from a darkened closet in the middle of the night.

It was Maculte, speaking through his robots.

"I've enjoyed watching you run around helpless," he said. "But now it's time to end this. Robots, initiate detonation protocol."

"Excuse me!" I said, waving my hand. Maculte's eyes, echoed six hundred and sixteen times on the robots' display monitors, shifted from glaring at Nate to looking at me.

"Yes?" Maculte said.

"I was just wondering, when you said that thing about 'detonation protocol,' were you talking about all the robots exploding?"

"Yes."

"Ahh, **piffle**. Okay, thanks." I turned to Nate and punched him in the shoulder.

"Sorry," I said. "Just stress. Okay, Nate, you're telling me there's no way to beat these robots, right?"

"Correct."

"But what I've been trying to say is . . . what if we didn't *have* to?"

"That *would* be better," he said.

"I'd vote for that," Wendy said.

"Me too," Stine added.

"Unanimous," Ventura said.

I said, "Isn't there some way we can turn them to *our* side? I mean, if there's going to *be* an unstoppable robot army, wouldn't it be better if it was on our side?"

Maculte laughed at my words as small panels slid open on all of the robots, revealing a transparent globe in each of them, no larger than an apple.

The globes were all pulsing.

Pulsing . . . red.

Remember how red *isn't* a good color?

"One minute to detonation," the robots said, speaking in unison.

"Time out!" I yelled.

"Fifty-nine seconds until detonation," the robots said, obviously not in the mood to play fair.

"Hmm," Nate said. It wasn't much, but to me it sounded like music, or like warm blankets on a cold day, or like cake on absolutely any day at all. It sounded *good* is what I'm saying, because it meant that Nate was thinking, and if Nate was thinking then everything was going to be okay.

Right?

Nate leaped to the nearest robot and tore away one of the panels, revealing a control board. One of the robot's tentacles grabbed his leg and tried to pull him away, but Nate refused to let go, so that for a moment he was being yanked apart, hanging between the robot and its tentacle like taffy.

"Karate *chop*!" I yelled, using the masterful karate chop that I learned on my training course, where I chop my hand into the pillow that Snarls, Mom's cat, uses to sleep on all the time. I'm not fond of Snarls, so I was quite pleased to steal his pillow.

"Karate *owww*!" I howled, because . . . as it turns out . . . a robot's tentacle is much harder than a cat's pillow. Still, my attack had the desired effect, if by "desired effect" you mean that the tentacle let go of Nate and grabbed me instead.

"Let me go!" I ordered the robot.

"Fifty-two seconds to detonation," it replied.

"Hah!" Nate said, staring at the robot's control panel. "You're right, Delphine! I was looking at the problem all wrong! When you can't *beat* them, *force* them to join you!" His fingers were working on the robot's interior, connecting wires, using a small blowtorch to weld them into different places, and doing all sorts of other things that I might have been able to understand if I wasn't currently being used as a flail, because the robot began using me to swat at Nate.

"**Guhh!**" I said, being slammed into him.

"**Guhh!**" he said, slammed into.

"**Gahhh!**" I said, as the roboctopus thumped me off Nate again.

"Oh," Nate said. "Dang." His tone of voice was . . . bad.

"What's wrong?" Ventura asked. It was the question I would've asked him, too, if I wasn't being helplessly flung around like a rag doll, because that does put a damper on conversation.

Nate said, "This . . . this robot has a *user agreement*."

"Huh?" I said. The roboctopus wasn't thumping me off Nate anymore, which I considered good news. The bad news (there was actually a wide range of bad news, but this one was immediately pertinent) is that it wasn't thumping me off Nate anymore because several of the roboctopi were now fighting over me, yanking me between tentacles, apparently fighting for the right to thump me off Nate, which they clearly enjoyed.

"A user agreement," Nate said. "Like, when you download a new application, you have to read and agree to all the rules of the user agreement."

"I do those *all the time*!" I told Nate. "But you don't have to *actually* read them! Just . . . check 'okay' and go on!"

"That would be a lie," Nate said. He trembled a bit. I did, too, partially because I could now see where this was going, and also because I was still being yanked back and forth between several robot tentacles, like they were dogs fighting over a bone.

"Just check it off, anyway," Stine said. "What's it matter?"

"He can't lie," I told Stine, trying to wriggle out of a robot's grasp. I was entirely successful in this, but I accidentally wriggled *into* a different robot's grasp, which I considered to be unfortunate. "Nate's currently genetically programmed so that he *has* to tell the truth."

"Thirty-two seconds until detonation," the robots said in tandem. I hoped they were lying.

"Here," Wendy said. "I'll click it." She brushed past Nate and was about to hit a button when a blast of electricity sizzled out from the robot. Nate pushed her back just in time, or else she'd have been caught in the blast.

"That won't work," he told her. "I'm already in past the robot's defenses. This has to be me."

"Then start reading!" I yelled out.

Maculte was still laughing.

Nate was still frowning. He said, "Maculte entered an enormous amount of material here. It would take me . . . hours to read all this."

"Twenty-four seconds until detonation," the robots said. The pulsing globes were no longer pulsing; they were absolutely *glowing*. Then, the robots each reached into their own chest cavities and plucked out their globes, holding them high above their bodies, casting an odd heat, like sunlight pulsing against my face and arms. The robot that had been holding me dropped me, and I rolled to a stop with all the grace of a seventh grade girl terrified of being *exploded* by robots, meaning I pretty much fell on my face.

"Twenty-two seconds until detonation," the

robots said. Maculte was still laughing and talking about how clever he was, how his amazing brain could *never* be defeated, that Nate and I were just children, and children deserved nothing but merciless taunts and swift extermination, which is why he devised this little game that we couldn't possibly win. I jumped to my feet and tried to push past Nate and click the user agreement button myself, but it sent out the same burst of electricity that had nearly charbroiled Wendy.

I didn't dodge it.

I trusted the nano-bots in my system to deal with it, and they did, to a small degree, meaning that I wasn't immediately burnt to ashes, but the sheer force of the electricity made it feel like I was being pummeled by baseballs. I was staggering backward, but *not* accepting defeat, *never* accepting defeat, gritting my teeth, stomping closer, my eyes on that user agreement button, and my eyes also on all the glowing globes that were nearing explosion, and on the robots that were talking about "eighteen seconds to detonation," and I could see that Nate was trying to hurry up and read the user agreement, but both of us knew it was hopeless, because he had *hours* of reading to do and there were now only six-teen *seconds* before . . .

"Hey," I said.

"Hmm," I said.

"Ah-hah!" I said.

Then I said, "Liz! Do you still have that vial of Nate's 'Speed Reading' potion?"

"Yes."

"Need it. *Now!*"

"Thirteen seconds to detonation," the robots said as Liz grabbed a vial from her pocket and hurled it down to me. I caught it, then immediately took out the cork and poured it down Nate's surprised mouth.

"Glug glug glug," he said.

"Eleven seconds to detonation," the robots said. But there was the first hint of unease in their combined voice, in *Maculte's* voice. His eyes, displayed on all the monitors, narrowed in concern.

"Ten seconds to detonation," he said.

But Nate's eyes turned to the control board, and I could see those brown eyes of his flickering and speeding through the lines, his fingers tapping on the tiny keyboard as an endless spool of pages went racing past, hundreds of pages at a time, with Nate's amazing mind capturing all the information, zooming along with the aid of the "Speed Reading" potion.

"Seven seconds to detonation," Maculte said. His

confidence was returning. There were so many pages, and so little time. I could feel sweat trickling down my back. Stine reached out and grabbed my hand. Together, we watched Nate read.

The pages were speeding past so quickly that they were nothing but a blur. There was a growing hum filling the room. The globes were beginning to vibrate. Stine was whimpering.

"Five seconds to detonation," the robots said.

The pages weren't even a blur anymore, they were just a gray haze, as Nate was reading thousands of pages in the blink of an eye. Unfortunately, we were running out of time, even for blinks of an eye.

"Three seconds to detonation," the robots said. The combined voice, Maculte's voice, was full of triumph. Melville came flying down from above and landed on my shoulder with a buzz of concern. Wendy took my other hand. My eyes wanted to close, to squeeze shut so that I wouldn't have to see all those hundreds of glowing globes, the bombs being held up by the robots, and I wouldn't have to see the seemingly endless views of Maculte, now with Luria standing next to him, the two of them grinning, the collective horde of roboctopi venting steam as they were reaching the moment when they would detonate and the entire room would be explosively—

"Agreed!" Nate said, tapping on the control board. Then, with his fingers flying, he typed at speeds that were comparable to how fast he'd been reading.

"Robots!" he yelled. "Cease detonation protocol!"

There was silence in the room.

Nate and I were holding our breath.

The hum had stopped. The robots were motionless, not even creaking their tentacles or hissing their steam vents. Liz wasn't making a single sound. There wasn't the merest buzz from Melville, or anything from Stine, or Wendy, or Ventura, and no sounds at all from Maculte or Luria on the display monitors, and nothing from—

"Pffft."

Okay, that was from Bosper, even though he was unconscious.

"Oh. Eww." That was from Liz, her nose wrinkling up, holding Bosper at arm's length.

"Robots!" Nate said. "Acknowledge new overlord!" Maculte's face, displayed on hundreds of robotic monitors, was red with rage. He looked very near to screaming, or to venting steam the way the roboctopi were all doing now, with their tentacles returning to life, writhing and twisting as they tucked their globes back inside their bodies, their knifelike tentacles stabbing into the floor for balance as they turned as one, hundreds of robots facing Nate, the hum of their mechanisms rising in volume, louder and louder, an acrid scent of burning tires carried along with the steam billowing from each of them, and a taste of metal in the air, which was crackling with electricity. I could feel my skin vibrating with the power emitting from hundreds of robots, their mechanisms churning and surging, and the entire floor was shaking with the impacts of so many tentacles shifting back and forth as the robots bent lower and lower, submitting to their new master, bowing to Nate for the space of a heartbeat before suddenly, in an intricately choreographed moment, the robots lifted higher on their tentacles and then pivoted.

To me.

"Acknowledging Delphine Cooper," the robots said, drowning out Maculte's voice and his rage. He was sputtering about Nate "cheating," about "revenge," and so on and so forth, including a few choice utterances of what was, without question, questionable language.

"What's happening?" I said. The robots had formed a circle around me.

Nate said, "It was one year ago today that we first became friends."

"Really?" I said.

"Really," Nate answered. For some reason, he was blushing. "And, so, because that was feasibly the most important day of my life, even though we're not dating, I wanted to get you a present."

"We are *not* dating," I said, not only because it was true, but because I didn't want any rumors to get started, especially when all of my best friends were in the room, because friends have a tendency to blow things out of proportion, like how the *only* reason I suddenly jumped forward and kissed Nate on the cheek was because he'd gotten me a present, and *not* because he looked so handsome. That's ridiculous. I looked up to Liz and saw that she was grinning, and she raised an eyebrow and nodded down to me in a meaningful way, and when I looked to where *she* was looking, I noticed I was holding Nate's hand. When had *that* happened? I quickly let go.

"So, you got me a present?" I asked. I still wasn't understanding, possibly because I'd been quite recently used as a flail and was more than a bit dizzy.

"I did get you a present," Nate said. "I got you robots."

So, thing is, I became the Queen of the Robot Octopus Army.

"You deserve being the one in charge of the roboctopi," Nate told me. "I was looking at the problem all wrong. Too focused on *beating* the robots, but you were the one who understood we could just . . . bring them onto our team." Nate nodded to my friends, to Wendy and Stine and Ventura, to Melville, and to Liz and Bosper above us. I could remember how it wasn't that long ago that he'd been afraid of being around my friends, nervous about having them around, about trusting them, and now he was calling us a team.

It made me feel . . . good.

Like I'd helped Nate to grow.

I gave his hand a little squeeze.

Oh, umm . . . yeah.

His hand.

We were holding hands again.

I seriously don't know why that kept happening.

I looked out over the room.

And took a deep breath.

What I was going to say next was very important.

Dad has told me that there's a moment in everyone's lives when *who* they are hangs in the balance, when what *kind* of person they are, what kind of person they *want* to be, is on a razor's edge. He says it's a moment when a person will know, deep in their stomach, or in their heart, and in fact in the very *core* of their soul, that the next words they speak will determine their fate, sculpting their personality, cementing it into place.

I was on the verge of that moment.

But I was ready.

I wasn't nervous.

I knew what I wanted to say.

It was, in fact, what I *had* to say in order to be true to myself, and to the person that I, Delphine Gabriella Cooper, want to be.

I looked to my friends, to the room as a whole, and mostly I looked to Nate. And then I said . . .

"Release the robot octopi!"

Chapter 11

And so Nate and I found ourselves charging down the hallways in the underwater headquarters of the Red Death Tea Society, leading hundreds of roboctopi into battle. The roar of the tentacles slamming against the walls was competing with me shouting orders to my robot horde, all but drowning out a series of beeps coming from a small mechanical device Nate was working on (it looked like a mechanical version of a half-peeled grapefruit, but smelled like a burnt match) and with Liz singing one of the first songs we wrote way back when we met in Rock Camp, a song called, "Rolly the Seriously Butt-Kicking Robot," which . . . as I'm sure you've rightly assumed . . . centered around a robot with a hobby of seriously kicking butt.

The song was currently pertinent. My robots were kicking butt. Occasionally, one of the Red Death Tea Society assassins would pop out from a room, firing those disintegrator pistols of theirs, but my robot hordes were forming an impenetrable barrier around me and my friends, with my robots completely immune to the weapons and quickly wrapping up the assassins in their tentacles before spraying a burst of sleeping gas into their faces.

It is lovely to have a robot horde. Everyone should do it.

In addition to protecting us, my robots were also energetically destroying any machinery they found. And any computers they found. And also *anything* they found. They were *really* into destroying things. Bosper was running along beside me, barking happily. Nate had given the terrier a pill to chew on (it was an "Un-Unconscious" pill, which immediately woke Bosper up) and then had given him a "Whiff Away" pill, because Bosper was still having his stomach troubles.

"Let's be biting things!" Bosper said, charging along with the robots, biting at things.

"Let's be biting Maculte," I answered, because the leader of the Red Death Tea Society was hiding somewhere, and as long as he was out there, he was dangerous, and very much in need of biting.

It was at that moment, just as we were discussing what other things we would all *prefer* to bite (Wendy was voting for pizza, I was going for cake, Liz was going for pie, and Nate was talking about a carbonated acorn he'd invented, which none of us understood), that we burst through a doorway and were confronted with somewhere in the neighborhood of a thousand members of the Red Death Tea Society, who are not actually the sort of people you want in your neighborhood.

"Welcome . . . to your *doom*!" Maculte said. He and Luria Pevermore were on a balcony high above the floor. The room was another vast Earthquake Cavern, this one even larger than the first.

"Oh," I said. "Is this our doom? My bad! I was looking for a different room." I tried to back out and close the door, but my robots were destroying the doors (and the walls, and even some of the floor), so there was no door to close.

"I'm impressed you were able to turn my robot horde against me," Maculte told Nate.

"You forgot to close the third tangent of the beta branch in the ninth subset of the phase space," Nate said. "Your Riemann surface allowed a fracture of the negative curve!" He looked back to me and rolled his eyes.

"What a dummy!" I told Nate.

"You actually understood that?" Liz whispered to me.

"Not a chance," I whispered back.

Maculte told Nate, "I didn't think you'd delve into the ergodicity."

Liz looked at me.

"Not a clue," I said.

"First place I looked!" Nate said. "You always mess it up. Your calculations are precise but have no *art* to them."

"Art?" Maculte said, his hands clutching at the balcony rails. "Art is for the weak! Nothing more than idle amusements for cretins! *Math* is the only thing that matters!" My robot horde was assembling in front of me, shielding my friends and me from the army of Red Death Tea Society assassins. The crystals of the Earthquake Cavern were beginning to vibrate, and the assassins were staring at us, full of menace but almost entirely unmoving, except whenever one of them would jog over to the tea dispensers at the edges of the room to refill their cups.

Nate told Maculte, "Math is merely a tool. You can build machines, formulate plans, grasp the secrets of the universe, but Delphine has taught me that you can't use it to make friends. And *these* are my friends."

He put a hand on my shoulder and said, "This is Delphine. She's my . . . she's . . ."

He paused, all but glowing red with a blush.

"Stupid honesty potion," he muttered. I could barely hear him.

"What?" I asked.

"This is Liz!" Nate shouted out to Maculte, moving quickly on, nodding to Liz. "She enjoys archaeology and writing plays."

"I do!" Liz said.

Nate said, "And the one holding on to Liz's hand so that she doesn't float away, that's Wendy. She loves animals and wants to be a veterinarian."

"That's . . . right," Wendy said. "How do you know all these things?"

"And that's Stine," Nate said, avoiding Wendy's question, likely because he didn't want to explain that he has a complete dossier on *everyone* in Polt. "Stine enjoys making clothes and wants to be a fashion designer, and she has a crush on someone but I'm not supposed to tell."

"Oh, you better *not* tell!" Stine said. She punched Nate in the arm, which made me a bit jealous, because Nate's arm is *mine* to punch, but it probably wasn't the best time to start any arguments between us, since the thousand or so weapons pointed in our direction seemed like more than enough trouble to deal with.

I *did* wonder about this *crush*, though, and how Nate knew about it. It was the first I'd heard.

"This is Melville!" Nate said. "She's a bee."

"Buzz," Melville said. She dipped in midair, taking a bow.

"This is Ventura," Nate said. "She's from Barcelona and wants to join the boys soccer team. She's better than most of them. I've already talked to the coach and got him to give permission."

"You . . . did?" Ventura said.

"And this is Bosper," Nate yelled, holding up the terrier so that Maculte could see him. "He's my best friend!"

"Bosper is the dog that bites!" Bosper said. Then, his tail slunk down as he asked, "Does it okay if the dog bites?"

"Sure," Nate said. "If you bite Maculte, I'll even give you some peanut butter. Five jars. No, *ten*." Bosper's tail began wagging so fast that it reminded me of Chester, who was another problem we needed to deal with, as soon as we survived the imminent battle with the Red Death Tea Society.

Assuming we did.

Nate walked forward, even past my robots, to stare up at Maculte. He gestured back to us and said, "Most of them started out as Delphine's friends, but

they're *my* friends now, and they're much more important than any math equation in the entire universe,
even Euler's identity equation, or the true calculation
of pi!" Maculte narrowed his eyes at this. I could tell
he thought Nate was being absurd.

"Did Nate say something about . . . pie?" Liz
asked, but I'd already predicted she would ask that,
and was ready.

"He means the ratio of a circle's circumference to
its diameter," I told her. "Not the yummy dessert that's
chock-full of fruit and makes me salivate nearly as
much as cake."

"Got it," Liz said.

"You've got *pie*?" Stine asked, hopeful.

It was at that moment, before I could break Stine's
heart by pointing out that we had a grand total of
zero pie, that Maculte started laughing. It wasn't the
laughter of mirth, but rather the laughter of disgust,
the type of laughter that only evil people laugh, and I
have to say that Maculte was particularly talented at
this type of laugh, and that he likely practiced it in
front of a mirror.

"Your *friends*," Maculte said. He'd stopped laughing. The room went deadly still. My robots weren't
even moving their tentacles. The hundreds of Red
Death Tea Society assassins were as motionless as

statues, all excepting one who was halfway to the tea dispensers at the edges of the room, and who stopped when he realized that everyone was staring at him.

"Oh, sorry," he said.

All eyes turned back to Maculte.

"Your friends," he said again, "are *nothing*. I don't have friends. I have no need of them. I have . . . an *army*!" As one, the Red Death Tea Society assassins raised their weapons.

"Me too," I said. Thousands of robot tentacles began to uncoil and writhe.

And the fight was on.

Here's the thing about fights. They're chaotic. It's hard to tell what's really going on, especially if you happen to have several friends with you, and they're the type of friends who are really terrific but have very little experience in any mass melee, barring only that of our weekly Cake vs. Pie meetings, which do feature some shocking violence, but only if you happen to think a well-delivered pillow is brutal.

So . . . the chaos.

My robots were tossing Red Death Tea Society assassins as if they were popcorn.

Nate was hunched over, working on that device

of his, the one that looked like a half-peeled grapefruit.

Disintegrator rays were blasting wildly about.

Bosper was biting.

I was kicking.

Liz was floating.

Maculte was bellowing.

Luria was standing on the edge of her balcony with a spray can, spraying something into the air.

My octopi were releasing clouds of knockout gas.

I was stubbing my toe when I accidentally kicked a robot.

The Red Death Tea Society members were putting on face masks.

The entire room was vibrating, and the earthquake crystals were starting to glow.

Stine was shoving over all the tea dispensers at the edges of the room, causing an outcry from the assassins.

I was hopping on one foot, because of that "stubbed toe" thing.

There were tentacles everywhere, and a man grabbed me by my hair and was dragging me along, and then Bosper was biting him, and then I was biting him, and then Bosper and I were bonding by biting the man together. The assassin yelled and let go of me, so I stomped him on his toes and then a robot tossed him almost fifty feet away and Bosper raced off to bite more things (yelling about how proud he was of my biting, which warmed my heart to hear such praise from an expert), and then Nate was walking casually through the fight, just touching assassins, and each time he touched someone (he was barely paying attention, working out an equation on his pants) there was this little spark of electricity and the person he'd touched would shiver for a moment and then fall unconscious, and then I noticed that the disintegrator pistols were now actually working against my robots, that piles of dust (meaning, *ex*-robots) were not that uncommon to run across, and then another man grabbed me from behind, and he was cheating because he was wearing steel-toed boots (thus negating my formidable toe-stomping skills), and then Wendy kicked him from behind in a not-socially-acceptable manner, and he fell on top of me, pinning me to the floor.

Where . . .

. . . there was a note.

One of Nate's.

With my name on it.

I started to open it, but then the assassin grabbed it from me, and he had a smirk for about a tenth of a second before Melville landed on his forehead.

"Buzz?" she asked.

"Yes," I said.

She stung him.

I grabbed the note from his hands.

She stung him again.

I opened the note.

She stung him again.

The note said . . .

"Delphine, we're going to need Chester. Immediately. Could you go get him? Also, there is a 74.78 percent chance of us not surviving this fight, so I would like to take this opportunity to point out that I've been unable to call you a friend when this honesty potion is in effect, not because you're not my friend, but because there's . . . something more. Some other word I should use. I'm not sure what it is. It's exciting to not know what's happening! And . . . one more thing, since we have a 74.78 percent chance of losing this fight, it probably won't come into play, but there's a 25.22 percent chance that I'll be hosting a victory party, in which case I'll need help planning the snacks. Do you think your friends . . . our friends . . . would like some carbonated acorns? Spaghetti with raisins? I've made some water-flavored ice cream, too. People like water, right?"

"Wow," I told the note. "You are *no* good at snacks."

I tossed down the note and called for Melville (I'd forgotten to tell her to quit stinging the man, so she was still merrily going overboard), and I called out for Liz (who was floating again, but able to navigate across the room by yanking on the hair of various assassins, pulling herself along), and we raced out of the room on a quest to find Chester.

Leaving Nate behind.

Chapter 12

Liz had parked Betsy in a room with a whole armada's worth of mini-submarines. The room was a natural cavern, and full of bats. I like caves. I do not like bats.

"Ooo," I said. "I don't like bats."

"Me neither," Liz said.

"Bzzz," Melville said.

"Seriously?" I asked my bee. "You *like* bats? Why would you *like* bats?" But there was no time for her to answer, because the bats came for us, swarming like a . . . like a . . . like a swarm of bats that I do not like.

"Bats!" I said, in case nobody else had noticed the bats, or because I knew the bats would get in my hair, because that's what bats *do*.

The bats came swooping down, and Melville swooped up to meet them, but before anything happened I saw two notes on the floor.

More of Nate's notes.

Both with my name on them.

I picked them up and read the first one. It said . . .

"Tell Betsy to use the friend gas."

"Betsy!" I yelled. "Use the friend gas!" She roared into life and came zooming closer, screeching her tires and honking her horn and then, with a quick 180-degree turn, she putt-putted a cloud of gas from her tailpipe, whooshing it up into the air.

The bats flew right through it. And then they swerved and fluttered wildly and seemed to lose all sense of direction. They did barrel rolls. They flew in loops. And then they all found perches and made bat noises that sounded like video game effects, but higher pitched, and they were all glinting with beads of the friend gas, like dew on morning grass.

And then one of the bats flew over to me and landed in my hair.

"Gahh," I said. I did not *scream* this. I *pronounced* it. Quietly. It would be best to consider it a horrified squeak.

"You have a bat in your hair," Liz said.

"Is it friendly?" I asked. The bat was flopping around in my hair, grabbing handholds. I was a statue. Shrieking on the inside.

"Hard to tell," Liz said. Then, "Delphine, you should quit shrieking on the inside."

"How did you know?" I squeaked.

"Easy to tell. And since bats can hear high-pitched frequencies, your internal shrieks might bother it. You do not want to bother the bat in your hair."

"I do not," I admitted. "I also do not want it in my hair. Could someone please shave me bald?"

"Friend Delphine," Betsy said. "Would you like me to translate what the bat is saying?"

"Is it saying good things?" I asked.

"Yes."

"Then go ahead."

"The bat is repeatedly saying 'friend,' and also questioning if you have any fruit."

"Fruit?" I asked. "Why would I be carrying fruit? It would be weird to carry fruit around."

"I've got these grapes," Liz said, taking some grapes from her pocket, because Liz is weird, which is one of the reasons we're friends. Why would anyone want friends who weren't weird?

Liz gave a grape to the bat in my hair, which is not a sentence I am comfortable with, but in all honesty if you have a bat in your hair you might as well get comfortable with it, because there is no known way to get a bat out of your hair. We were going to have to take it along with us on our mission to bring Chester back to the underwater headquarters of the Red Death

Tea Society. So, Melville flew in through Betsy's open window and landed on the dash, and then Liz helped me to the car, because I was walking stiffly, like a mummy in the movies, owing to how I was scared of the bat in my hair. Once we were all inside the car, Betsy drove herself into the water and then dove down past the mini-submarines, acting like a submarine herself, speeding through the waters while I, in case I have not mentioned this, had a bat in my hair.

"What's on Nate's second note?" Liz said, tapping on it. The tapping noise intrigued the bat in my hair, causing it to shift around so that it could crawl forward, lean out over my forehead, and peer down to the note.

I unfolded it.

It said . . .

"Delphine, in case this becomes pertinent, I should let you know that there is no possible way to get a bat out of your hair."

"I know that, genius," I whispered to the note.

We whooshed through the lake waters at a good speed, which is easy to do when there are no traffic lights. Meanwhile, the bat in my hair kept shifting to get a better view of what was happening, and Liz kept

feeding it grapes, so that there was grape juice trickling down my forehead, which is only one of the many
unfortunate things about having a bat in your hair.

Melville, however, was making friends.

"Bzzz," she said at one point, hovering in front of
my face.

"Oh yeah," I said, sarcastically agreeing with
her. "Having a bat in my hair is super-keen and I like
him, too!"

"Bzzz!" Melville said, happy that I was happy,
which likely meant that my bee was taking sarcasm-
detecting classes from Nate.

It was only a couple of minutes before we
surfaced, shooting several feet from the water like
a dolphin. My stomach did that roller-coaster thing
twice. Once for the sudden weightlessness. Once for
the way the bat in my hair tightened its grip.

"Nice!" Liz said, grinning, lost in the adventure
we were having. "Delphine, your life is incredible!"

I gave a nauseated thumbs-up while the bat in my
hair made a series of high-pitched noises, like a tiny
guitar solo in my ears.

"Would you like me to translate?" Betsy said.

"Sure," I said. "What the heck. Go for it."

"Twibble says that your hair smells nice."

"Twibble?"

"That's his name."

"Okay," I said, resigned to my fate, because there was no time for further introductions. We'd reached the shore by then, and I couldn't help but notice that the weather was bad. *Horribly* bad. There were drifts of hailstones as thick as snow, and everything was dented and battered. The hail was coming in gusts, with the sky almost blue one moment, and in the next it was a series of grays and reds and swirling blacks. The air smelled of burning candles. The wind was so strong that it was swatting us. Lightning was constantly flashing. Thunder was continually rumbling.

"Chester has to be around here somewhere," Liz said, looking at the clouds in the sky. "Didn't you say he was causing these weather patterns?"

"Yeah. He's running so fast that—**GAHHHHHH!**"

I was moving.

So very fast.

A boy was holding me.

Chester.

We were running across the lake. On top of the water. It went by in the blink of an eye, and then there were some mountains and some vague flashes of buildings and a long stretch of an interstate highway with cars that I thought were parked at first, but I soon came to realize they were actually driving at normal speeds, which was the tiniest fraction of the speed Chester and I were moving.

"How do I stop?" Chester asked. He was more than a bit frantic, which was still a bit less frantic than I was.

"Not sure!" I said. We were back on the lake again. For the fifth or sixth time. "But Nate says you need to come with us. There's something you should know about Nate. He's super-smart and—"

"I know!"

"You know?"

"I've been running around listening to you guys. I've heard everything you said since I started running. And if I missed it, I could just go back and hear it again."

"Go back?" I asked.

"Check it out! I'll show you!" Chester put on a burst of speed. We were running across the lake again, with the waters churning and boiling wherever Chester touched. There were chunks of hail that, because we were moving so fast, seemed only suspended in midair, pushed aside by the tremendous force of Chester's speed. Liz and the others were only just realizing that I was gone, with frowns beginning to show. Melville had a look of fury. The bat was still in my hair.

Of course.

"You know?" I heard. It was my voice.

"Go back?" I heard. My voice, again. But I wasn't actually speaking. So where was my voice coming from?

"Did you hear it?" Chester said. "I caught up to the sound of your voice. Sound moves really slow." Chester took a long curving arc, up and over a hill and back down the interstate highway and then he swooped back almost to where we'd just been.

"You know?" I heard again. We'd caught back up to my voice and were running alongside the sound, so that I could hear myself on repeat. *You know? You know?* Again and again.

"So I haven't missed anything you've said since you had me swallow that pill," Chester said. "I know that Nate is super-smart, and that you're his girlfriend, and you fight against the Red Death Tea Society, but I can't stop *running*! Delphine, how do I *stop running*! I'm getting *tired*! It's starting to *hurt*! I mean, *really hurt*!"

"What did you say about me being Nate's *girl-friend*?" I asked. Honestly, I felt bad about it, because we really *did* need to figure out a way for Chester to stop running, and Nate *had* seemed very serious when he'd asked me to bring Chester back to the under-water headquarters, and there *was* the little matter of the Red Death Tea Society having several of my friends at the mercy of an army, and the entire city of Polt at the mercy of an earthquake machine, and also there was a bat in my hair, which was *not* an insignificant threat to my sanity, and yet . . . with all that . . . I was questioning Chester about why he thought I was Nate's girlfriend.

"Oh," Chester said. "It was because of . . . uh . . . something Nate said." Lightning was crackling all around us, but it was too slow to catch us. I could feel the bat in my hair trying to steer us, like a cowboy steers a horse, with Twibble pulling the hairs on the right side of my head, or on the left side of my head, or yanking my hairs back when he wanted me to slow down, even though *I* wasn't the one doing the running. No, I was only being held in the arms of a sixth grade speedster who believed Nate was my boyfriend.

"So, what did Nate *say*?" I asked.

"Something about you. And about being a girlfriend. You weren't around and he was talking to himself, working out an equation on his pants just before he went down into the water."

"He mentioned me by name?"

"Yes."

"And he said 'girlfriend'?"

"Yes."

"That's weird," I said, because Nate and I aren't dating, so for him to consider me his girlfriend *had* to be some sort of joke, except, *except* . . . Nate was still under the effects of having to tell the truth about *everything*.

It must have been the friction from how fast we were running, because suddenly everything felt incredibly warm.

"Did he say anything *else*?" I asked.

"Something about having to make sure you were okay, and then having to stop the Red Death Tea Society, and he was talking about a white poodle."

"A white poodle?" I asked.

"Yes."

"Nothing about this makes sense," I said. Why was Nate talking about white poodles? And about me being his *girlfriend*? I mean, he'd never even asked me out, so how could he be my boyfriend? And if Nate *had* asked me to be his girlfriend, I would've turned him down, of course. I want my boyfriend to be handsome, or at least interesting to look at, sort of the way Nate is. And I would want him to be considerate, like the way my mom takes cares of her clients whenever they need help, or I guess the way Nate always tries to help people whenever he can. And I would want my boyfriend to be heroic, the type of boy who is willing to sacrifice himself for others, the way Nate is willing to do in order to stop the Red Death Tea Society. And I would definitely want my boyfriend to be mysterious, full of surprises, so that life would always be an adventure. And of course I would want my boyfriend to be very smart, because I find that fascinating.

So you can clearly see that Nate isn't what I'm looking for in a boyfriend.

And speaking of looking for things, Chester and I were racing across the lake again, and I caught a quick glimpse of Liz and her worried face and it reminded me that I was on a mission.

"Chester," I said. "Nate and some of my friends are trapped in the Red Death Tea Society's underwater headquarters. Can you get us there?"

Chester dove into the lake.

He wasn't swimming.

He was still running.

The three of us were encased in a big air bubble that was surrounding Chester, a bubble of air that was swept along with us, like a leaf caught in the wake of a passing car. Incidentally, by "the three of us," I mean me, Chester, and Twibble . . . the visiting bat in my hair.

"Which way?" Chester asked.

"I'm not sure!" Everything was moving too fast and I couldn't catch my bearings.

It was then that I felt a bat tugging on my hair. And while it's true that I'd been feeling a bat tugging on my hair for *quite* some time, it was now more insistent. And always in one direction.

"Hold on," I said. "I think Twibble is trying to tell me something."

"Twibble?"

"The bat in my hair."

"Oh. I'd noticed you had a bat in your hair, but I didn't think it was nice to tell girls they have bats in their hair."

"I get that. But for right now, Twibble thinks we should go to the left."

"Okay," Chester said, veering to the left. Twibble tugged a bit of my hair to the right.

"Not that far left," I told Chester. He eased down on the curve.

And so it was that Chester ran us through the depths of the lake water, with me in Chester's arms telling him where to go, thanks to a bat in my hair telling *me* where to go. In no time flat we'd reached the underwater cave where Twibble had befriended my hair, meaning the huge cavern with the mini-submarines and the seven heavily armed guards that had certainly not been there before.

"**Piffle**," I said, looking at the guards.

"Fire!" one of the guards yelled.

"Huh?" he then said, only a millisecond later. His gun had gone missing. *Everyone's* guns had gone missing. Well, they weren't so much missing as jumbled together in a smoking pile on the floor. It was only at that moment that I noticed Chester had tossed me up into the air. And then he'd raced around and disarmed everyone. And then he caught me.

Almost.

I fell on him.

Because while Chester *is* fast, he's *not* all that strong, and his plan of catching me was optimistic at best. The two of us thumped down onto the floor, and for once I *didn't* knock anybody out (hurrah!), but it still gave the members of the Red Death Tea Society (boo! hiss!) a chance to run up and grab us both.

Which is when the bats descended from above.

I suppose I can understand the bats' enthusiasm. After all, it's exciting to make new friends, and for a time all you want to do is hang out and get to know one another. And since Betsy had sprayed the bats with friend gas, they were all my friends now, despite the ongoing objections from my hair. Unfortunately for the bats, I'd left immediately *after* we'd become friends. The bats had undoubtedly missed their new friend, but now they were thrilled to see me again, except . . . I was being threatened.

Friends, of course, stick up for friends.

So suddenly there was a chaotic swarm of friendly bats, although they were only friendly depending on your perspective, and it was a terrible perspective if you happened to be a member of the Red Death Tea Society, because they were being attacked. More precisely, they were being buffeted and scratched and bitten, and there was a fair amount of high-pitched screeching from the bats, and even more high-pitched screaming from the assassins.

"Let's go!" I told Chester, taking advantage of the distraction. We ran out into the hall, where more assassins were waiting, but Chester managed to disarm them all in the space of a heartbeat, even before I'd really even seen them, so I could not for certain tell you if they'd been wearing pants in the first place. I *could* say that they *certainly* weren't wearing pants as we raced past. They were only wearing underwear with "teacup" designs, and they were also wearing expressions of concentrated confusion.

"Did you do that thing with the pants?" I asked Chester. By then we were several hallways past the assassins, having run through a series of intersections and even stopping in the kitchen so that Chester could grab a quick snack (several cupcakes and six bowls of oatmeal) owing to how he was burning up so many calories with all his running. It had been less than five seconds since we'd left the first room with all the submarines and all the bats, and by "all" the bats I mean all of them except the one in my hair.

"I *did* do the thing with the pants," Chester said. "I don't like those assassins."

"Look out," I said.

"What?"

"Look out!" I yelled. We were running right for a wall at the end of a T intersection, and Chester was still eating cupcakes and had *globs* of cream frosting on his face, and also a thick layer of chocolate sprinkles, making me worry he couldn't see.

"You mean the wall?" Chester said. "No problem. I can easily avoid it, because my *GAHHH!*"

So . . . that terrified scream of his?

I should explain.

It turns out that having cream frosting and chocolate sprinkles on your face is enticing to bats.

Which is why Twibble had leaped out from my hair and landed on Chester's face.

And when you're running at speeds well over a

thousand miles per hour, it's an unfortunate thing to suddenly have a bat's wings cover your eyes while it's licking your nose.

"**GAHHH!**" Chester repeated, apparently feeling it needed to be stressed.

"*Piffle!*" I yelled, expressing my own opinions on the matter.

"**Eeeeeee!**" Twibble screeched, which I'm just going to assume meant, "I sure am enjoying this cream frosting and chocolate sprinkles, Delphine, but I miss your hair!" Because he leaped back into my hair.

But by then it was too late. Chester, still holding me in his arms as he ran, stumbled and staggered and lost a bit of his balance, and then . . .

We fell.

At a thousand miles per hour.

We bounced and tumbled and thudded against the walls and the floor, banging against the ceiling and against each other, with Chester holding me tight in his panic and Twibble burrowing deeper into my hair. And then . . . there was the wall.

It was concrete and over two feet thick, because the walls in the Red Death Tea Society's underwater headquarters were reinforced to help support the weight of an entire lake suspended above. What the architects *hadn't* planned on, however, was a seventh grade girl who quite often . . . and possibly *too* often . . . indulges in her hobby of dramatic accidents.

We burst through the wall, surrounded and protected by a bubble of pure force that had formed around Chester as he was running.

And then we soared out above an immense cavern, where Maculte and an entire army of Red Death Tea Society assassins were fighting against Nate and the rest of my friends.

And as we began to fall amid the rubble of the destroyed wall, the concussive blast was blowing people over like brittle trees in a strong wind. Maculte and Luria were diving for cover. An army of roboctopi were flailing their tentacles in an attempt to protect themselves from the incoming debris. The vast horde of assassins were collectively gasping in surprise, because who could have *possibly* predicted that Chester and I would burst through a concrete wall fifty feet above the floor? Then, as Chester and I were still flailing and plummeting, and when we were still high above the floor . . . I looked down and locked eyes with Nate.

"Ahh, Delphine," he said. "Just as I expected."

"Robots!" I yelled out. "Catch your queen!"

This was perhaps the most amazing thing I've

ever spoken, and it was equally amazing to see all of the roboctopi scurrying to catch me, so that I was soon landing on a sea of cushioning tentacles.

"I brought Chester!" I told Nate, sliding down a tentacle to stand next to him. "He's over there!" I pointed to a colorful blur that was still arcing through the air, as Chester . . . with his blue shirt, yellow pants, and intensely red socks . . . smashed into the row of tea dispensers at the edge of the Earthquake Cavern, smashing them to bits.

A collective groan shivered through the Red Death Tea Society assassins.

"Good work!" Nate said.

"What's happened since I left?" I asked. Looking around, I couldn't see Wendy, Stine, or Ventura any-where. Not even Bosper.

"Our friends have been taken hostage."

"That's horrible!" I said.

"That's great!" Nate said. "I counted on it."

"You counted on it?" Maculte said, interrupting our conversation. He and Luria had floated down to the same level as the rest of the Red Death Tea Society. His army parted as he walked forward, bowing with respect and also jealousy, because he was the only one who still had any tea, now that the dispensers had been destroyed.

"I did!" Nate said. "I have a spy in your organization, and having our friends getting taken hostage was the only way for our side to meet up with my spy and sabotage your headquarters."

"Uh, Nate," I said. "Should you be telling them this?"

"Nope! But I can't help it. Because of the honesty thing."

Maculte walked closer. He was glaring. His usual scowl was in place, and it made me wonder why he was so intent on taking over the world. After all, I'd *never* truly seen him happy, and if you're not doing what makes you happy in life, then why do you keep doing it? Instead of trying to take over the world, why not try to become a painter, or a scientist, or lead guitarist for a cool band that serves cake at all their concerts?

But instead he was looming over two seventh graders who were the last line of defense against the entire city of Polt being annihilated in an earthquake. Maculte's fingers were clenching. His teeth were gnashing. He cocked his head to one side. Then he stared at me. Right in my eyes. It was a stare down, and it meant that Maculte wasn't very intelligent, because I have *never* lost a stare down. I'm basically the Wild West Gunfighting champion of stare downs.

I've defeated my brother Steve, who finally had to admit that it *was* his turn to do the dishes. And I've defeated my dad, who ultimately had to admit that cake existed before the universe was formed (this is a scientific theory I've devised, and it is flawless), and I've defeated Liz, who actually fell asleep, because it was four in the morning and we'd just finished watching the entire Carrot Cake Master martial-arts movie trilogy, where a chef who has mastered the art of carrot cake must defend her recipe against zombies in the first movie, a giant gorilla in the second movie, and an army of intelligent porcupines in the third. I've even won stare downs against Snarls, my mom's cat, who quickly pretended he hadn't meant to get into a stare down in the first place.

So, clearly, Maculte was out of his league.

He just kept staring at me.

And I stared back.

And Luria was staring at me, too.

I could feel it.

But I wasn't going to look aside.

"Nate," Maculte said, all the while staring at me. "*Who* is the spy in my organization?" Even as he was speaking, he was reaching into the vest of his suit and pulling out a red box about the size of a candy bar, and not one of the humongous candy bars my grandmother used to bring back from Switzerland and that tasted like chocolate fireworks going off inside my mouth, but one of the smaller American candy bars you can find in the checkout lanes at grocery stores, right next to the magazines that pretend celebrities aren't real people.

"Don't tell him, Nate!" I said, keeping my eyes on Maculte. My neck was starting to hurt. I had to look way up, because the leader of the Red Death Tea Society is quite a bit taller than I am, even when I have a bat on my head.

But there was no need for Nate to tell Maculte, because at that moment our friends arrived.

Wendy. And Stine. Ventura. And Bosper.

And a white poodle.

They all rushed out onto the balcony where Maculte and Luria had been standing. Everyone looked up.

Wendy said, "Hi, Delphine!"

Bosper said, "The dog has done some escaping!"

The white poodle said, "Arf!"

Luria, her face gone white, said, "No. The . . . spy? My poodle? It cannot be." Her words were whispers full of despair. I tried not to smile at her anguish, because it is a rude thing to do. I failed, though. I had a big rude grin.

"Her?" Maculte said, nodding up to the balcony.

"Her," Nate agreed. He looked to me and said, "The poodle's name is Minty. She's Luria's pet. Bosper has been dating her, and also learning all of the Red Death Tea Society's secrets."

"Minty!" Luria said, calling up to the balcony. "How could you?"

"Arf!" Minty said.

"The Bosper has a girlfriend!" Bosper said. He sounded giddy.

Nate told me, "Bosper's been meeting Minty for the last few weeks. I'm sure you've noticed."

"Of course!" I said, thinking of Bosper's mysterious meeting in the bookstore, and his equally mysterious meeting in my yard, and hoping that Nate wouldn't detect my lie that I'd known what was happening, especially when *he* was being constantly forced to tell the truth.

"This is meaningless," Maculte said. "What secrets could you possibly learn that would do you any good?" Incidentally, I would like to point out that when we'd all looked up to the balcony, Maculte had looked *first*. Which meant that I was still the undefeated stare down champion of the world.

In response to Maculte's words, Nate gave that little smile of his. It's a smile that makes me as giddy as a terrier dating a poodle. It's a smile that means Nate has a situation well under control.

"It was *quite* informative," Nate said. "For instance, I learned that your favorite meal is oatmeal."

"Really?" I said, aghast. "That's weird."

"Unflavored oatmeal," Nate added.

"No way!" I said. "At least put in some *fruit*! Or some pizza. Or some cake."

Nate told Maculte, "I also learned that you wake at precisely four thirty in the morning, every day."

"What?" Ventura yelled down from the balcony. "That's *insane*! I hope you don't make everyone *else* get up that early!" There was a rumbling swell of discontent from the army of assassins in the room. It was the first time I'd ever felt sorry for them. I'm pretty sure that if I had to get up at four thirty in the morning, *every* morning, then I would be a villain, too.

"And Minty told me that your favorite music is not to listen to music at all."

"**Gahh!**" Ventura said from the balcony. "How can you not like *music*?"

"*And* I learned that you haven't solved how to link quarks with high-density gravitational singularities," Nate told a scowling Maculte.

"That's so easy!" Wendy laughed from the balcony. We all looked up at her. Her face went red.

"Sorry!" she said. "I was just getting into the spirit of things."

"None of these things will help you," Maculte said. "You've been playing games, like the child you are. *This* is what you should have been paying attention to." He held up that little red box of his. And then he flicked it open.

To reveal a big red button.

That he pushed.

It made a clicking noise.

And the room began to hum.

"In two minutes," Maculte said, "the city of Polt will be destroyed."

"No," I said. It was a whisper. Of horror.

Maculte looked at me. He grinned. My heart was clutching and my stomach was roiling and my legs felt weak. Two minutes until the entire city of Polt was destroyed? I could feel sweat beading up on my forehead, and even in the palms of my hands, so I could only hope that it wasn't grossing out Nate, since at some point I'd apparently grabbed his hand and was clutching it *tight*.

The crystals in the walls were humming louder, beginning to glow. The army of Red Death Tea Society assassins were all scurrying out of the room in horror as the vibrations began. It felt like we were standing in a heavy rain, with high winds, but there were no rains or winds, just the vibrations of the room growing ever more powerful.

"Robots!" I yelled. "Destroy the walls!"

Immediately, my robot army began fanning out toward the walls, striding through the panicked tide of the escaping Red Death Tea Society assassins.

"Override," Maculte said. "Robots deactivate."

The robots all crumpled to the floor.

"Did you think I wouldn't devise an override to your override?" Maculte sneered. "You've learned nothing." He had to raise his voice over the high-pitched whine of Chester's shoes as Chester fought for traction on the tea-slickened floor, his legs a blur and the tea dissipating into flavored steam, and then there was the ever-increasing roar of the earthquake crystals, but it still wasn't much of a problem for Maculte to be heard, because he's one of those people who's always raising his voice, like the men who can't order a hamburger without yelling about it, or tie their own shoelaces without going on a tirade.

"You're actually 5.3 seconds *behind* when I thought you would deactivate the robots," Nate said. "You're slipping." His smile was still in place, making me not worry *too* much about how violently the Earthquake Cavern was vibrating. Bosper was whining, covering his ears. Minty, the poodle, was doing the same. The sound was painful. But if *Nate* wasn't worried, then *I* wasn't worried. Too much.

"And *you're* twenty seconds behind saving your beloved city," Luria said. "Because once Maculte pushed that button, there was nothing you could possibly do. The whole of Polt will be destroyed, along with you, your friends, and that *traitor*." With the last, Luria looked to Minty, the poodle. Minty and Bosper had leaped over the side of the balcony, sliding down the tentacles of one of the inert robots that had been clutching the side of the wall. My friends were climbing down after them. Ventura had her eyes closed because she is afraid of heights.

"Nate," I said. "You have a plan, right?"

"I do," Nate said. Maculte's eyes narrowed, because he *knew* that Nate was being forced to tell the truth. If he *said* he had a plan, he had a plan.

"There's nothing you can—" Maculte said. But Nate held up his hand and stopped him.

"You keep saying I can't do anything," Nate said. "But I *can*. Because I'm smarter than you. Because I plan ahead. Which is why I've had a spy in your army." Nate reached down and petted Minty. Luria took a step forward but the poodle growled at her, and I could see the anguish in Luria's eyes.

Nate said, "And *through* Minty, I learned about how you teach a three-week course on why it's important for socks to match."

"Three weeks?" I said. "Seriously?"

"It's important!" Maculte told me. We had to yell, because the hum of the earthquake crystals was now as loud as a jet engine. Everything on the floor, the robots and the shattered tea dispensers, was jiggling and vibrating, and of course since *we* were all standing on the floor the vibrations were making us shiver and tremble, like we were being electrified. Soon, the growing vibrations would be released in a jolt powerful enough that the fault line beneath Polt's lake would be ripped asunder, and the very earth would shake and crack, and the city would be shattered. I wasn't sure if the nausea I was feeling was because of all the vibrations, or the disturbing hum, or the thought of so many people just . . . gone.

"I've also learned that you've been kidnapping children," Nate said. His voice had turned grim. His fingers clenched into fists as he faced off against the man who was the second smartest person in the entire world, and by far the most evil. "You've been brainwashing them, turning them into assassins, into members of your Red Death Tea Society."

"It's an effective method of recruiting," Maculte said, adding an insolent shrug. "And it's best for sheep to be led." Crackles of electricity were forming in the air, spontaneously bursting into existence due to the gathering power in the cavern. It cast us all in an eerie light, with the sharp crackles of illumination piercing the pulsing green glow that had pervaded the entire room.

"Twenty seconds until the power is released," Luria said. "Time to take our leave."

Maculte looked to her. Nodded. Then, without a word, with only one solitary sneer back to Nate, he and Luria began to walk away and leave us to be torn apart by the powerful forces at the heart of a machine that was about to destroy an entire city.

"One other thing I learned . . ." Nate said.

Maculte stopped. But he did not look back.

"I've learned the *exact* frequency of your earthquake machine," Nate said, and his smile turned even more whimsical and . . . I'll just go ahead and be honest . . . attractive, and it made me feel like holding his hand again, but I couldn't do that with everybody watching, so instead I punched him in the arm.

"You . . . *what?*" Maculte said. He still hadn't turned around.

"Chester!" Nate yelled. "I need you to stomp your

feet on the floor *precisely* seven hundred and thirty-two times a second!"

"Okay!" Chester said, and he immediately started stomping, as if he'd been just *waiting* for a chance to do some excellent stomping, which . . . as I understand it . . . is basically a boy's natural state.

The room's hum began to warble.

Chester's feet were stomping down on the floor, sending out vibrations, and it felt like we weren't standing on solid footing anymore. The floor felt . . . *liquid*. Like standing atop a series of small waves. Minty began barking at the floor. Bosper was trying to console her, and meanwhile Chester's feet just kept stomping, and stomping, and the hum of the crystals was going up, and up, then plummeting down. Then the cycle would begin again, and my ears were doing that thing like when you're in an airplane and it starts to descend, and the air pressure makes your ears feel like they're underwater.

"That was only seven hundred and thirty-*one* stomps," Nate told Chester, so . . . I guess Nate was counting? It all seemed like one big stomp to me, and the floor where Chester was stomping began to glow with heat, so that he stomped to another area. The crystals were shimmering, blurring, the hum reaching a crescendo but then going abruptly silent, and then again soaring louder and louder . . . louder each time, with the immeasurable power on the very verge of being violently released, but canceled by the vibrations of Chester's stomps, so that the power was being contained, but still growing, and growing, to the brink of bursting.

"That's better," Nate told Chester, who I guess had stomped the proper number of times in the last second.

"I'm getting the hang of it!" Chester said. He was a blur of blue and yellow, and *especially* red, as his bright red socks were just a haze of color as Chester stomped, and stomped, and *stomped*.

"Stop it!" Maculte ordered. He was a man accustomed to his orders being obeyed, and it showed in his voice.

"Stuff it!" Chester said, still stomping, because there are very few people in our Polt Middle School class who get their names written on the "misbehaving" blackboard list more often than Chester. He's nowhere near *my* level, of course, but he shows promise and I respect him for that.

"The knockout spray," Maculte said, to Luria. She instantly produced a small spray can and depressed the nozzle, sending a misty spray in Chester's direction.

"My Knock Out Knockout spray," Nate said, spraying a second mist in the middle of the mist that Luria had sprayed. Together, the mists hardened, then sank to the floor. And Chester kept stomping. The whole room felt distorted and my eyes were beginning to hurt. The hair on the back of my neck was standing up. There were flashes of light in the room, like flashbulbs going off.

"The Friend Ray," Maculte said, firing a beam of light at Chester.

"The *No-Way* Ray," Nate said, firing his own beam of light at Chester, who stuck out his tongue at Maculte, and kept stomping.

"Sleep powder," Luria said. She held up her hand and puffed blue powder toward Chester's face.

"This cheap fan from the dollar store," Nate said, holding up a tiny fan that blew the powder away from Chester, who just kept stomping, and stomping, hundreds upon hundreds of times a second. The crystals were pulsing, shaking, almost breaking free of the walls. The air smelled like tires. Like oil. Like burnt fur and spent matches.

"Disintegrator ray!" Maculte yelled. His voice was growing desperate as he pulled a pistol from inside his suit jacket and aimed it at Chester.

"A dog bite," Nate said.

"Huh?" Maculte said. Then, "**Gahhh!**" he screeched, dropping his gun, because Bosper had chomped on his leg.

"The dog has bitten!" Bosper said. His head swiveled to me. "Bites more?" he asked.

"Sure," I said. "Bites more."

"**Gahh!**" Maculte soon yelped, bitten again.

And Chester kept stomping. The hum had again reached what seemed to be a breaking point, with the sound so loud that we were all skidding along on the floor, pushed back from one wall, and then another wall if we got too close. I heard an explosive crack and saw a fault develop in one of the crystals. They were starting to burst. And Chester kept stomping. The dogs were howling. I was holding Nate's hand. The walls were layered with electricity, with a sea of sparks flowing over the walls like water. I couldn't catch my breath. My hair was standing on end. There were more cracks in the crystals. Maculte was enraged. The room felt like the inside of a giant drum, and some gargantuan drummer was pounding, and pounding, and *pounding*. There were pulsing flashes of blue, and then blackness, and then blue again. I felt like I was almost floating. But at the same time I felt like I was being crushed in some monstrous grasp. More crystals began cracking. The hum was like the screech of a hundred million drill bits. And then . . .

Chester fainted.

"**Uh-oh**," I said.

"Ah-hah!" Maculte said.

"No," Nate said. "I planned on this." And then he lifted one leg, holding it up, and he stared in Maculte's eyes for one long moment and then he said . . .

"Wait for it."

"What?" Maculte replied.

And then . . .

Nate stomped down.

And the crystals on the walls all shattered in a cataclysmic explosion of shards, like it was suddenly raining broken snow.

"I'd calculated that Chester's energy would run out when there was only one stomp remaining," Nate said. The shards were falling all around us, crashing to the floor like a not-very-comfortable rain. I reached up to my hair and covered Twibble, so he wouldn't get injured. He squeaked a high-pitched noise that was probably a thank-you, and also an expression of delight that he wouldn't have to leave my hair, apparently *ever*.

"That's . . . an amazing calculation," Maculte said, looking to Nate. For the briefest of moments there was admiration in his eyes, but then it was replaced with his usual hatred, with a veneer of arrogance and a stew of pomposity, intolerance, and in all probability a bit of stomach troubles, such as you would suffer if the only thing you ever ate was unflavored oatmeal.

"I had Bosper help me with the math," Nate said, gesturing to the terrier, who was shaking shards from his fur like they were water.

"Bosper is the dog that did the biting on your leg!" Bosper told Maculte, who did not appear as if he had forgotten.

"See *that?*" I told Maculte. "Nate had a *friend* help him. *That's* what friends are all about."

Maculte just glared at me.

"Friends like me," I said, tapping my chest.

"And friends like Bosper," I said, petting the terrier.

"And friends like Chester," I said, pointing to Chester, who had staggered back to his feet, finally drained of the "Speed Runner" pill's effects and now completely normal again, although somewhat exhausted and entirely soaked by spilled tea, and with sneakers that were smoldering like they were about to burst into flame.

I told Maculte, "Maybe if *you* had friends, then you wouldn't be so evil. Did you know that you are evil?" Maybe he didn't. Evil people don't seem to know when they're acting evil. It's very evil of them.

"Friends are a weakness," Maculte said, reaching down into the shards that were covering the floor, sinking his hand into the broken crystal fragments that went several inches deep.

"Friends distract you from your goals," he said. He was up to his wrist in crystal fragments, sorting through the remnants of his crazed dream of destroying Polt. The Earthquake Cavern had no power now. It was just a big room filled with inert robots, and with Nate and the rest of my friends, and Maculte and Luria, the defeated leaders of the Red Death Tea Society. Maculte's hand was sifting through the fragmented crystals, like a boy twirling his fingers through a puddle, or a man sifting through a box of old photographs, dreaming of what might have been.

"Ah-hah," he said.

"Ah-hah?" I questioned.

"Ah-hah!" he yelled, and he stood up, and now he was holding his disintegrator pistol again, and he reached out and grabbed me by the hair and put the barrel to my cheek.

"Oh," I whispered. "It was *that* kind of 'ah-hah,' was it?"

"It was," he said. And Luria did a little clapping,

and Bosper did a little growling, and my knees did a little tremble. I'm not overly fond of disintegrator pistols. Okay, I *did* ask Nate if he could make one for me, but *only* so that I could disintegrate my brother's workout clothes, which he tends to leave hanging over the shower rod in our upstairs bathroom, and which tend to smell like donkey farts, except with more pepper. A disintegrator pistol comes in very handy during "stinky gym clothes" situations, but are decidedly *not* as fun during "pointed at your head" situations.

"Friends," Maculte said, with the raging sneer returned to his voice. "Nate, tell me . . . how *valuable* are your friends? How important are these *weaknesses* of yours?" Twibble came crawling out of my hair, peered down at the disintegrator pistol pointed at my cheek, and then hid deep in my hair. I could hardly blame him.

"They're . . . the most important thing in the world," Nate said. "Especially Delphine." I felt a little flush of . . . something . . . when Nate said that. After all, he *could* have said that his *inventions* were the most important thing in the world, that *science* was the most important thing in the world, but . . . no. When forced to tell the truth, Nate had just said that I was the most important thing in his world.

"See?" Maculte said. "A weakness."

Nate was reaching into his shirt, obviously about to produce some amazing technological device that would do . . . something. I wasn't sure what, but then . . . that's why Nate is the genius.

"Don't," Maculte said, pressing the barrel of the pistol even tighter against my cheek. "Put your hands to your sides, Nathan." I could see in Nate's eyes that he was doing furious calculations, working out probable outcomes if he made a move. There were little flashes of light in Nate's eyes, but . . . one by one . . . they dulled. And he put his hands to his sides.

"That's better," Maculte said. "Now then, I admit that I've been once again impressed by your intelligence. It would be a shame to deprive the world of your genius. So I will make you a deal."

"No deals!" I blurted. "Nate, don't make any deals!" We'd made a deal once before with Maculte, and he'd gone back on his word almost immediately.

"I'm listening," Nate said. He wiped a bit of sweat from his forehead. I'm not sure I've ever seen him sweat before.

"Swear that you will become a member of the Red Death Tea Society," Maculte said. He had one hand on my neck and the other hand holding the pistol. It was quite difficult to squirm, but I think I did an excellent job under the circumstances.

"I swear," Nate said.

"Say it," Maculte ordered. He poked the pistol at my cheek, and I have to say that it *was* uncomfortable, but Nate was besting me in the "squirming uncomfortably" category.

"I swear that I will become a member of the Red Death Tea Society," Nate said. It came out as a hiss. His entire body shuddered. He was having trouble swallowing. I was having trouble breathing. Even the disintegrator pistol aimed at my head didn't seem so bad now.

"And swear that you will obey my every command," Maculte ordered. I could practically *see* the triumph spitting out of his mouth, and I definitely *could* feel the spit that was spitting out of his mouth.

"If you let Delphine and the rest of my friends go," Nate said, "then . . . yes, I swear I will obey your every command." Bosper was barking, too angry and too shocked to speak. Ventura was crying. Luria had picked up several crystal shards and was pitching them at Minty, who simply let them bounce off her back, staring at what was happening. And then there was me . . . held in Maculte's grasp, listening to what Nate was saying, knowing . . . just as Maculte knew . . . that every word Nate was speaking was the truth.

"For the rest of your life," Maculte said.

"For the rest of my life," Nate said. "I swear."

I was sweating. Like, *bad*. Like I'd been turned into a human fire hose. I was hoping Maculte was getting his hands soaked in my gross sweat. I couldn't seem to breathe anymore, and the whole world was turning gray.

"Heh," Maculte said. Not even a word. But it was the worst thing I'd ever heard. Because *he* knew what we *all* knew.

He'd won.

The Red Death Tea Society had won.

For like, two minutes, all I could do was stare.

I wasn't staring at anything.

I was just staring.

I was listening to the sounds of my feet shifting in the broken crystals that covered the floor.

I was listening to the beating of my heart, which sounded like a drum, and felt like a clenched fist.

I was listening to Bosper. He was barking, barking, barking.

I was crying.

"That's that, then," Maculte said, and he shoved me away from him so violently that I fell down into the crystal shards, which cut against my hands. Stine helped me to my feet and, together . . . with Nate and Ventura, with Wendy and Chester and Bosper and Minty . . . we all stood facing Maculte and Luria.

"Come here, Nate," Maculte said. I immediately grabbed Nate's hand. Nothing bad could happen as long as I didn't let go. I was *clutching* his hand, holding tight.

But Nate's hand slid away from mine.

And he walked over to Maculte.

"Stand there and watch what happens next," Maculte said. "Don't interfere." I began to get a bad feeling. Like, *another* bad feeling. Bad feelings were stacked on top of one another like pancakes, like a huge stack of pancakes with no butter or syrup, and I've probably lost control of my analogy but what I'm trying to say is that I had a *very* bad feeling and then I had that disintegrator pistol aimed at me again, only this time it was aimed at all of my friends as well. All of them except Nate, who was standing next to Maculte, with one of Maculte's hands on his shoulder.

"What are you doing?" Nate said.

"Disintegrating your friends," Maculte said.

"No," Nate said.

"No," I added, in case I got a vote.

Nate said, "You *said* you would let them go."

Maculte told him, "I lied. But *you* can't. I know you, Nathan Bannister. You *never* go back on your word, and with the honesty potion working in your system you're *incapable* of lying. So . . . stand there and watch while I disintegrate your friends."

"No," I said, again. I know you're not supposed to vote twice, but I went for it, anyway.

"Can I . . . can I say goodbye to Delphine?" Nate asked. There were tears in his eyes, and that only made mine worse.

"Hmm," Maculte said.

"Oh, let him," Luria said. "It will be poignant. It makes for a good laugh."

"Very well," Maculte said. "Say your goodbye."

Nate walked over to me. He stared in my eyes. I was waiting for him to make one of his last-second rescues, *hoping* for one of them, but the moment I looked into those eyes of his I knew it was hopeless. I'd never seen such sadness in his eyes before. And, I guess I never would again.

"Sorry," he told me. His hand reached out to hold mine. I was compulsively wiping the sweat away from my hand, repeatedly back and forth against my pants, and then I all but grabbed Nate's hand and squeezed tight. He squeezed back. He was still looking in my eyes. We were both crying. Luria began clapping, applauding us.

"You couldn't help it," I told Nate. "With that honesty potion, you can't . . . you can't . . ." I didn't know what I was trying to say. I didn't know *anything*.

Nate's hand left mine and rose up to my cheek, wiping away my tears. "I'm sorry," he said again. "But . . . this is the only way."

His hand moved farther up, brushing some hair out of my eyes. Then, after touching gently on the side of my face, his hand moved even farther up, up into my hair, where, with a single finger, Nate poked down at Twibble.

Hard.

"**Eeeeeeeeeeeeeeee!**" Twibble shrieked as Nate pressed down. It was easily as loud as an opera-trained elephant screaming in my ears, so if that ever happens to you then you will know how I felt.

Maculte's gun shattered.

"There," Nate said, taking his finger off the bat in my hair and restoring a sense of peace to the world.

"What?" Maculte bellowed, outraged, staring at the shattered remnants of the pistol in his hand. "How could you *do* this? You *swore* that you'd obey my every command! That you would *serve* me! You . . . you lied! You *can't* have lied!"

"I was wondering about that myself," I said. Well, I whispered it, because I didn't want to make it sound like I was agreeing with Maculte in any way whatsoever.

"That?" Nate said. "Didn't you see me shudder when I was giving you my vows, when I was swearing to obey you for the rest of my life? That was when my honesty potion finally ran out, allowing me to lie if I wanted. And frankly, I wouldn't have had to lie anyway, since you'd promised to let my friends go, and went back on your word."

"And my pistol?" Maculte asked. "How?" He was still clutching the shattered disintegrator pistol, but it was obviously useless.

"Easy," Nate said. "As you all know, a disintegrator pistol works by using a series of sonic waves to upset the balance of an atom, to disrupt the interplay between protons, neutrons, and electrons . . . causing the atoms to fly apart from one another due to the resonance feedback."

"Duh," I said.

Nate looked to me.

I blushed.

"Okay, go on," I said.

Nate, turning back to Maculte, said, "But I happened to know that there was a bat in Delphine's hair, and not *only* a bat, but one that had been subjected to *friend gas*. And bats that have been affected by friend gas are particularly ticklish."

"Duh," I said. I actually *did* know this one, because Twibble had been giggling in my hair for quite some time, though it *had* taken me a bit to understand it was laughter, because a bat's laughter sounds like a series of miniature gas leaks.

Nate looked to me.

"No, seriously," I said. "I knew that one. Every time Twibble moves in my hair, he giggles."

"Oh," Nate said, blushing.

He turned back to Maculte and said, "Knowing that I had access to a ticklish bat, it was only a matter of pressing it in just the right tickle-spot to produce an extremely high-pitched giggle, in effect a sonic disruption that would cause a feedback in your pistol's resonance chamber, in turn causing an explosion much like the one we used to destroy your Earthquake Cavern." Nate kicked at the crystals covering the floor the way you kick at a puddle. The crystals made a pleasant sound, like the shifting of sand combined with the ringing of bells. To be honest, though, the most musical sound I could hear was Nate's voice.

"You lose," Nate told Maculte.

"Do I?" Maculte said. I was suddenly uncomfortable at how resolutely his sneer was in place. I wanted to grab Nate's hand, just for reassurance, but I found out that I was *already* holding his hand. Weird how that happens sometimes.

"There's one thing you forgot," Maculte said. "You see, Nathan, while I admit that you were able to best me, *this* time, from a *scientific* standpoint, you are still only a child trapped in my underwater headquarters, and where *science* has failed me, brute force will win the day." He made a fist. It looked very unscientific.

Maculte took a step forward.

Nate smiled.

Maculte took another step.

Nate smiled an even more impressive smile, and Maculte's third step wavered.

"I didn't forget," Nate said. He gestured to the room and added, "Really, Maculte? Did you think that I wouldn't devise an override to your override of my override?"

"Huh?" I said.

"Ooo!" Bosper said.

362

"Can we get ice cream after this?" Ventura asked.

"Robots, arise!" Nate shouted.

And all of the roboctopi suddenly shuddered into life. Their tentacles began whipping back and forth, clanging against one another as they stood.

"Two minutes until explosion," Nate ordered the robots. "Begin the countdown."

There was silence in the room from everyone but the robots. I think we were all too stunned by what was happening, though it's possible that Bosper was stunned by how Minty was standing so close to him, and also I'm reasonably certain that Ventura was dreaming of ice cream, but the rest of us were simply stunned by how we were watching the robots once again bring forth their bombs, holding them at the tips of their tentacles, high above their heads.

"Stay and fight me if you want," Nate told Maculte. "But, a better calculation would be for you to . . . run."

"Hmm," Maculte said.

His fists unclenched.

"Your calculation is correct," he said.

And he and Luria ran.

"Yay!" I said. "We win!"

"We should run," Nate said.

I'd been going for a high five, or a hug, or possibly even a kiss on the cheek, which would've only been out of *friendship*, because Nate and I are not dating, and even if I'd been about to kiss him on the lips, it would've been *only* because I was swept up in the relief of not being disintegrated, so there wouldn't have been any reason to start any rumors.

"Seriously," Nate said, as I unromantically-spur-of-the-moment kissed him. "We should run."

We ran.

Bosper and Minty were leading, because dogs run faster, and also because Minty knew the way. Nate and I were close behind, and there was Ventura and Wendy, and Stine, and Chester, who was stumbling with exhaustion and complaining about not being able to run very fast. I suppose the world *did* seem much slower to him, because he could now only run at about fifteen miles per hour, which is not very fast compared to his previous speeds, and which felt *extremely* slow owing to the series of explosions happening right behind us.

Oh, I should mention the explosions.

There were explosions happening behind us.

The explosions were making explode-y noises, and we were all yelling and panicking and wondering which way to go as the underwater headquarters of the Red Death Tea Society began collapsing all around us, with the ceilings caving in, and the walls crumbling, and the lake waters rushing down through gaps from above. Bosper and Minty soon abandoned their lead positions and began running around us like herd dogs, making sure everyone stayed together and went in the right direction.

"We did it!" I yelled, happy that we had once again beaten the Red Death Tea Society.

"Your life is awesome!" Stine yelled. "I mean, as long as we don't end up trapped in a watery tomb, this has been fun!"

"We should get ice cream!" Ventura said. We were still in danger of being crushed by the falling debris, or drowned by the rushing waters, so it was a very silly time to be thinking about ice cream, or even about cake, although it wasn't *that* far away from the time when ice cream and cake would become a priority, and it doesn't hurt to plan ahead.

But, first things first. We needed to *escape*, because the walls were cracking and crumbling, with hallways beginning to fill with rubble and water, so that we had to make detours, taking us farther out of our way, with the headquarters shuddering and shaking and collapsing, rocks bursting under the growing pressure and alarms blaring loudly and the dogs barking at us, nipping at our heels if we went the wrong way, tiny bites that were understandable under the circumstances but that we'd be discussing later.

There were fires as machinery exploded. There were menacing rumbles more intense than thunder. There were never-ending avalanches of building materials and even of the bedrock the headquarters had been built within, and there were showers of mud, which is not a shower I would advise.

Finally, we made it to the cavern with the mini-submarines. Without Chester to run us through the waters, and without Betsy to help us, we needed to grab one of the submarines. We raced across the docks to the nearest one. The cavern's ceiling was collapsing, with rocks falling down from above to make *blooping* sounds in the underwater lake, and with boulders falling down from above to make *BUHH-LOOOSHING* sounds in the water, and even one boulder making a *KEEE-RANNGG* sound as it smashed into one of the submarines, violently tearing the vessel in half. The alarms were still sounding and bats were flying everywhere in panic and one of the walls collapsed into a big sliding avalanche of rock and mud, causing a small tsunami as it slammed into the water, a wave that washed up over the docks and sent us all tumbling. But we scrambled back to our feet, needing to hurry, needing to *escape* before the entire headquarters came crashing down upon us.

Stine yelled, "Delphine, I totally take back my earlier comments on how your life is awesome! This is scary!"

Ventura yelled, "I'm sticking with my earlier comments on how I want ice cream! I completely still do!"

We raced across a wooden dock that had been partially destroyed by the wave and the avalanche, having to wade somewhat, as the dock was beginning to sink, but we managed to scramble up onto the submarine and then, helping Bosper and Minty, we opened the hatch and crawled down inside.

We were safe.

Unless one of those huge boulders fell on us or unless the entire cavern collapsed so there was no escape route and we'd be trapped down here forever.

So . . . we were not *so* safe.

And not so *roomy*, either, because the submarine was only built for three or four people at the most, and there was me, and Nate, and Wendy, and Stine, and Ventura, and Chester and two dogs. So, we were past maximum capacity, with little room to move around. Nate immediately went to the controls and started hitting buttons and entering commands on a keyboard, flicking switches and generally acting comfortable in his role of a submarine commander, as if it was something he did every day.

"Let's go!" I yelled, scrunched into one corner.

"Agreed!" Ventura said, basically hanging from an overhead pipe in order to find room.

"Full speed ahead!" Stine yelled, sitting on a control board, trying to find space.

"**Eeeeeeeee!**" Twibble said, frantically pulling at my hairs.

"**Eeeeeeeee!**" I said, because there was a bat frantically pulling at my hairs.

"Why's your bat going crazy?" Wendy said. She was pressed all the way up against a wall, because the submarine was *cramped*.

"Not sure!" I said. "Maybe she's frightened of watching her old home be . . . be . . . oh dang."

"What?" Stine asked.

But by then I was already scrambling up the ladder, hurrying back up to the hatch, which I opened. Then, with a look back down to the already horribly cramped conditions of the submarine, I told my friends, "Sorry about this."

And I *was* sorry. I was *so* sorry.

Then, looking up to the cavern's collapsing ceiling, with boulders falling everywhere and with the vast lake above us starting to burst through, I yelled out, "C'mon, guys! Let's get out of here!"

I was talking to the bats.

Instantly, the immense swarm of hundreds of bats dove for the submarine, flying down past me through the hatch, brushing up against me, of course, so that it felt like I was taking a shower of bats, which is another type of shower I would advise against.

Then, when all the bats were inside, and with Twibble now pleased, I resealed the hatch and climbed back down.

"I invited some bats to come with us," I said. There were bats clinging to every wall. There were bats hanging from every pipe. There were bats clinging everywhere, which of course meant they were clinging to Stine, and Wendy, and Chester and Ventura, and even Bosper and Minty.

"I noticed," Stine said, twitching. She probably had thirty bats hanging off her.

"**Guhhh**," Wendy said, trembling. I'd say . . . fifty bats on her.

"There!" Nate said, stepping back from the control board. "We're ready to go!" There were *zero* bats hanging off him. Not a single one.

"Why aren't there any bats on you?" I asked.

"'Bat-block' lotion," he told me. "It's like sun-block, except instead of protecting me from sunburn, it safeguards me from bats."

"And, was there enough of this 'bat-tan' lotion to *share*?" I asked, while possibly narrowing my eyes and definitely being covered in bats.

"Oh, I *should* have made enough for everyone!" Nate said, obviously considering the notion for the first time, despite how it's *always* time to think of protecting your friends from becoming encased in bats. Bosper, currently looking like a pile of bats with a terrier's tail sticking out, let out a muffled murmur that *he* would've appreciated some lotion as well.

"Oh well," Nate said. "Here's this instead." And he leaned closer and kissed me right on the lips, or at least partially on my lips because one of the bats on my face didn't manage to shuffle aside in time.

"What was *that* for?" I asked in shock, sputtering in surprise after barely returning his kiss at all.

"Because I'm happy, I guess?" Nate said, seeming like he was as puzzled and shocked by the kiss as I was, since we are definitely not anything more than friends. "It's just that, for a while there, I thought I was going to have to join the Red Death Tea Society, and then I wouldn't have been able to be with you, and . . . strange as this sounds . . . I was glad when Maculte said he was going to disintegrate you."

"That *does* sound strange," I said. I looked over to Stine. She nodded. Yep. Definitely strange.

Nate continued, "Because that meant that Maculte was going back on his word. My vow to join the Red Death Tea Society was conditional on him letting everyone go, which he wasn't doing. So, I was released from my promise."

"Oh," I said. "Right. I suppose it was actually a good thing, me nearly getting disintegrated."

"It was wonderful!" Nate said. "Now I don't have to join the assassins! And, Delphine, I'm sorry I kissed you out of the blue, but I was just so happy, and, uh, I suppose there's something important I should tell you, right now." He was suddenly looking very serious. Staring at me. Staring right into my eyes. Unwavering. His own eyes held a wealth of importance and knowledge. I'm forever fascinated by Nate's eyes, but this time they seemed more magnetic than ever, drawing me closer.

"Yes?" I said. He leaned closer.

"Delphine," he said. "I've been thinking, and, well, there's something you should know."

"Okay," I said. He'd moved in even closer. His lips

were so close to mine. I could feel all my friends staring at us. I could feel all the bats clinging to me. I could feel my skin tingling. I wondered if Nate was going to kiss me again. It wouldn't be a surprise, this time, but it would still be a shock. If he tried, I was going to have to remind him that we were only friends. But I'd do it after the kiss, I guess. Just in case.

"Delphine," he said. Nothing more than my name, but it sounded like everything, to me.

"Yes?" His lips were almost on mine. I could feel his warmth. I could feel my heart beating. I could feel—

"If we don't leave right now," Nate said, "I predict a 98.49 percent chance that we'll be crushed when the cavern collapses."

"Oh," I said, a bit stunned. I looked to Wendy.

"Oh," she said, equally stunned.

I looked to Stine.

"Oh," she said, a bit bewildered.

I looked to Bosper.

"Pfft," he farted, and that was enough to finally shake me from my daze.

"OH!" I yelled. And I leaped for the submarine's controls as, down at my feet, the bats all fluttered away from Bosper. "Nate! What are we *waiting* for? Let's *go*!"

Chapter 13

Weeks passed.

My obstacle course had new regulars. Liz and Wendy and Stine and Ventura came over all the time, hurtling and balancing and throwing and holding their breath and punching and doing all the other things necessary to pass the increasingly difficult challenges I presented, because they wanted to get into shape for any further adventures, and also because they couldn't have any cake or pie until they'd passed their daily tests.

Bosper and Minty romped all over Polt, snuggling and barking and doing all the other things that dogs in love do together, such as one of them talking about math while the other one chomps on banana peels she found in a garbage can.

I spent a lot of time wondering if I should ever tell my parents that I was fighting an international society of genius-level assassins, and decided that it probably wasn't the wisest course of action. I spent an equal amount of time wondering if I should turn my brother Steve back into a zebra forever, and decided that I should definitely go for it.

Meanwhile, somewhere out in the world, I knew that Maculte and Luria and the Red Death Tea Society members were planning more plans, scheming more schemes, and drinking thousands more gallons of truly terrible tea. Maculte, with his ego, was undoubtedly confident that he could defeat us the next time around. He *wouldn't* have been so confident, though, if he'd known that Stine could now hold her breath for over three minutes, or that Wendy could walk across a tightrope on her hands, or that Ventura's quick mind had memorized all three hundred and twelve ice-cream flavors available in the entire city of Polt. Plus, Melville was practicing stinging, and Twibble was learning new evasive maneuvers, and Bosper was in such a good mood that his mind was racing in all directions, solving math problems that even Nate was struggling to understand. Liz, meanwhile, was organizing all of the inventions that Nate had ever made, including several hundred that he'd totally forgotten, such as a bottle of "Earlobe Enlargement" pills and a toothbrush with octopus tentacles instead of bristles, so that it could sneak into your bedroom and scrub your teeth while you slept.

In other words, the Red Death Tea Society would be foolish to challenge us.

That said, for a group of geniuses, they'd proven to be plenty foolish in the past, so I was always ready to go, alert for Nate's call, with my adventure bag fully stocked with everything I could possibly need.

When my phone rang, I was in the kitchen with Mom, having just baked an experimental strawberry cake with pineapple frosting. I had a freshly sliced piece on my plate and my fork in hand. I dropped the fork and grabbed my phone.

"You're choosing a phone call over cake?" my mom said, amazed. Then she glanced at my phone and saw who was calling, and she smiled and added, "Oh. I see. It's Nate." There was . . . a certain *way* she said it.

"What's *that* supposed to mean?" I said.

"Oh, it's just, you know, Nate." She *still* had that certain tone in her voice, but I couldn't worry about that. I answered my phone.

"Delphine!" Nate said. He *also* had a certain tone in his voice. It was the very specific Nate Bannister tone that meant something had gone horribly wrong, and I suppose that there must be something horribly wrong with *me*, because I found it very exciting.

"What's going on?" I said, hurrying to my room for privacy.

"I may have done something . . . not so smart," he said. "But I didn't think my latest invention would escape, and also there's a Red Death Tea Society robot attacking my treehouse, and I made these new pills that, umm, well . . . have you seen today's date?"

"Of course," I said, putting on my jetbelt while looking at the calendar on my wall, the one where Friday the thirteenth was circled several times, and where I'd added a huge exclamation mark.

"I'm on the way," I told Nate.

Acknowledgments

No book gets written in a vacuum. At least not until we have space-authors floating alone through the universe, drifting through galaxy after galaxy while tapping on a computer keyboard and wondering how far it is until the next decent place to buy a cookie. For now, though, we authors are always part of a vast group of people who help bring our stories to life and novels to print. For me, first off, big thanks to Cindy Loh and Allison Moore at Bloomsbury, who are always there for me, championing my work. And high fives to all the others at Bloomsbury as well, for all their help in editing, proofing, nodding their heads when I needed it, shaking their heads when the book needed it, and for loving the craft of writing as much as I do.

Thanks to my agent, Brooks Sherman, for his always sage advice, and for dressing so nattily. You are an inspiration, sir.

Shout-out to all those at Rocking Frog and Floyd's

and at all the other cafés where I write. Without those sandwiches and cookies, I would probably starve. Although, would it hurt you to put some pancakes on the menu? Think about it, guys.

Big thanks, most of all, to all my readers, whether for my Genius Factor series, or my Bandette or Plants vs. Zombies comics, or any and all of my other projects, because without readers I would just be a crazy person writing in an alleyway, instead of what I am today, a crazy person writing two stories above an alleyway.

**DON'T MISS NATE AND DELPHINE'S
FIRST ADVENTURE IN**

HOW TO CAPTURE AN iNVISIBlE CAT

**BY
PAUL TOBIN**

**ILLUSTRATED BY
KATIE ABEY**

NATE AND DELPHINE
SAVE THE WORLD IN

How to Outsmart A Billion Robot Bees

BY
PAUL TOBIN

ILLUSTRATED BY
KATIE ABEY